ADORE

COOPER & JESSE

A.D. ELLIS

ONE
COOPER SCOTT

"COOPER," Bev said my name in that exasperated tone that made me realize she'd likely been speaking to me for several moments while I spaced out. "Calm your fidgets and give me a hand with these veggies."

I forced my fingers to stop tapping and turned to see Bev washing a bowl full of vegetables at the sink. "Sorry." I grabbed the cutting board and a knife. Starting in on the carrots, I immediately calmed down and focused on the repetitive movements and not chopping off my fingers. "But did you see him? He's hot, right?" I waggled my brows as Bev laughed.

Bev wasn't my biological mother, but she definitely held a top spot in my heart. Luckily, I had a good relationship with both of my parents, but at the age of twenty-five, I was grateful to Bev for providing me with my own space.

Mom and Dad didn't really understand why my brother, Dalton, and I were so insistent on moving out, but then we moved into a boardinghouse of sorts. Neither Dalton or I wanted to hurt our parents' feelings, but living with your actual family at twenty-five and twenty-nine was a lot different than living with friends and a seventy-year-old woman. Bev's home allowed us to be on our own, independent—mostly—and away from home which was necessary for both of us. Dalton and I loved our parents, but we'd lived with them long enough. After we both did stints in the dorms, and Dalton attempted to get his own private place, Bev's was the perfect option.

"Boy, you need to focus more on those veggies and less on what's in that man's jeans." Bev chuckled as she popped me on the back of my head. "And I never know what you're going to think qualifies as *hot*. The older guy, silver fox look doing it for you these days?" she asked as she snuck a peek out the window at the new neighbor. "Can't say I'd kick him out of bed for eating crackers." She shrugged. "But I'm not looking for a bedfellow. Jerry was enough for a lifetime. Long as I have my children here at the house, I'm satisfied." She gave a little wink. "Nothing I can't take care of by myself," she added.

"You go, girl." I laughed. I hoped to be as vivacious and amazing at age seventy as Bev was. I threw another glance out the window. "He's moving into Spinks's Garage so he's likely a mechanic and not at all gay." I sighed dramatically. Honestly, guys my dad's age usually didn't do it for me, but this guy was completely drool-worthy. Silver streaked through his light brown hair, broad shoulders, trim waist. Poster boy for the *dad bod* physique. And when had I ever found that hot?

"Since when can mechanics not be gay?" Bev bumped my hip.

"Okay, okay, I'm stereotyping." I finished the carrots and moved on to the tomatoes. "Mmm, gay or not, he's definitely better visual stimulation than old man Spinks ever was."

"Don't go stimulating anything in my kitchen, child. Not in front of my salad. You keep that to yourself." She chuckled at her little joke.

Dear Lord, had she seen a meme or gif with the salad quote? I wouldn't put it past her. And right at that moment, I was reminded exactly why living at Remington Place was the perfect situation for me.

For all intents and purposes, Bev was our landlord, but she lived in the house too. *The house* was an amazing old Victorian style home which Bev had bought with plans to turn it into a bed and breakfast. But she'd changed her mind when she realized how many college kids were looking for safe and affordable places to stay. So, she turned 69069 at the corner of Remington Way and Pleasure Boulevard into a boardinghouse of sorts. No shit, there was no way I could make up that house number and those street names.

Dalton and I, plus our best friend, Spencer, were Bev's first boarders at Remington Place—the name of her house—about three years ago. Dalton's girlfriend, Gabby, had recently moved in as well. For the time being, Dalton and Gabby shared an upstairs room, Spencer had the largest single room—which meant he would eventually have to have a roommate. I had the smallest room and it was best set up for a single occupant—but two twin beds could squeeze in if needed. Bev had the downstairs bedroom and bathroom combo. There was one room upstairs that could house two renters.

Bev had bought the house before her late husband, Jerry, passed away, but she didn't do anything with it until about five years ago. She'd been accustomed to moving from place to place with her parents as a child because they moved a lot for their jobs. Then she married Jerry at age seventeen and became an instant military wife which meant she continued moving around a lot.

Having a permanent place to call her own and *kids* like Dalton, Spencer, and me to fill it—she and Jerry had never been able to have kids—meant the world to Bev. She didn't *need* the money, but she charged us a fair rent to cover our room, utilities, and meals. We helped with upkeep as needed—or actually, Spencer helped with upkeep mostly. He was in construction and could fix just about anything that needed fixing.

Dalton and Gabby both had some sort of office jobs. I wasn't completely sure what they did, but I knew it had to do with numbers and they'd met at work.

Numbers were something I hated. I'd been born premature and spent most of my childhood being labeled *behind* on developmental milestones. With a preschool teacher for a mother—and being held back to repeat Kindergarten—I eventually *caught up*, although math still haunted me—much to the chagrin of my math teacher father. While several labels dropped away as I got older, I still carried around dyscalculia and ADHD. Basically, I sucked with numbers, had no filter, never shut up, and never sat still.

"We should make plans to go welcome him to the

neighborhood," Bev said as she slid a lasagna in the oven. "Let's do a casserole, salad, and cake. We'll take it over tomorrow." She nodded as if it was all decided.

I knew I'd be the one helping with the meal for our new hot neighbor. Dalton and Gabby worked long hours and spent most of their down time hiding in their bedroom on the third floor. Spencer worked long and sometimes odd hours depending on what projects he had. If he was around, he'd hang with me and Bev, but he also opted for solo meals at his favorite diner and a lot of quiet time.

Spence had a lot of pain in his past that carried over to his present. I really wished the guy would believe that he could count on Dalton and me— wished he'd stop being so hard on himself and believe that he was worthy of good things.

I had a feeling that Spencer wouldn't learn to love himself until he found that perfect someone to show him it was okay. And honestly, I sometimes wondered if that person was out there for my broody and broken friend.

I tossed the tomatoes into the salad bowl and started on the broccoli and cauliflower. Bev and I would eat dinner and she'd make plates for everyone else with the leftovers. I loved our tiny little clan of chosen family, but I wasn't against growing our crew with new boarders as long as everyone could be respectful. Living with a large group of friends-turned-family was sometimes just as frustrating and hard as living with parents.

"How's the job hunt going?" Bev asked as she poured two glasses of sweet tea and gestured toward the large, open veranda where we often sat on the facing swings.

I took the glass and we made our way to the porch. Hoping to not be too obvious, I took the swing that would allow me the most glimpses of the hottie next door. Bev wasn't fooled though and she rolled her eyes and chuckled as she took the other swing.

"Job hunt continues. I'm almost considering going down to the Wishing Well to see if they'd be interested in a dancer." I took a sip of tea. "Hell, at this point, I'd be willing to give blow jobs on the corner outside of the bar if it earned me some money."

Bev groaned. "Child, don't *even* with me. First of all, you know I'm flexible on the rent."

"I know," I interrupted, "but you already charge the lowest rent in town for one of the most amazing spaces. I'm not going to short you."

She waved off my concern. I *did* know that she'd let me slide if I couldn't come up with rent, but my entire life had left me feeling dumb and irresponsible. I'd never felt successful and that was my biggest goal at this point in my life.

"Second, I don't really think giving oral on the corner outside the Wishing Well bar is the best way to pad your resume if you're still wanting to open up your own preschool." Bev's short, ample legs swung from the swing, her usual day dress and apron fluttering in the breeze. She was sharp and witty, but definitely had never left the era of housewife fashion.

I laughed. "Truth. I'm guessing most families would prefer their preschool owner *not* pimp themselves out for rent money if at all possible." Pushing back with my toes, I let the swing fall as I enjoyed the back and forth movement. Swinging was something I could always count on to calm my fidgets. Yes, the medication I took for ADHD helped a lot and I was glad I had that as an option, but keeping my hands busy, swinging, and dancing were all good non-chemical techniques as well.

"What's the issue with the job?" Bev asked and I forced myself to stop staring at the house next door hoping that the silver fox daddy would make another appearance. He'd moved in a few days ago and then disappeared, but he was back today and looked to be trying to break a world record for how much work one man could do in a day.

I sighed. "The hours. I need early morning and late afternoon, could do some evenings. But with my school work and practicum hours, I can't work a regular eight-hour day." I ran a hand through my messy bleach-blond hair. "I know I could try to get overnight shifts or work whole weekends, but I kinda already struggle to keep up with school work and lack of sleep messes with my brain."

Bev stood and made her way to my side. "I'm going to check the lasagna." Her deep brown skin felt like a warm hug against my pale complexion as she patted my arm. "Now about those hours. I'm going to say no. I'll put my foot down on that one. You aren't working overnight or weekends. School is too important." She took my empty glass. "And don't think I won't call Robby and Celeste to let them know you need some money."

I gasped and pretended to be offended. "You wouldn't!"

"I would. I know those parents of yours don't completely understand your need to live here and do things on your own. I *do* get why you want to be independent and prove you can be responsible." She reached up and brushed a strand of hair from my forehead. "But your main goal right now should be getting through school. Robby and Celeste don't want to see you struggle any more than I do. You'll figure something out. And if you don't, I'll either pause your rent or contact your parents. Your choice."

I huffed. "You're an evil old woman."

Bev cackled as she walked back into the house.

Letting the swing continue to calm me, I watched as the man next door carried boxes into the house as if he was racing a time clock.

I'd grown up helping my mom in her preschool classroom and all I'd ever wanted to do since I was old enough to know about jobs was be a preschool teacher. But lately, my goal had extended to owning a preschool. I wanted to be sure the children my school served were treated with dignity and respect no matter their struggles or labels. I never wanted a kid to feel less than because they were different than other students. And I wanted the children who faced challenges—whether the same as I faced or one of a million other obstacles—to know they were loved and good enough no matter what.

My parents had shown me nothing but love and support my entire life. I'd had a few great teachers. But I'd also had some terrible ones. I never wanted children in my care to feel like their inability to sit still or be quiet or make sense of numbers was their fault or something that made them bad.

But in order to open my own preschool one day, I

needed to finish my double major in early childhood education and business. To do those things, I needed to keep up with my homework *and* gather the required number of on-the-job training hours at the preschool where I was doing my practicum for the school year.

Then I could look into starting my own school.

But until I conquered all that, I needed a job with early morning and afternoon hours. Even the occasional evening hours would work. But nowhere I'd applied around town had the right options for what I needed.

I stared at the house next door where old man Spinks used to live and run his auto repair shop. Was the new guy going to keep the business going? Too bad I didn't have a mechanical bone in my body or I could see if he'd need some part time work. I snorted. The last time I'd taken my car to get the oil changed, I'd been unable to answer the question *What kind of car is it* with anything other than *A white one*. A job working with vehicles and tools was likely *not* the best option for me.

When hottie-potottie next door paused to pull up his shirt and wipe his face, exposing the perfect dad-bod abs—not super defined, but definitely not flabby —sprinkled with salt-n-pepper hair, I bit my lip.

Maybe a job next door wasn't in the cards for me, but I damn sure needed to meet the man.

He's probably married.

Definitely not gay.

I rolled my eyes at myself and shrugged. Who cared? He didn't need to be single for me to gather plenty of jerk-off material. Not like I was looking for a marriage proposal anytime soon anyway.

With a laugh and a final longing glance next door, I went inside to help Bev finish preparing our dinner.

TWO
JESSE THOMPSON

"HEY, MAN," I answered when I saw my best friend's name on the phone screen. I accepted the call and popped the phone into my shirt pocket. "Gotcha on speaker phone. Trying to get as much done as possible while Hadley naps."

My just-turned-five-year-old granddaughter, Hadley Nicole, didn't often take naps anymore, but I was determined to take advantage of her exhaustion from the long drive. If I was figuring right, I likely had about another hour before she would wake up and my production rate would drop like a brick.

"I'm coming over later," the voice I'd known as well as my own for the past thirty-ish years filled the air as I carried boxes from the truck. Some into the shop, some into the house, making sure to never be too far away from the baby-monitor in case Hadley needed me. "Save some work for me. You know I always wanted to see inside Old Man Spinks's house. And I've got a surprise for you."

I laughed. "Not sure surprises are what I need right now." Five years of grief, guilt, and extreme fatigue made me see surprises with anxious eyes.

"Well, what *do* you need?"

"A full night of sleep? All of these boxes unpacked? Spinks's clients to stay on and keep me in business." I sighed and stretched my back after a particularly heavy box. "Someone to help with Hadley—but the hours are shit."

"I can help with boxes. No problem. I've already heard talk around town; Spinks is giving you a lot of praise, I think most of the customers will stay." He chuckled. "You need me to rock you to sleep and stroke your back? Not sure I can help with the sleep issues. Speaking of Hadley, you ask about some night shifts at the Wishing Well?"

"Yeah, I think they're going to use me as a bouncer a few nights a week, maybe a couple weekends—they said they could possibly do evenings so I'm not gone super late. Not tons of money, but any extra helps. Just have to find someone to cover Hadley—maybe dinner, but mostly bedtime and be there while she sleeps."

It seemed somewhat counterproductive to take a

side job that would require me to pay a babysitter for my child. But Hadley needed the socialization and *I* needed the break.

Sometimes I felt selfish for it, but I'd learned early on that I was a much better parent when I took care of me as well as Hadley. Plus, bouncing at the bar gave me the chance to meet people in town— yeah, I was moving back to my hometown of so many years ago, but there were *a lot* of new people around these days. The bouncer gig would also help me feel like I was doing *something* to assuage the guilt and anger I lived with.

"Well, that's kinda part of my surprise. I'll tell you more about it when I get there." The pause in the conversation told me I wasn't necessarily going to like the next part. "How are you doing? Your therapist give you recs for someone to see here? You know I'll help in whatever way I can and I'm so damned glad you're back. But I know moving here isn't the answer to all the hurt."

I hefted another box, feeling every one of my fifty years and then some. "Moving here is for the best. I needed away from the memories. I need a fresh start to give Hadley new memories; hell, she was an infant, she doesn't have any memories of Nicole or Lauren." I tossed the box on the work bench with a little more force than necessary. "Selfishly, I'd like to think the guilt and anger will magically disappear now that I'm back; all the pain will just go away." I knew it was stupid to think that. Grief was a bitch no matter which way you sliced it.

I paused outside the shop door, standing on the little patio and walkway that led between my new auto repair shop and the house. The house sat facing the street, the shop farther back from the road, and a large apron of asphalt for parking and three bays in the large garage.

Old Man Spinks had owned the repair shop back when I was a teen. When I heard he was selling, I made a split-second decision to put in an offer and move back to my hometown. He sold me the house, the garage, and his portfolio of clients—I could only hope I was as successful as he'd always been.

I glanced toward the huge Victorian house next door and caught a glimpse of a kid with wild blond hair, a tight tie-dyed t-shirt, and ripped skinny jeans. I chuckled. Even if that had been the style when I was a teen, I never would have been able to pull it off —especially not the earrings or the stud in his chin just under his bottom lip. Although, I'd been able to make a mean tight-roll on my jeans and I'd always rocked my Converse—funny how certain things were coming back in style.

And making me feel old as fuck.

I pulled up my shirt and wiped the sweat from my brow.

"Therapy still helping with working through the issues with Nicole?"

I groaned. "It's really hard and shitty to try to fix a marriage when one of the participants is dead."

"Can't imagine it's easy; you kinda got hit with a double—no, triple—whammy."

I laughed with no humor. "Yeah, it sucks. Talking about Lauren sucks, but sometimes it seems like I'm working through that section of this shit a bit easier. Maybe. And it's hard enough to sit and talk to a stranger about Nicole's infidelity, her accusations of my detachment and disinterest, and her constant questioning of my sexuality. But try doing it when she's dead—it's like she's blaming me for her cheating, but I can't even defend myself or work through it because you can't argue with a damn ghost." I let out a long breath and went back to the truck. "We were supposed to have our first couples session the week after they died." I pinched the bridge of my nose. "I guess I can see the importance of working through the issues for myself, but it's really hard to not feel guilty when you're angry at a dead person."

"Fuck man, I'm sorry."

That's what I'd always appreciated about our

friendship. Ever since we were sixteen, we'd been able to talk—like *real talk*—and I never felt judged. We knew shit about each other that *no one* else knew and we'd take it to our graves.

"I'm pretty damn sure we were heading for divorce. She was right about me being detached. It felt like we'd lost whatever spark we *did* have a long time ago. Not even sure we ever *had* a spark, maybe just the friendship." Nicole and I had been high school sweethearts, but we broke up when she went off to college and I went to trade school. We met up again years later and picked right back up where we'd left off. She'd always been a good friend and I did love her. Our struggle to get pregnant—when I'd never been *sure* I even wanted kids—had taken a toll. But when Lauren was born as Nicole and I neared our thirties, it had seemed like maybe things were looking up.

My therapist had encouraged me to talk about my feelings for Nicole. She was a friend, a partner, a good mom to Lauren, and I enjoyed seeing her being a grandma to Hadley. Had she ever been the love of my life? My soulmate? Someone I *craved*? No. We were comfortable, but it was never that soul-searing, electric type of heat and attraction that fictional stories make you think are real.

My daughter, Lauren, had been my little buddy

from the very beginning. She and I were inseparable and never really had any parent/child issues. However, Lauren and Nicole went back and forth from the time Lauren was about eleven. We all three loved each other, but the dynamic between the three of us was very different. When Lauren got pregnant at seventeen, she and Nicole had a huge blow-up which ended in Lauren blurting out that Nicole was cheating on me.

My wife of twenty-years had recoiled as if she'd been slapped, but she didn't deny the accusation—it was more like she was pissed Lauren didn't keep her secret or take her side. She'd gone to stay with her mother for a while.

I'd been left at home with a teenage pregnancy and a very emotional daughter; but Lauren and I bucked up and made it through the rough patch. Looking back, I probably hadn't been the best dad in the world during that time. I was facing marital issues that had been growing for a while and the emotional upheaval that came from watching your baby become a parent when you weren't ready for them to be grown up.

During one of our heart-to-hearts, Lauren provided some truths and insights I maybe at the time hadn't been ready to hear. "Dad, I love you both, but neither of you have seemed *happy* for a very long time. I didn't recognize it when I was little, but I see it now. You and Mom are friends and get along fine, but you're not in love." Lauren had picked at her bedspread while I sat on the desk chair in her room.

"Couples grow and change. Not every couple will be madly in love their whole relationship," I'd argued, although, I did wonder what it would be like to have that breathless excitement about someone.

"I screwed up and got pregnant. I'm keeping the baby even if Jack isn't going to stick around." She'd snorted. "And let's be honest, it's for the best if he hightails it out of here and never looks back. He's already saying he wants to sign over his rights." She'd waved her hand. "But finding myself in this situation has given me the chance to grow up a lot in these last couple months." She'd pursed her lips. "And I'm sorry I kept it from you and Mom for so long. I was scared." She sighed and continued to pick at the thread on her bed. "I think you and Mom can be friends, but you both need something the other can't give."

I'd been able to do nothing but stare at my kid as she went on.

"I know, I know. Where was this mature, smart girl when she was getting mixed up with Jack and pregnant at seventeen?" Lauren had scoffed at herself.

"You're one of the best and smartest people I know," I'd defended.

"You have to say that, you're my dad. But my point is, I think you and Mom owe it to yourselves to say goodbye—not forever, just let go of the marriage —so you can each find what you need." Lauren had shrugged and given me a sad smile.

"Well, according to you, your mom has already found what she needs," I'd groused. I didn't like the idea of Nicole with some other guy—mainly only because it meant I'd been distracted enough not to even realize she'd been sneaking around and unhappy. But the fact that I wasn't devastated should have been a huge clue that things were over between us. If I'd been being honest with myself back then, things had been over for a very long time.

Nicole had eventually come home to be with Lauren.

I'd moved to a little apartment next to the repair shop where I was working.

We'd agreed to a trial separation at least until we got Lauren through the pregnancy and gave her the first few months of settling into motherhood. Nicole and I weren't dumb enough to think having a newborn in the house along with a teenage mom was going to make things with our marriage easier, but we did agree that we'd put off our problems for so many years, another little bit wasn't going to make a difference.

Lauren had turned eighteen and three months later, Hadley Nicole had come into the world and made me a grandpa at age forty-five.

When Hadley was six months old, Lauren and Nicole wanted to go on a family outing. I'd recently seen Nicole on a date with her newest boyfriend—despite the fact that we'd said we'd at least give therapy a shot—and I had no desire to fake my way through a family outing despite the fact I'd been faking my way through my marriage. So, I'd offered to keep a fussy Hadley at home and let my wife and daughter have a girls' day.

They'd never come home.

Hit by a drunk driver.

In the blink of an eye, I'd become a widower and the father of an infant.

Friends had come to help during that first few weeks. A few nice people from a church in town had helped with meals and babysitting Hadley—when I didn't have her strapped to my chest what seemed like twenty-four-seven. She'd gone with me to therapy which had been planned for marriage counseling, but suddenly morphed into grief counseling.

I'd somehow made it through the process of cremation and gathering my wife and daughter's ashes, filling out the proper paperwork to claim their life insurance benefits, and speaking to a lawyer to make sure Hadley was legally my daughter so that her biological father could never take back his signed away rights and try to take her.

I moved back into the home we'd all shared together, took the spare room, and reverted back to the man I'd been when Lauren was a baby. Hadley became my little shadow whenever possible and pretty much my only thought was to make her happy.

For five years, I'd survived on autopilot. Hadley was my only focus. I'd been making good money at the shop so hiring a nanny wasn't an issue. Hadley and I got by just fine. We were together every hour of the day if I wasn't working and the baby loved Miss Margie who cared for her.

Until one day, I realized I couldn't live in that house any longer.

The guilt. Was it my fault Nicole had been so unhappy? Was it my fault they were dead because I pushed them to go by themselves that day?

The memories. Pictures of Lauren with Hadley at

the park, on the porch swing, with Nicole on a walk. Those were hard. Harder still were the pictures of the three of us back when it was easy to pretend we were a happy family, a couple in love, rather than just two friends who probably had no business ever getting married and bringing a kid into the world.

The ghosts. It felt as if I saw Nicole and Lauren everywhere. It was easy to stay mad at Nicole. But I missed my baby girl. I found myself talking to Lauren a lot and hoping she was okay with the way I was taking care of Hadley.

The anger. It was too much and I didn't know how to process it on top of everything else.

The emotions were eating me alive and I needed out.

Spinks's house and garage being for sale were like a beacon of hope, a life saver in a storm I wasn't even sure I wanted to be saved from—but I had no choice. Hadley was my child and I wouldn't leave her alone. She'd already lost so much. I'd made the offer, signed the papers, packed up, and moved all within a week.

I chuckled. Which was likely why I was so damn emotionally and physically exhausted.

A voice prodded through my fog of memories. "You give any more thought to Nicole's questions about your sexuality?"

While we could usually talk about anything and

everything, I wasn't going there with him—not right then and maybe not ever. I clenched my jaw. "No. Moving through the grief and doing right by Hadley is my biggest goal right now."

He made some sort of noise that could have been an argument, could have been agreement. "Well, just don't think your moving here means you've come here to wither up and die. You and Hadley have us now, and I'm making it my damned personal goal to make sure you live your life. I'm not going to play matchmaker—I realize that's going to take time and be something only *you* can decide the who and what you're ready for—but I'm not going to have you come here convinced you deserve to live like some shell."

Not really having an answer for that, I kept quiet for a moment. As I took a final box into the house, I heard movement on the baby monitor.

Saved.

For the time being.

"Hey, could you save the surprise and the visit for tomorrow? Hadley's awake and I need to take the moving truck back. Need to look into a few more possibilities for a nanny or at least a babysitter, too."

"Sure. You have any shop appointments tomorrow?"

I snorted. "Not yet. I'm hoping to be up and running next week."

"Good. I'll be over around lunchtime."

Once the call ended, I made my way to Hadley. Sitting in the middle of her new room playing with a doll and a truck, looking like the perfect mix of her mom and grandma with her dark brown curls and green eyes, she turned to look at me with a smile. "I woked up. Can we have snacks?"

I laughed and sat down next to her. She climbed onto my lap and snuggled against my chest. How had the guy who wasn't even sure he wanted kids become a father and grandfather and actually loved it? I wanted to be the best I could be for Hadley. Lauren had been a great kid, but I worried a lot of that was Nicole's doing.

Maybe I hadn't been strict enough.

Maybe I hadn't set up enough routines and procedures.

What if I screwed my granddaughter up?

I couldn't find it in myself to be super strict with Hadley or force her into routines and procedures.

Hell, she was *five*. She was a good kid and pretty much went with the flow. Maybe she wasn't the type of kid who needed strict or routines.

She'd already lost so much—granted, she didn't have any memories of Nicole or Lauren, only what I helped to keep alive in her mind—would I be able to make sure she had all the love and support she needed as she grew up?

I kissed the top of her head and pushed down the wave of anxiety. I sure as hell hoped so. I knew I'd devote the rest of my life to making sure that little girl had what she needed.

And what about you? What about that soul-searing, electric heat, madly in love feeling you've never had? Will you ever give yourself permission to have that?

I cleared my throat and took a deep breath.

Even contemplating *that* meant opening up a whole box of issues I didn't have the emotional or mental strength to deal with.

Not then.

Maybe not ever.

So, no.

I'd make sure I got breaks and kept up with friends for socializing so I'd be the best me for Hadley.

But there was *way* too much going on in my life—Hadley being the most important—for me to even allow thoughts of a love life to take root. Plus, who in their right mind would want a relationship with a fifty-year-old, single grandfather?

"Let's get you a snack. Then we'll go on a drive to

take the truck back." I brushed Hadley's sleep-mussed hair from her face.

"Can we get cheeseburgers and French fries with ketchup?" she asked, her big green eyes blinking hopefully.

"We need to eat healthier," I said, but sighed. Cooking sounded like a total bitch since I had no idea which boxes held pots and pans. Plus, I needed to make a grocery trip. "But until we get settled, we'll go for easy."

"Yay!" Hadley hopped up and rushed to the kitchen.

At least I could get some fruits and veggies in her for a snack. Thank goodness I'd thought to pack a little cooler for the drive.

"Apples, carrots, and milk for a snack. Then we'll drive the big truck." I found the cooler and started preparing the snack. If my head and body longed for a nap and a beer, they were just going to have to get over it and remember that we had a little girl to take care of.

THREE
COOPER

"I THINK cheeseburger noodle casserole will be the best," Bev said as she gathered the ingredients for one of her dishes that I particularly loved. "I saw a little one over there earlier this morning. If he's got a child, cheesy noodles are always a good bet."

"No way he's got a kid. He's like fifty." I wrinkled my nose.

"Grandchild maybe?" Bev shrugged and set a pot of water to boil. "I think some green beans and a chocolate cake with vanilla cream icing, too," she spoke to herself as she puttered around grabbing utensils and measuring cups. The woman could make the entire meal in her sleep, she simply let me *help* because I liked to be in the kitchen with her.

"A mechanic *and* a grandfather? Dang," I

pretended to pout. "My chances are getting slimmer and slimmer."

"You know, for a smart, young gay man, you sure do have some preconceived notions. We already talked about the mechanic part. And a grandchild doesn't mean hetero, not necessarily." Bev swatted at me with a spatula. "Now, don't get me wrong, I'm not saying I know anything about the man's sexuality one way or another. I'm just saying don't make assumptions."

"I'm not looking for a husband, just some eye candy. And if he's gay and wants a fling, all the better," I teased.

"Hookups with neighbors can only lead to messy situations," Bev said with a shake of her head and a smile that said she knew I'd never listen.

"Look, all I'm saying is that he can lube my shaft and dip his stick anytime he wants and we'll be good. Not like the guy has to be more than just a neighbor."

"My Lord, child. I don't even want to know what you're talking about," Bev said sternly, but I saw her biting back a laugh.

"What? He's a mechanic, things in that profession sound dirty even when they aren't. I know a dipstick is for oil changes. I have no clue what a mechanic actually *does* when he lubes a shaft, but the term makes for a lot of fun fantasies." I dumped the noodles in the boiling water.

"If he's got a child, he likely doesn't have a lot of time for dipsticking or shaft lubing." Bev turned on the mixer as she poured flour into the cake mix.

I laughed. The woman was amazing. She'd call me on my shit *and* join in at the same time. I'd been blessed to find her and I was beyond grateful to call her a friend. "Too bad he doesn't have a kind, caring neighbor lady who likes children and may be available to help him occasionally free up his evenings for hot and heavy sex with the young twink next door." I batted my lashes and smiled innocently.

Bev cackled. "Maybe he should hope he's got a snarky yet caring neighbor boy who loves children and needs odd hours of employment."

"I'm not so sure Spencer loves children," I deadpanned.

Bev laughed and patted my cheek. "Let's just meet the new neighbors. He may be a jerk and all of this speculation and planning for clandestine meetings and shaft lubing will be for naught."

I glanced out the window and saw the man in question walking from his backdoor to the shop. "Jerk or not, have you *seen* him?"

"Cooper James Scott," she unleashed my full name and I actually cringed. "You will have more respect for yourself than that. I don't care if a man is the most attractive person on the face of this earth, you will *not* put yourself in a position of being mistreated just because he's hot. Despite what the brain between your legs may think, there is much more to life than good sex." She frowned at me. "I know we joke, but you need to put yourself on a higher pedestal and not allow for anything less than the best."

I sighed and gave a little nod. Bev was right, of course. And if I was looking for long term, I'd likely be a bit pickier. But I was young and independent. If I wanted to lust over a hot new neighbor and fantasize about dropping to my knees to suck him off in the bay of his workshop, I would.

When lunch was ready, Bev piled it all in a basket, removed her apron, and washed her hands. "Come on. Bring those pretty gray eyes and smile; let's meet the neighbors."

I took the basket from Bev's hands and followed her out the door. I would have procrastinated for at least an hour if left on my own—maybe it was a bad time, maybe the guy didn't like cheeseburger casserole, maybe he was a total hermit—but Bev marched right over to his patio with a wave.

The man was even hotter up close—like seriously, I wanted to snake my hands under his shirt and lean in to lick his nipples—and he paused in his efforts of setting up a patio set to smile.

"I'm Bev King, I'm your neighbor." She reached out a hand and I had a split-second of worry that maybe this guy wasn't friendly.

But the way he shook Bev's hand and gave a gracious welcome proved me wrong just as quickly.

"I'm Jesse," he said.

"Hi, I'm Cooper," I said, balancing the basket and sticking out my free hand.

Jesse threw a glance over his shoulder to the little girl playing with chalk on the garage apron. "That's my granddaughter, Hadley."

Hadley looked up at the mention of her name and came over with a curious look on her face. "I'm five."

I put the basket on the table and knelt down to Hadley's level. She was quite possibly one of the cutest kids I'd ever seen. "Five? Wow. So, you'll be going to Kindergarten soon?"

She nodded, big green eyes wide. "Daddy says I'll make friends and learn all my words."

I covered the confusion on my face with a smile. Jesse had said granddaughter, but Hadley called him daddy. Interesting. But likely not my business.

"Oh yeah, Daddy's right." There was something seriously wrong with my head that I could be chatting with a five-year-old and still lusting over said *Daddy*. I didn't have a Daddy/boy kink, but the thought of what that sexy silver fox could do to me was definitely turning my crank. "You'll learn colors and shapes and numbers and words."

Hadley laughed. "I know my colors and shapes. And lots of numbers. I want to read. Daddy says I'll learn at Kinnergarden."

I smiled. "You sure will. I bet you'll be able to read me a book by Christmas time."

Hadley giggled. "What's your name?"

I held out my hand. "I'm Cooper."

She shook my hand very seriously. "My name's Hadley Nicole."

"Very nice to meet you, Hadley Nicole."

The little girl soon lost interest in the conversation and went back to play with her chalk.

"We brought lunch. Didn't want to intrude, but I knew you'd need to eat. Moving is a big chore." Bev patted the basket.

"That's so nice of you," Jesse said with a tired smile. "Can't say I'm not exhausted. Would you like to sit? I need a break and I'll need to feed Hadley pretty soon."

"There's sweet tea in the basket. I put some cups in there too. Do you have ice?" Bev popped open the lid and pulled out a large thermos.

Jesse's eyes lit up. "*That* I actually do have. Let

me go get a bowl." He headed into the house after a quick check on Hadley.

"Put your tongue back in your mouth and stop panting like a dog," Bev muttered next to me as she set up the cups.

"I can't help it," I chuckled. "He's *hot*."

Jesse came back with a bowl of ice and we settled in at the table to drink tea and visit. I wasn't sure I'd ever be able to live in a super tiny town *or* a large city, but Remington was the perfect size. You didn't know *everyone*, but you could be friendly with neighbors and count on a close circle of friends and family if you wanted them. Chatting on a patio with sweet tea in hand was just one of the things I loved about the easy-going town.

"I love your house," Jesse's eyes traveled over Remington Place. "Can't imagine the history inside those walls. How long have you lived there?"

"I bought it a while back, but didn't move in until about five years ago. I was going to make it a bed and breakfast, but found out I was pretty good at running a boarding house."

"A boarding house? What does that entail?" Jesse sipped his tea.

Bev smiled and patted my arm. "Pretty much the exact same as if I lived there by myself, but I've got this one, his brother and his girlfriend, and their friend, plus room for a few more. They pay a set rent and help me around the house. I give them a safe and loving place, a bed, and food."

"Kinda like a house mother?" Jesse cocked his head. "That's great. I love it. From the smells coming from that basket, your boarders are very lucky to have you cooking for them."

"You like to cook?" I asked.

"I like to eat," Jesse joked with a smile.

Something about the man made me feel as if I knew him, but I couldn't put my finger on it. *Probably because you've been stalking him since he first showed up.*

"I can cook the basics. I like to grill. Luckily, Hadley was raised on my cooking so she's used to it." A loving smile filled his face as he gazed at the little girl. "She's been loving the fact that we need to get groceries and I've got to unpack the kitchen boxes because we've been eating more fast food. Nothing that kid loves more than fries with ketchup. She's always been a good eater, though. She usually won't *pick* to eat veggies, but she'll tolerate them when they're put on her plate."

"Well, I love to cook and do it daily. We'd love to have you and Hadley as dinner guests from time-to-time." Bev smiled fondly at Hadley who was now dancing around the asphalt with a ribbon. "Are you new to Remington or just this part of town?"

Jesse cleared his throat. "Actually, grew up here, so it's a homecoming of sorts. I've been gone for a long time, looks like a lot has changed."

"Probably some, but I can guarantee a lot has stayed the same." Bev swatted at an insect flying by her head. "I used to move all over with my parents and then my late husband. Moving to Remington was the best thing I ever did. When Jerry died, I sold our little house on the other side of town and made Remington Place my home. It's where I'll die."

"Oh, that's not morbid or anything." I deadpanned.

Bev chuckled. "I just call it like I see it. Don't worry, I've got several more years to keep you in food and chores."

I whispered to Jesse. "The food is so good, I'd do double the chores if she asked. But don't let her know. I don't particularly like to clean the toilets."

Hadley came rushing over, pushing her dark curly hair from her eyes. Her dark hair didn't match Jesse's caramel brown with silver streaks and her green eyes were a far cry from his deep brown ones. I couldn't help but wonder about their family situation. It did *not* bypass my attention that Jesse wasn't wearing a ring and the conversation so far had indicated it was just him and Hadley.

"Daddy, I'm hungry."

"Well, that's my cue. I need to clean up the kitchen and I've got a date with a cup of tea." Bev stood up. "You enjoy the meal and just return the dishes when you have a moment."

I panicked, not wanting to leave, but not sure how to earn an invite to stay. "Hadley, do you like cheeseburger noodles?"

The little girl's eyes went wide. "I like cheeseburgers and noodles."

"You're going to *love* Ms. Bev's lunch she made for you." I stood and launched right into getting the plates and silverware out. "Can you go wash your hands, please?"

Jesse gawked at me, his face a mixture of *Who the fuck are you, get off my property* and *You're my knight in shining armor, where have you been all my life.* "You're good with kids."

"Should be. I'm an early elementary major, work at a preschool, and plan to open my own preschool at some point." I shrugged at his look of surprise mixed with curiosity and scooped up casserole and green beans. "Sorry, I didn't mean to just take over. I can leave."

"No, no. Stay. Hadley loves to have visitors. We

don't know many people in town yet." He smiled sadly. "One of the things I worry I've short-changed her on is socialization."

"School will be great for her. I'm not officially licensed yet, but I can tell she's going to do well. She's bright and eager. She'll make friends in no time and you'll be planning playdates before you know it." I put the plate of food on the table.

Jesse looked horrified. "Oh shit, I never thought about playdates. I've barely survived my own, I can't take care of other people's kids."

I laughed. "One step at a time. Maybe you'll luck out with a super cute neighbor who would be more than happy to help with a playdate." *And more than happy to help with* anything *you might need. Seriously,* anything.

Jesse sputtered. "Yeah, maybe." Seemingly attempting to ignore my comment, he turned and hollered toward the house. "Hadley!"

"Can I ask..." I started, but Hadley came busting out the backdoor.

"Cheeseburgers and noodles!" she exclaimed with a giggle.

I had to do some persuading when she realized the lunch wasn't actual cheeseburgers and noodles, but after I took some bites and Jesse declared it one of the best things he'd ever tasted—and he wasn't even putting on a show—she took a little bite and a smiled filled her face.

"See, I told you it was delish. Eat some cheesy noodles and green beans first, and I can let you in on the secret of where there's some amazing chocolate cake." I made a silly face and Hadley laughed as she gobbled up more noodles.

Jesse offered me a plate, but I shook my head. "Nah, thanks. You guys keep the leftovers. I'll eat with Bev later." I gestured toward the garage. "Are you keeping the garage open?"

Jesse nodded around a bite of casserole. "Yeah. Spinks had the garage back when I was a teenager. Hadley and I needed a new location for—well, for a lot of reasons—so, when I saw he was selling the house and the garage, I jumped at it."

"Did you get to keep the customers?" I poured some more tea.

"Yep. Well, he included his client portfolio in the sale. I guess it's up to me to *keep* them as customers. I'm hoping most will at least give me a chance." He savored a bite of green beans. "Why do my green beans never taste this good?" he groaned and I immediately knew I needed to hear that sound over and over again.

"It's the lard. I swear, it sounds gross, but Bev

uses a bit of lard in a lot of her dishes and it's totally a magic ingredient." I shrugged.

"That should turn me off, but these are so good, I can't help it."

We enjoyed the nice day and comfortable silence for a moment until a thought hit me. It was definitely crazy, but…

I was crushing on Jesse big time, no doubt about that. Gay or not, I knew without question that I wanted to spend time around the man. Would it be setting me up for heartache? Maybe. But the main thing I had going for me was I wasn't looking for love or anything serious. If Jesse was straight, I'd enjoy a friend's company and have some material for my fantasies. If he ended up being bi or gay or pan, maybe I'd luck out with a friends-with-benefits situation. Either way, I wasn't going to get the chance if I didn't jump right in.

I cleared my throat. "So, you have a babysitter for Hadley? How does your schedule work?"

Jesse, finished with his food, placed his plate on the table and sighed. "Well, aside from being a single parent, moving to a new place, opening a new business, and dealing with a ton of other stuff I won't bore you with right now…" he paused to take a drink.

No, no, please bore me. I want to hear it all.

"Childcare is my biggest conundrum right now." He helped Hadley wipe her hands and face and told her she could have cake when her tummy wasn't so full. She giggled and patted her tummy before running off to play again. "When she was a baby, I either took her everywhere I went or the nanny watched her. The move was the best thing for us, but we left behind Miss Margie and now I'm stuck in my hometown—where I basically know no one anymore—with no nanny, no babysitter, and no clue how I'm going to make it work."

My gut clenched for the guy. I could tell he was stressing. "What hours are you needing?"

"Well, that's the biggest issue. I need someone who can be here in the mornings to get Hadley either on the bus or dropped at school and then do pick up or be here when the bus arrives in the afternoon. Help with afterschool time. Maybe help with dinner if I'm working late in the shop. And I may work down at the Wishing Well as a bouncer a few nights a week so I'd need someone to do bedtime and be here while Hadley sleeps." He ran a hand over his face. "Not many people have hours like that available. And I'm paying over minimum wage, but it's not like the position is rolling in dough. A retired person would maybe have the time, but likely not be available every single day. But I can't trust just some kid, you know? And I'd kinda like to have *one* person to give the kid some consistency."

I took a deep breath to calm the butterflies in my stomach. "This is crazy, almost like fate brought us together."

Jesse frowned. "Huh? Why?"

"I've been looking for a job, but I've not had any luck. You know why? Because I need early morning and afternoons, plus I have some evening hours available."

He stared at me for several moments almost as if he was waiting for me to say I was joking. "Are you serious?"

I nodded. "Completely. There are three things I don't joke about."

He cocked his head.

"The need for employment, good sex, and good food."

He chuckled. "I can't believe you just said that."

"I'm a greedy bottom, I never joke about good sex." I shrugged and gave him a wink over my cup.

Jesse choked on his tea. "Okay, moving on." But the flush on his neck had me *very* intrigued. "Before I get too excited about this."

"The good sex?" I deadpanned.

He pinched the bridge of his nose. "The possible position."

"I like pretty much any position." I bit my lip.

He clenched his jaw and fought back what appeared to be a grin mixed with a grimace. "Can you be serious for a moment?"

I started to tell him I was *very* serious, but even my lack of filter knew when to stop. I gestured for him to continue.

"What are your available morning hours?"

"I could be here as early as six and stay until nine if needed. I have a nine-thirty to three-thirty shift at the preschool in the next town over where I do my on-site practicum hours. It's a pretty sweet gig—I get very little pay, enough maybe to put gas in my tank, but I get the hours and the experience. So, it's pretty much like a very poorly paid internship." I pulled the cake from the basket. I wouldn't cut a piece for myself, but if it was offered, there was no way I was turning it down.

"Hadley's bus is scheduled to pick up at nine o'clock or she can be dropped off at nine-fifteen." He pulled out his phone and scrolled through something. "And she can be picked up from school at three-forty-five or the bus drops off here at four o'clock," he read from his phone.

I smiled broadly. "That's amazingly perfect timing. Do you know if she wants to ride the bus?"

He chuckled. "She's *dying* to ride the bus."

"That would likely be the best set up as long as you're okay with it." I attempted to stop my knee from bouncing, but it was useless. "What do the evening hours look like?"

"The Wishing Well said I could probably have three evenings a week. Their Friday and Saturday nights are covered, but they said I had my pick of Monday through Thursday. The offer was seven to eleven or eleven to three."

I grimaced. "I could definitely do the seven to eleven. Eleven to three would mess up my sleep too much."

When he narrowed his eyes, I shrugged. "I have ADHD." I nodded toward my bouncing knee and the way I'd shredded a napkin. "Sleep can be very hard for me—shutting down my brain and all, but I have to have sleep or I'm a mess. The meds help a lot, but if I'm exhausted, I can't function."

"No worries, the earlier shift sounded better anyway. Would Monday, Tuesday, Wednesday work?" He took the cover off the cake and cut three slices. "Hadley goes to bed around eight so you'd have time to do homework or whatever."

I liked the sound of *or whatever* and my mind let a

little fantasy scene play out. Would sex on a car in his shop be considered inappropriate? I chuckled to myself and shook my head. "Yeah, that works." I twisted the other napkin in my hand. "Not to sound greedy, but what's the pay?"

He took a deep breath. "I've been doing the math and right now, all I can do is ten an hour for the before and after school. And eight an hour for the evenings." He winced, waiting for my response.

I frowned. "So, something you need to know about me, aside from the ADHD, I have dyscalculia so numbers are difficult—like, that's an understatement. I can't figure out in my head exactly what that amount would be, but it sounds fair. I know a lot of places I was looking for jobs were between eight and ten an hour. It's not a career salary, but Bev charges me a very fair rent and I don't have a lot of bills outside of my phone, car, and insurance."

"I'll pretend I didn't say this if you want," Jesse lowered his voice as if getting ready to tell me a deep, dark secret, "but I can pay the evening hours in cash only so you don't have to worry about taxes."

My eyes went wide. "You'd do that?" I wasn't completely sure about skirting taxes, but tax-free money was a definite bonus.

"I can claim the daily pay on my taxes, evening pay can be unofficial."

Why in the hell did my stomach flip-flop at the idea of what other unofficial pay we could set up for the evenings?

"Hadley starts school in a few weeks, right?"

Jesse nodded with a groan. "Yeah. So much to do between now and then."

"What do you say we spend the next few weeks getting to know each other." Yes, I totally meant any possible innuendo that may have been read into that. "Hadley and I will get into a routine. Then we'll all three be ready for the first day of school. And you can ease into your shop work and the Wishing Well." I wrinkled my nose. "Just out of curiosity, why a bouncer at a bar?"

Jesse's eyes clouded. "So, while we're being honest, there's something you should know. My old therapist—by the way, I'm in need of a new one if you've got recs—was working with me on talking openly about the past."

I fought the urge to put a hand on his leg. Probably wouldn't have the comforting effect I was going for, so I just waited.

"Hadley's mom and grandma were killed by a drunk driver five years ago." Pain washed over his face. "So, bouncing at a bar is two-fold. Keeps me sane with adult interaction *and* allows me to hopefully stop people who have had too much to drink. Kinda like my little bit of making it up to them and Hadley."

At that point, I couldn't stop myself and my hand moved to his knee as I leaned forward in my chair. "A drunk driver wasn't your fault. You know that right?" Something niggled at the back of my brain as if there was something I was missing. "But I can see why you'd want to do it." My hand felt as if it would catch fire; I didn't want to move it, but the uncertainty on Jesse's face as he stared at where we touched was too much so I jerked my hand away.

"Hadley, come eat some cake," he cleared his throat and called to his granddaughter.

My phone buzzed.

DAD: *I'm coming over. I have a surprise for you.*

FIVE MINUTES LATER, as I pretended to eat Hadley's cake—because I'd already inhaled my own —I heard my dad's voice as he came up the driveway.

"Well, damn. You ruined my surprise."

Jesse's eyes went wide right before he groaned.

"Robby," he said as he stood up with a look of—was that resignation?—on his face.

My brain attempted to make sense of what was happening.

"How did I ruin the surprise? I don't get it." Sometimes it felt as if I was still that kid who could never catch up despite my brain running a thousand miles an hour. I stood to hug my dad and then watched in absolute confusion as he moved to pull Jesse into a hug.

"I was going to introduce you two, but you've already met. Should have known Bev would send you over with food," Dad said as he slapped Jesse on the back. "CJ, this is my oldest and best friend, Jesse. Jess, this is my son, Cooper."

Jesse's face went a bit pale. "I don't think you've ever called him anything but CJ."

"Yeah, it's a nickname he hasn't appreciated since he was young, but it's a hard habit to break." Dad put an arm around me. "But I'm working on using *Cooper* exclusively."

"I should have put two-and-two together," I mumbled. All of a sudden, Dad's story about his best friend losing his wife and daughter came back to me and slotted in perfectly with Jesse's story and timeline.

Holy shit.

Jesse was my dad's best friend.

The silver fox daddy hottie I had just agreed to work for and wanted to climb like a tree was *my dad's best friend*.

I settled in to listen to Dad and Jesse catch up while my mind whirled with a mixture of thoughts and emotions.

By the time I told Hadley and Jesse goodbye and walked my dad back to his car, I couldn't decide if all of my previous fantasies about Jesse needed to take a flying leap or if the challenge that was Jesse just got a whole lot bigger and more exciting.

I waved to Dad and headed back toward the house as an argument played through my head.

Jesse was now essentially my employer.

He should be off limits.

Jesse was a single father with a shit ton of baggage.

He should be off limits.

Jesse was Dad's best friend.

He should be doubly off limits.

Yet, as I climbed the stairs to my room, I bit back a wicked grin. All of a sudden, I couldn't help but feel like *off limits* was just another word for *hell yeah*.

FOUR
JESSE

My phone buzzed.

Robby: Shit, I got so distracted by you and Coop meeting, I forgot to see the house and help out. I'm coming back over.

Robby: How cool is this shit? You're back in town and I can come over any damn time I please. I hope you know you better stock the fridge with beer.

Me: I'm here. Can't get drunk, have to do bedtime later, but come on over.

I laughed at my best friend.

He'd never change.

He'd been scattered and distractible as fuck ever since we met way back during our teenage years. He struggled with reading. Not because he couldn't read, but he couldn't stay focused on the story long enough to follow it. He never sat still. He could come talk to you five times and never actually remember to tell you what he needed to tell you.

But he was a genius in math. I wasn't exactly sure how he made teaching middle school math work, but I knew numbers were totally his thing.

"Numbers make sense. When I'm working on math problems, it's like everything just falls into place. Like I get this calm over me," Robby had told me once.

I wondered briefly if his wife, Celeste, had trouble with numbers like Cooper. The kid had gotten his dad's fidgets for sure—maybe his scatteredness, too. Was Robby's *love* of numbers and Cooper's dyscalculia a point of contention between them?

I thought back to Cooper's bouncing knee and shredded napkin. He'd pretty much moved the entire time we talked, but I hadn't been bothered by it. Maybe because I'd gotten so used to it with Robby all those years ago.

It was really overwhelming to be dealing with the move and all that had led to it, but I was feeling so damned relieved to be back in town with my best friend so close. We hadn't seen each other in years and years, but we'd kept in touch almost daily and nothing had changed between us. We were still Jesse and Robby, best friends from way back when. I trusted him with my life and knew he felt the same. I'd known Celeste in school, but they hadn't started dating until college, so I wasn't super close to the woman. I had a feeling anyone who had put up with and loved Robby for this long would be an easy person to like.

I trusted Robby and, by extension, I trusted Celeste. Did that mean I could also trust Cooper?

I sighed as Hadley squealed when I pulled her bike out of the garage. "Helmet and pads, stay here by the garage," I told her.

I'd had an immediate *something* with Cooper. He was great with Hadley, seemed responsible, and made me smile. If I was being honest with myself, I liked the kid. Like *really* liked the kid. Yes, I needed to keep reminding myself he was a *kid* because at least *part* of the something had been an attraction.

And that needed to be nipped in the bud right away.

I hadn't *ever* let myself see any guys as attractive. Not because I didn't find myself in that situation, but I was married, I was *straight*, and I wasn't going to mess anything up by exploring something I didn't even completely understand.

If I was younger and single *and* I'd had time to allow for a curiosity—I was sure that was *all* it was—

maybe I'd have contemplated the way Cooper made my stomach flutter and how I wanted to call him on his flirting and see what he'd do.

But me liking Cooper beyond a friendly neighbor/nanny type relationship was a bad, bad thing.

Out.

Of.

The.

Question.

For several reasons.

Cooper was twenty-five.

Twenty-five.

Fuck. Lauren would have been twenty-three this year.

I pinched the bridge of my nose as I took a seat to watch Hadley. She looked so much like Lauren—loved riding her bike just like her mom—that my heart clenched.

I could *not* have any sort of *anything* with a kid who was basically my dead daughter's age.

Lauren wanted you to be happy. You know she knew you and Nicole were having a rough time of it. She straight up told you needed to find what you needed to be happy.

I pushed the thought away. I didn't think my late daughter had been trying to tell me to discover my bisexuality and bone my best friend's son.

A deep groan filled my chest.

Even if Cooper's age and the fact that he was soon going to be my employee wasn't a problem—along with the part about me not being gay or bi or whatever—he was Robby's son.

My best friend's son.

Robby and I had been friends for well over half our lives. We knew everything about each other—the good and the bad—and would do anything to help the other out. I loved him like a brother.

There was *no way*—even if I could look past all the other stuff—even if I could admit to myself that I'd spent over two decades ignoring the fact that an attractive guy could turn me on as much if not more than a pretty girl—there was *no way* I could get involved with my best friend's kid.

That was sacrilege.

A major violation of the friend code.

Just *asking* to lose the person who had been by my side for over three decades.

I mean, how would that even work? I scrubbed my hands down the thighs of my jeans. *"Hey, Robby. Just thought you should know that I think your kid is fucking sexy as hell and I'd really like your blessing to bend him over my workbench and fuck his brains out."*

A choked laugh tumbled from me, causing Hadley to look my way and wave.

I waved back and ground my teeth together.

I needed to find someone else to do the nanny thing.

I needed to stay as far away from Cooper Scott as possible.

No one had ever stirred longings in me the way that kid did. I'd *never* allowed myself to imagine sex with a man.

Until Cooper walked into my life and unleashed decades of thoughts and feelings and curiosities I thought I'd locked away for good.

But he needed the hours. I needed the help.

Maybe we really were brought together by fate.

Fine. I was a professional. I could keep things between us completely on the up-and-up. Plus—and I needed to keep reminding myself of the fact—I had a shit ton of baggage from my marriage and the death of Nicole and Lauren. I had no intention, no *right*, to be thinking about involving another person in my life.

And what the hell would I even know about being with a man.

My cock stirred as if to say it had plenty of ideas.

I coughed and stood up, stalking to the garage to tackle more boxes.

Like Cooper would even be interested in an old

man I thought as I sliced open the flaps of a box labeled *bathroom*.

He seemed pretty damn interested by the way he flirted.

With a growl, I tossed the box cutter down and yanked the box off the table. "Hadley, let's take a bathroom break while I unload this box. I'll get you a drink and then you can ride some more."

Thirty-minutes later, a knock sounded at the door as I put a lid on a cup of apple juice. I'd used the last of the jug I'd brought with us. *Damn.* I really needed to get to the grocery store.

Robby stood on the other side of the door with a huge grin. "Let me in. I wanna see the place." He bounced on the balls of his feet looking very much like Cooper, except the younger Scott man had gray eyes and crazy blond hair while Robby's hair was buzzed short and his eyes more of a blue.

He slapped me on the back as he walked through the door. "Hey, Hadley," he said as he gave her a wave and a smile.

She gave a little wave.

"This is Robby, remember my best friend from when I was little?" I threw my arm around Robby's shoulders. "He's Cooper's dad." *Fuck.* Why did I have to put that out there?

She smiled a bit and nodded. "Can I go ride my bike?"

One thing I loved about the new place was that Hadley had a huge amount of play area and it was fenced. I'd already shown her where she wasn't allowed to go, but I wasn't hesitant about her being outside for a bit without me. I was slowly learning to let go, which I knew was good for both of us.

"Yes, stay where I told you." I helped her put her safety gear back on. "Robby and I will be out in a minute, he wants to see the house."

About twenty-minutes later, after Robby had seen the inside of the new place, we headed outside. I checked on Hadley and motioned to the shop.

As I tossed him a box cutter, Robby continued his chatter about the house. "Used the think Spinks was the meanest fucker in town, figured his house was all dark and dismal." He laughed as he tore open a box. "But I really like the place. I guess a few things could use updating, but it looks like he did quite a bit not too long ago. It's not nearly as old as Remington Place," he gestured toward Bev's house, "I think I've heard a story about how the original house burned and this was the one built to replace it. The upstairs is great; Hadley can have her own space while you have your own place downstairs. And that basement is totally livable if needed." He cocked his brow. "Not pushing or anything, but it's good that as Hadley gets older she'll be able to have her area and *you* can have your area—like to be on your own with a *friend* or someone who may come visit." He winked and laughed. "You should totally check with Cooper about how to make the upstairs area kid-friendly. He's amazing with kids. He can help at least decorate it and help Hadley make it feel like *her* space."

I gave a little nod. "Really glad he's good with kids," I hedged. "We were talking earlier and I think we may have stumbled upon a mutually beneficial situation."

Robby paused long enough to frown in confusion. "How's that?" *Shit.* Was I imagining that he seemed defensive and protective?

"Well, I've been struggling to find a nanny to help with Hadley because the hours aren't great."

Robby's eyes went wide. "And CJ has been all over town looking for a job that could work with his available hours. That's great, man; I was actually going to suggest that he could babysit, but I hadn't thought of a full-on nanny position. You're going to *love* him. Always wished we'd stayed in the same town so we'd have known each other's kids." He grimaced. "Would have loved to know Lauren."

I blinked my stinging eyes. "Yeah, you would have loved her. Hang with Hadley for more than a few minutes and you'll get a good picture of her mom. She's so much like Lauren at that age it hurts sometimes just to look at her."

Robby gestured toward the refrigerator in the back of the shop. "You got any beer in there yet?"

I laughed as the pain in my heart eased a bit. "Man, I have ice and a roll of toilet paper. I'm in desperate need of a grocery trip."

Robby held up a finger and rushed from the garage. "Hadley, go ask Gramps if you can have a juice box," I heard him ask from the driveway.

She giggled. "He's not Gramps, he's Daddy!"

I rolled my eyes at the name. Robby loved the fact that he was half a year older, but *I* was the grandfather.

"Can I have a juice box?" Hadley asked as she sipped from her half-full cup.

I laughed. "Sure. Can you run inside and put your cup in the fridge?"

Robby returned with a cooler. "I came prepared. Six-packs for all!" He pulled out a six pack of beer and then waggled his brow when he produced a six-pack of juice boxes.

"You know the way to both our hearts." I laughed. "Cold, too? Impressive."

Robby pulled a box off for Hadley and two cans for us before placing the rest in the refrigerator just as Hadley came running back into the shop.

"Here ya go, Hads," Robby said as he handed her the box with the straw already popped through.

"Thank you," Hadley said shyly before taking a drink and running back to ride her bike.

"So, when is CJ—sorry, Cooper, hard habit to break. He says he doesn't mind since it's just the nickname we always called him, but I'm trying. When does he start working for you?"

I explained the set-up Cooper and I had talked about, including the Wishing Well shifts in the evenings.

"That sounds perfect. I can't help much with the school hours, but if Coop is ever not available for the evenings, give us a holler. Celeste and I would be happy to babysit." Robby took a long swig of his beer.

I shook my head. "I don't want to get in the habit of taking advantage of people."

"Shut up," he scoffed. "Celeste and I *love* kids and we miss little ones. Dalton and Gabby *may* have kids someday, but it's a while off, I'm sure. And Cooper *loves* kids and may want some of his own, but he's too focused on getting his degree and having a whole school of preschoolers right now. We'd *love* to hang with Hadley and get to know her; give us a little experience with what being grandparents will be like." He poked a finger at my chest. "I'm not joking. You better have us babysit."

"The pay isn't great," I hedged.

"Damn, man. You're a total buzzkill these days. Like we'd accept *pay* for playing with your kid? I know Coop needs the money, but Celeste and I would be doing it just to help. No worries." He took another drink before opening a box. "I seriously can't tell you how glad I am that you're back. Plus, you and Cooper are going to be friends. I love it. I think you'll be really good for him."

I swallowed a groan with a swig of beer.

"He's a really good kid. Struggled a lot as a kid if you can remember my stories. But he's resilient and determined as fuck. Never been more proud of someone. We had a few go-rounds when we were figuring out his dyscalculia; I had a hard time understanding how anyone couldn't find numbers natural." He grimaced. "But I eventually learned a lot about it and realized his struggles with numbers are as frustrating and real as my struggles with words." Robby tossed his empty beer can in the trash. "Honestly, his issues with numbers was harder for me to wrap my head around than him being gay. Remember when he came out to me?"

I nodded and took a deep breath. "Yeah, you were like *Okay, we love you. What do you need from us? You* took it all in stride. I'm glad you and Celeste could be that for him."

Robby cleared his throat. "Not sure how any parent could *not* accept their kid for who they are." He gazed at the house next door. "It's almost harder to know *both* my kids choose to live with Bev than to live with Celeste and me."

"Nah, I don't see it that way." I grabbed two more cans from the fridge and handed one to Robby. "Think about when we were their ages. We wanted to be on our own more than anything, but sometimes having that built-in circle of friends and safety was a lifesaver. They love you guys, but living with your parents is different. You're lucky you get to see them so often. What they've got with Bev is the perfect set-up. On their own, a parental figure, learning responsibility, yet *not* doing it under your thumb."

Robby frowned. "Sometimes I've got to admit that I hate they'd rather live with Bev. Don't get me wrong, she's an amazing person and I trust her from here until forever with my boys. But why do they like to be around her, but can't bring themselves to live with us?"

"Dude," I elbowed him, "they're twenty-five and twenty-nine. *We* definitely didn't want to live with our parents at those ages. Hell, we were both getting married and becoming parents around that time." I took a drink. "I think Bev's place gives them the chance to save money, live with friends, be on their own, still be close to you guys, and figure out what they need and want without being completely on their own. Except for Bev living there, too, it's really not that different than living in a house with multiple roommates." I tipped my can toward Remington Place. "I doubt they'll be there more than a few more years at the most. And you can only hope they stay nearby; don't miss out on this time of having them near."

Robby groaned. "Shit, man. I'm sorry. I'm bitching because my kids don't live with me; I should be grateful I have them around." He slapped my shoulder.

I shrugged. "See things differently when you've lost a child."

We unpacked things for a while, chatting easily as we carried items to the proper places in the house.

"So, um, about Cooper," I started. "He's responsible? Not a big partier? Not going to have to worry about him having random guys around Hadley?"

The thought of having to see Cooper romantically involved with any guy made me want to launch my beer at the wall.

"Nah, he's snarky as shit and has no filter, but he never really got into the party scene. He's dated a lot, but has never had any inclination to settle down from what I can tell. He's gotten a lot more focused on his schooling and career in the last year. I think he's so close to the end he can *taste* it and it's got him super determined." Robby did a few squats— always on the move. "I think between the job with you, his hours at the preschool, and homework, he'll be too busy for too much dating. Remington doesn't really have a huge gay scene, but the neighboring towns have bars Coop's talked about." He shrugged and swung his arms in circles. "Kinda weird to think about your kid hooking up, but I'd assume he's got those apps for when he's needing some physical shit."

I laughed at the look of *ugh* on Robby's face— mostly because if I didn't laugh, I'd likely bite through my tongue thinking about Cooper hooking up with some guy from an app. One, because imagining him having sex was so very wrong, but so very hot. Two, because if I was going to be a total perv and think about my best friend's son having sex, I sure as hell was going to have it be with me. Which meant I was going to burn in hell.

Fuck.

An hour later, it was time to get Hadley washed up and fed.

"Man, thanks for your help." I slapped Robby on the back. "I'm so damn glad to be here. Let me know what Celeste says about therapists I should maybe look into."

Robby ruffled Hadley's hair before giving me a hug. "This is good. Take care of Cooper for me. If I can't be there, at least I know you'll be by his side to make sure he doesn't screw up with something stupid."

As I watched Robby walk toward his car, I couldn't help the moan that escaped my lips. "Who's going to keep me from screwing up and doing something stupid?" I mumbled.

You are, you asshole. You're a grown man. You can push away curiosities and urges. This is a friendly professional relationship, nothing more. You will not let it become anything more.

Three hours later, dinner cleaned up, Hadley's bath and bedtime routine finished, I found myself showering away the exhaustion of the day.

And thinking about Cooper.

The kid's face hadn't left my mind since the moment we met.

His flirty chatter ran on a loop through my head.

And despite cursing at myself, I found my fist

wrapped around my cock, stroking hard as I imagined Cooper on his knees in front of me. His gorgeous gray eyes staring up at me, his soft pink lips stretched around my shaft, his fingers playing with my balls.

With a groan, I shot my release against the shower wall.

Jacking off hadn't been on the list of my top priorities since losing my wife and daughter. Not that I didn't do it from time-to-time, but it was more just a means to an end.

Not an imaginative fantasy.

Even when I did give in, I'd never let myself imagine being with another man.

And I'd never come so hard in my entire life as I did with Cooper starring in my fantasy.

I pressed my forehead against the cool tile as I caught my breath.

When I walked from the bathroom into the main bedroom downstairs, wrapped only in a towel, I glanced out the window toward Remington Place.

A light was on in the kitchen and a room on the second floor.

The second-floor window had the blinds open.

And a nearly naked Cooper stood framed in the window as he stared down at me.

We were far enough apart that I couldn't see

specifics, but I could easily make out his slim build, pale skin, and the bulge in his bikini-cut underwear.

Fuck. I was so damned screwed.

After nearly swallowing my tongue, I gave a little wave and yanked down the blind on my bedroom window.

How in the holy fuck was I going to work with Cooper and *not* let something happen?

Be a damn professional and push it out of your mind. The kid can't be interested. You're twice his age and his dad's best friend. Get over yourself.

I wanted to believe what my mind was telling me.

Then why did it feel like Cooper was an animal, his sights locked on me, ready for the attack?

And I wasn't sure I was strong enough to outrun him.

Not even sure I wanted to.

FIVE
COOPER

THE NEXT MORNING, I pulled on a pair of jeans and a t-shirt with my Cons and hurried down the stairs.

Bev met me in the kitchen. "You want French toast?" she asked with a wave of her spatula as she stood at the stove.

"Mmm, yes, please." I poured a cup of coffee.

"You seem bright-eyed and bushy-tailed this morning," Bev said with narrowed eyes. "What's gotcha in such a good mood?"

I shrugged. "Jesse and I talked after you left. He needs someone to watch Hadley before and after school and my hours work perfectly." I took the plate she handed me and made my way to the table just as Spencer walked in.

"Smells good, any left?" he asked Bev with a kiss to her cheek.

"Of course, grab some coffee and sit down."

Spencer smacked the back of my head lightly as he walked by with his cup of coffee. "Morning. What were you saying about a job?"

"New neighbor has a kid starting school. He's going to be reopening the garage and needs someone to help with Hadley before and after school. My available hours are perfect." I slathered butter on the French toast.

"No shit? That's great. I was going to offer you some hours with my crew, but I knew you'd hate it." Spencer stirred cream into his coffee.

I laughed. "Yeah, not only would *I* hate it, you'd regret it within five minutes and likely get fired when I demolished something." I gestured toward myself. "This perfection may be beautiful and fabulous, but I'm not exactly mechanical."

Spencer snorted. "So, who's the guy next door?" he asked just as Dalton walked into the kitchen with Gabby by his side.

Dalton and Gabby were super cute together and were pretty much the picture-perfect couple. I was glad my brother was happy and in love.

Even if I had no desire for the same.

Okay, *happy* yes. *In love?* Not necessary.

"His name's Jesse Thompson," I answered around a huge bite of buttery, syrupy bread.

Dalton frowned. "Why does that name sound familiar?"

I nodded. "I thought so, too. Maybe not so much the name, but there was *something* about him that made me think I should know him."

"And?" Dalton pressed.

"Turns out the new neighbor is Dad's old best friend," I said with a shrug. As if feigning nonchalance would make it no big deal.

Bev's head whipped around and her wide eyes stared at me. "You don't say."

I nodded and ignored Bev. I knew she'd have a lot to say about me horn-doggin' over the neighbor now that I knew he was Dad's friend.

Dalton nodded. "Yeah, that's right. We never met the guy, but Dad always talked about him." He handed a cup of coffee to Gabby before holding out two plates for Bev to fill with French toast slices. "He's the one whose wife and daughter were killed a while back, right?"

I pressed my lips together. "Yeah. Hadley is five. She calls him Daddy, but he introduced her as his granddaughter. I don't know the whole story, but I think she was just a baby when the accident happened." I washed down a bite with a swig of coffee. I knew the others around the table didn't understand it, but they drank coffee to wake themselves up, I drank it to calm my fidgets before my medicine kicked in. "I'm going to be spending the next couple weeks getting to know Hadley and figuring out the new routine so when school starts we're ready."

Spencer cocked his head. "You going over there today?"

I swallowed thickly knowing either or both my brother and best friend would easily see through me. "Yeah, thought I'd offer to go to the store with them. Hadley seemed okay with me, but the better buddies we can become, the easier her first few days of school will be. Dad texted me something about how I needed to help Jesse set up the upstairs so it would be something Hadley could call her own."

"Let's plan on beers and cards tonight," Dalton said, leaving no room for argument. "Gabby's got plans with friends." He leaned over and kissed her cheek. "We'll have a guys' night."

My stomach flipped. Shit. Dalton and Spencer would see through me or badger me until they got it out of me. Then they'd spend the whole night telling me why I was an idiot to think I could have any sort of crush on my new employer.

I wasn't saying they were *wrong*. I just didn't want to deal with them.

But there was no way out and I knew it.

So, I nodded. "Sounds good. I'll be here." I stood and took a final sip of my coffee before rinsing my dishes and putting them in the dishwasher. "Gonna head over and see what kind of help Jesse might need. See you later." I gave a wave and bounded down the back steps.

Pausing outside of the house where I was hidden from prying eyes inside both houses, I did some squats, ran in place, and swung my arms in circles. I was my normal fidgety, but also nervous.

Not only was I barging into Jesse's personal life and inviting myself to go shopping with him, I had *clearly* not given enough thought to the ramifications of last night's little window peep show.

I'd found myself wired and unable to settle even after a shower and swinging. When I'd stripped from my clothes, determined to go to bed even if it meant lying there for an hour while my brain unwound, I'd danced around my room for several moments and worked through some yoga poses. When I'd stood to stretch, I'd noticed a light on at Jesse's place and wondered which room it was. Without much thought, I'd caught the top of the window frame with my fingers and leaned into the stretch as I imagined all the deliciously dirty things Jesse could do to me.

Soon, I'd had my answer about which room it was when Jesse—holy fuck, wrapped only in a towel—had entered the room.

I should have ducked out of sight right away.

But I'd found myself mesmerized as I watched him, hoping he saw me and praying he didn't.

I swear there was definite interest in his eyes when he'd seen me.

He may have thought he hid it well with his little wave and quickly closing the blinds, but I'd seen that flash of something on his face.

Interest.

Curiosity.

Panic.

Stubborn determination.

And now I was going over to his house to do grocery shopping while wondering if he'd bring up the window.

My head was fucked up because I wasn't sure if I wanted him to act as if nothing had happened or if I wanted him to do or say something about it.

I took a deep breath.

My mind had been ping-ponging between my two options all night long.

Option A- the smart, responsible, rational

decision would be to be Hadley's babysitter, help Jesse as I could, and stay focused *only* on my school work and plans for a future.

Option A sounded safe and comfortable.

And boring as hell.

Option B- the daring, up-for-a-challenge, you-only-live-once decision would be to be Hadley's babysitter, help Jesse, focus on my school work and future plans, *and* work my way into Jesse's bed for as much fun as we could have while it lasted.

Option B sounded dangerous and unwise.

Potentially awkward and definitely irrational.

And exciting.

Thrilling.

Promising.

Option B and the possibilities coursed through me with such electric anticipation I actually shivered.

Maybe Jesse would squash me like a bug.

Maybe I'd end up regretting my decision when I inevitably faced disaster—hello? This was my dad's best friend we were talking about. His assumed straight best friend.

But from the moment I'd shaken Jesse's hand to that split second of connection we shared at our windows, I'd not been able to shake the feeling that there was *something* between us.

Yeah, idiot. You're his employee. His nanny. Nothing more than a babysitter. Hired help.

I shook my head and bit my lip to keep from grinning like a fool. Nope, no one who'd see me as just an employee would have that much fiery interest in his eyes when he caught a glimpse of me nearly naked.

I shook out my arms and did a few more squats, glad to feel the effects of the coffee and meds beginning to calm me. "Calling it right now," I mumbled to myself. "Jesse Thompson is at least bisexual." I ruffled my hair, hoping it wasn't looking too wild. "Maybe doesn't know it, maybe has never admitted it, but he is."

I wasn't the type to force a guy out of his closet or put him in an uncomfortable position. But I definitely wasn't going to ignore the spark between us.

Smiling as my plan came together in my head, I headed toward Jesse's door.

I'd be a friend and offer exactly what Jesse needed —whether he wanted to need it or not—and see where things went.

And what about your dad?

I shrugged. No worries. Friends with benefits, no strings—those types of relationships had a time limit. *If* something panned out between us, Jesse and

I would reach the end of our mutually satisfying interaction long before Dad ever needed to know.

I knocked on the door.

Now, I just had to convince Jesse.

I had a feeling *that* wasn't going to come easily.

The door swung open and Jesse greeted me with a confused smile and a look that screamed *You're interrupting*.

"Morning. Hope you're of the mind that backdoor friends are best," I blurted. When Jesse narrowed his eyes, I continued. "And I mean that in the most literal way. You know, since I'm standing at your actual backdoor likely interrupting your morning." I bounced on the balls of my feet. "Unless you want to take it figuratively, then we can definitely discuss the unintended innuendo of my perky, round *backdoor*." I waggled my brows. "I'm going to shut up now. Good morning."

Jesse snorted. "Good morning. What can I do for you?"

"Well, Dad texted that you may need help setting up a space for Hadley and I *know* you need to go grocery shopping. Thought I'd tag along. Get to know Hadley, help with groceries. We could get a few pieces for her room or whatever."

For a split-second, Jesse looked as if he was going to refuse, but Hadley came to the door. "Cooper!"

she grabbed my hand and pulled me inside. "Daddy said you could help me make a special place."

I bit back a triumphant smile. Jesse had been talking about me? Interesting. "I definitely can. Can you show me your space?" I glanced toward Jesse to make sure it was okay.

He nodded. "You want some coffee or anything?"

"I'm good, thanks." I let Hadley pull me to the stairs and smiled as Jesse followed.

"This is my room," Hadley said proudly as she showed me a room with a mixture of toys and clothes strewn about.

Jesse cleared his throat. "I need to straighten it up, sorry," he mumbled as he began picking up shirts and putting them on hangers.

"No worries. You just moved in." I ruffled Hadley's hair. "This big girl can help with clean up, too."

Hadley wrinkled her nose and Jesse looked at me as if I had no clue what I was talking about.

I shrugged. "We'll work on it. So, are we looking for decoration for the room?"

Jesse gestured around the room. "Thought maybe colorful pieces that are functional for storage? The little foyer area is going to be her spot. Wanted to make it fun and something that can grow with her; use it for a homework space as well as a relax and unwind spot." He cleared his throat. "Robby suggested this space could be Hadley's and maybe I could do some finishing in the basement and make that mine."

Ohhh, the ideas I had about what Jesse could do in that basement.

I cleared my throat. "Sounds like a great idea. Having a dedicated space for homework—free of distractions—is a good habit to get into. And a space just for you is important, too." I turned to watch Hadley dump a tote of toys—we were definitely going to work on clean-up skills. "Hadley, what colors do you like?"

She shrugged. "All the colors. But not brown." She pushed hair from her face as she pushed a truck around in a circle before plopping a doll on top and taking it for a ride.

"Okay, sounds good. Let's clean up our toys and if Daddy says it's okay, I'll braid your hair before we go shopping." I raised a brow at Jesse.

He nodded, but the look on his face said *good luck*.

Fifteen minutes later, Hadley—albeit reluctantly—had picked up all the toys from her floor and tossed them into the tote and I'd done a quick braid to keep her hair out of her face.

She giggled as she raced down the stairs.

"How the hell did you do that? I can't get her to

clean anything." Jesse rubbed a hand over his face. "And I'm all thumbs when it comes to her hair."

"It's different when it's someone other than Dad, but a no opt-out approach is best. We'll work on it." I patted his arm. It was meant to be comforting, not flirty, but the heat of his skin zinged through me. "And I've been braiding hair since I got my first Barbie way back when. I can teach you a few simple hair-dos to at least keep it out of her face."

We headed down the stairs.

I grinned to myself as I wondered if Jesse was watching my ass.

"I love that she's got trucks *and* dolls. Hate the way toys are so gendered. It's good for kids to play with a variety of toys and not learn that things are *boy* or *girl*." We stopped at the kitchen island.

Jesse cleared his throat. "Yeah, Lauren was adamant that her kid wouldn't have gender forced on her. She wanted lots of colors for the baby, not just blue for a boy or pink for a girl. Lauren always dressed Hadley in whatever colors she was in the mood for; drove Nicole crazy because she always wanted Hadley in frilly pink." His eyes glistened. "Nicole and Lauren had a lot of differing opinions." Then he made a scoffing sound. "And not just in the baby color department."

I smiled softly. "Sounds like there's a story there."

He waved his hand as if to dismiss the subject. "Hadley, grab your shoes. We're going shopping."

"Can I stay here with Cooper?" the little girl whined.

"Not this time," Jesse answered as he plopped her onto the island and tied her shoes.

"Hadley, you want me to teach you how to tie your shoes?" I asked.

"Yes!" Hadley exclaimed. "Daddy tried, but he gets puffy."

Jesse groaned. "I may have gotten a bit frustrated. I don't remember teaching Lauren how to tie her shoes."

"Lauren is my mommy. She and Mimi Nicole died," Hadley informed as she waited for Jesse to finish her shoes. "I got pictures."

I swallowed thickly. "I'd like to see those pictures someday. Are you okay with me going shopping with you and Daddy?"

She smiled broadly. "Yes! Daddy gets grumpy when we go shopping."

"I do not," Jesse defended, but then he ducked his head sheepishly. "Sometimes it's just hard to keep track of a kid and make sure I get what we need. And the other shoppers are irritating; stopping in the middle of the aisle to talk is just rude."

"Maybe we'll set up a rotation. Sometimes I can go, sometimes you can go, sometimes the three of us can go. Shopping trips are good ways to teach colors and numbers and words."

"I want to learn words so I can read," Hadley interjected.

"Then we better get going." I helped her hop down from the island. I turned to Jesse and whispered. "Does she know about me watching her?"

He nodded.

"Hey, Hadley, would it be okay if I helped out in the mornings and after school? I'll watch you while Daddy works." I dropped down to her level.

"And I can ride the bus to school?" she asked.

"Yep, I'll be here to help with breakfast and getting ready and I'll make sure you get on the bus. Then, when the bus drops you off, I'll be here for snack time after school and homework. Maybe supper and bath time. Sometimes bedtime if Daddy has to work late." Weird how excited I was for the position. Not just because I needed the money. Not just because I wanted to spend time around Jesse. But because I genuinely liked this kid and was glad to be able to help. Jesse had done an amazing job raising her—something I had a feeling he didn't feel super confident about—but I knew I'd be able to offer support and make things easier for both of them.

"Okay!" Hadley agreed. "Will you braid my hair for school?"

"Definitely."

"I like bananas on my Cheerios," she advised seriously.

"Noted. We'll be sure to get Cheerios and bananas at the store."

"Daddy says we can go school shopping soon. I need a backpack and a lunch box and scissors and crayons..." she continued listing supplies as she skipped toward the door.

"Do you have the supply list yet?" I asked Jesse.

"Yeah, I figured next weekend maybe? I have a feeling I'll be a ball of grumpy anxiety with the crowds and the prices and the lump in my throat as I think about that little baby going off to school," he said gruffly.

"I'll go with. Back-to-school shopping is not for the weak," I teased.

"Hey, thanks for your help. I know you're doing this to make things easier on everyone, but I also know you don't *have* to help us until your job officially starts." Jesse winced. "I wish I could pay you already, but I didn't budget for that money to start coming out until the week school started." He ran a hand over the back of his neck. "Should have done better planning."

"No worries." I shook my head. "These couple weeks of getting to know Hadley and helping set a routine will make it easier for all of us. I wouldn't have been bringing in money just sitting at home, so I'd rather be hanging with her and setting us all up for success. Money or not."

Jesse glanced toward the door where we could see Hadley drawing on the driveway with a chunk of chalk.

"Hey, um, wanted to say sorry for the peep show last night," I hedged.

Jesse turned my way looking like a deer in headlights. "Oh, um, no big deal. Should have had my blinds closed."

I bumped against him as we walked to the door. "I mean, *I* didn't mind what I saw. You're welcome to keep them open and lose the towel."

Jesse snorted. "Noted."

"Just so you know, I don't make it a habit to stand nearly naked in front of my window. But I don't usually close the blinds. So, you know, if you're ever in the mood for a show, feel free to take a peek."

I turned and gave him a wink before walking over to Hadley.

The most gorgeous flush traveled from Jesse's neck to his cheeks.

Did he not protest because Hadley was within earshot?

Or was it because he didn't know what to say?

I had a feeling it was a combo of the two.

Guess I'd be making sure I had my nice undies on when standing in front of my window from now on.

Was I setting myself up for disappointment?

Gee, you think? Flirting with and pining over a straight guy?

Jesse was *supposedly* straight. No conversation had been had. And why was the default always straight? Why couldn't we assume a person was just a person and liked who they liked?

I pushed a piece of hair from my forehead. Honestly, I wasn't out to convert straight guys, but the way Jesse had looked at me through that window seriously hinted at an interest that wasn't at the one hundred percent straight end of the spectrum.

Deciding to ignore my jumbled thoughts, I helped Hadley climb into the truck.

Fifteen minutes later, the three of us piled out of Jesse's truck at the local grocery store.

The moment we entered the place, Hadley started

whining about wanting to ride in the cart. *Not* the little cart seat up front, the back of the cart. Where the numerous amounts of groceries Jesse planned to buy would need to sit.

"Hadley, do you want to practice for Kindergarten?" I interjected mid-whine.

The little girl perked up right away. "Yes!"

"Okay, in Kindergarten, you'll need to walk in line. So, we're going to practice our walking— keeping our hands and feet to ourselves and our eyes forward—and staying in a line." I took her hand and we fell into step beside Jesse.

"Thank you," he whispered. "Grocery shopping is always a nightmare; I don't have enough hands."

"No worries, we've got this."

I kept Hadley busy with walking in line while Jesse grabbed items from shelves as if he was on Supermarket Sweep. Sometimes he eyed the list, sometimes it looked as if he just reached for whatever might be good to have in the cabinets.

"Dude, you don't have to hurry. I've got all day. Take your time, use your list, think about what meals you want to make." I covered his hand with mine on the cart handle.

A mom with a baby in a carrier smiled indulgently at us as she passed. "Your daughter is gorgeous. Surrogate?"

Jesse cleared his throat and blinked.

"Granddaughter. And I'm the nanny," I offered in a way that didn't invite more conversation and gave Jesse's hand a reassuring squeeze. I was surprised he hadn't shaken my hand away. I kept telling myself he was distracted and likely didn't even realize what he was doing.

Once the lady had moved to another aisle, I whispered, "Oh my God, did she really just ask that?"

"You'd be surprised at what people will ask. It's insane the number of times I've had to prove I have custody of Hadley. Wouldn't be shocked if someone asks Hadley if she's okay." Jesse glanced around somewhat nervously and my heart hurt that he'd had to deal with losing Nicole and Lauren *and* suspicious people insinuating that he'd put Hadley in danger. "It seems a little better right now." He scoffed. "Probably because you're with me; I think people see us and assume family of some sort. When they see me alone with Hadley, they often assume the worst."

"That's insane. People need to mind their own business." My heart gave a little lurch when Jesse finally pulled his hand out from under mine.

"I guess I'm glad that the well-intentioned people are probably just looking out for Hadley's best interest. But it sucks that anyone would see me with her and assume she's in danger." He reached across to take a bottle of ketchup from the shelf. "I honestly didn't give a lot of thought to what meals needed made. I was more concerned about necessities. Now I see I should have had more focus." He nearly gave me whiplash with his subject change—dang, I thought *I* was the one who couldn't keep up with my brain sometimes.

I snorted. "Story of my life." I picked up a jar of pickles and raised my brow in question. When Jesse nodded, I put it in the cart. "Speaking of meals, Bev wanted to know if you and Hadley could make Thursday dinners at Remington Place a thing. Figured since you're working at the Wishing Well Monday through Wednesday, maybe Thursday not having to cook would be a nice break."

Jesse was definitely going to turn down the offer, but Hadley piped up. "I want to eat at Cooper's house."

He smiled wryly. "I guess we'd love to make Thursday dinner at Remington Place a thing."

"Perfect. She'd be cooking anyway—it's what she does—so don't think it's an imposition. She'll be thrilled to have guests."

We made our way to another aisle—where a woman sneered at us and a man mumbled something definitely unsavory under his breath. I'd dealt with enough homophobes throughout my life to take it in stride, but I knew it had to be bothering Jesse.

"Sorry, when you grocery shop with a sexy twink, you get read as gay," I said quietly as Hadley studied a display of cookies. "Does it bother you?"

Jesse's brows shot up. "Nah, not really. Better than being read as a pedophile who's abducted a child."

I snorted. "Yep, fabulously gay is definitely better."

Jesse laughed lightly before staring at me for a split second too long. "Kinda weird, though. I would have *thought* I'd be uncomfortable being read as gay." He shook his head. "But with everything Hadley and I have been through, I guess I've started to understand there's worse things." He cleared his throat.

My eyes went wide. "So, you're..."

"No, I'm not. Just saying that before I lost them, I would have been pissed if someone thought I was in a same-sex couple. Now? Doesn't even seem worth fighting over."

I pursed my lips and gave a little nod. "I can see that. Priorities change and you've definitely been through enough to have completely rearranged yours."

We continued our shopping.

But that little radar that had been pinging in my head since last night was definitely making more noise. I wasn't looking to manipulate a man out of whatever closet he'd made his home in, but I was for sure interested in giving him a little taste of whatever he'd maybe been curious about, what he'd been missing. Jesse deserved that, deserved to have some fun.

Hadley was doing a great job walking just like she'd need to do in school. Making a game of things —instead of a chore—always helped. I started pointing out words when it looked as if she was starting to tire of the line-walking game.

"I know that word!" Hadley exclaimed as she pointed toward the huge sign proclaiming *milk* over the dairy section. "That says milk!" And then she was off, hunting for letters and words, throwing in colors and shapes as she found them.

"Never been able to keep her this occupied *and* get the groceries. Thank you," Jesse said in a grateful and weary voice.

"Probably easier when she was still bound to the infant carrier or wearable in a pack, huh?"

"So much easier. Even when she could ride up front in the cart, I could keep her busy and quiet for a shopping trip. Now though? It's tough." Jesse scanned his list and grabbed a few boxes of cereal.

"She's a big cereal fan?"

"She is, but so am I. I eat a lot of cereal for snacks." Jesse smiled sheepishly. "Not because it's all we've got or I can't make something else, I just like it."

"I like cereal, I just don't love the milk. Or rather the milk doesn't love me. Makes my stomach all weird." I laughed at the rack of bananas strategically placed in the cereal aisle. "Product placement at its finest." I plucked a bunch of bananas from a hook and placed them in the cart. "Wouldn't want Hadley to miss out on her Cheerios and bananas."

We walked a few more aisles, Hadley calling out everything she recognized, Jesse mumbling to himself about meals he could make.

"Hey, I can help put together some casseroles. Mom always liked to make a few casseroles for the week and have them ready for nights when she wasn't in the mood to start a big dinner. Keep some rolls and a veggie option on hand and you've got a meal." I began to think of easy casserole type dishes I could help with.

"That's actually a good idea. Maybe make three a week and have some other easy meals planned." Jesse grimaced. "I kinda hate that you're going to be the one getting meals prepped and ready. Makes me feel guilty."

"It's my job. I'm down with it, no worries."

I took the list and pen from Jesse and jotted down items we'd need for the few casseroles I'd watched Bev make enough times that I knew I could handle them. I'd need to get more recipes from her. Lasagna, chicken pot pie, and cheeseburger noodles —Hadley had enjoyed that one so we'd do it again.

By the time we'd gathered all the ingredients for the newly-planned dishes, staples for the cupboard, a large bag of frozen chicken, a bag of Hadley's favorite frozen French fries, and an air fryer—because Jesse's had been on its last leg before the move—Hadley was getting tired.

"Hop on," I said as I knelt down. "You can ride piggyback while we finish up."

Hadley giggled as she climbed onto my back and I hefted her into a comfortable position.

After grabbing the final few items on Jesse's list, plus a few impulse buys, we made our way to the checkout. I popped a coin into the mechanical horse and let Hadley ride while Jesse unloaded the groceries onto the conveyer belt.

I noticed the frown on his face when the total rang up. Grabbing Hadley's hand, we fell into step beside Jesse after he'd paid and taken the receipt.

"Groceries are always such a chunk of change," I hedged.

He sighed. "Yeah. I've got money from a few sources due to the accident, but those all have to be used for certain things. I *really* need the garage business to boom. The Wishing Well will help, but it's more just for my sanity than extra income."

"Old man Spinks was crotchety, but he had a loyal customer base. I don't think he would have sold to just anyone. The fact he trusted you with his home and business tells me he knew you'd do a good job; I'm positive he's told his customers about you. You have any appointments yet?"

Jesse nodded as we reached the truck. "Yeah, I've actually got a pretty full week starting Monday. Just need to bring them in and keep them coming back."

"No worries, I have a feeling business will be booming before you know it." I let Hadley climb up onto my back again while I helped unload the groceries. "Gotta say, I'm impressed. A cooler and freezer bags? Who says you don't plan ahead?"

Jesse smiled. "Can't afford to have anything melt or spoil. We still need to stop for the storage items for upstairs."

By the time we got back to Jesse's place and unloaded the groceries, Hadley was zonked.

"I'm going to put her down for a nap. She's

growing out of needing them, but today was a lot, she needs one," Jesse whispered as he held the sleepy girl.

"I'll start unboxing the pieces. You can decide where you want the food to go and I'll help put it away." I checked the time. "We've got plenty of time, we should go ahead and get the casseroles made." A thought hit me. "Shoot, do you have baking dishes?"

Jesse laughed. "Yes, a neighbor gave me a set of three as a going away present." He shifted Hadley in his arms. "We can use the basement for building those; they shouldn't be too heavy to carry upstairs when we're done. I'll bring the monitor down."

I made my way down the stairs with the storage items we needed to put together then went back to the kitchen to unload the cold items. I figured getting them into the fridge and freezer would be the best, then Jesse could make decisions about which cabinets and shelves the dry goods would go on.

"Okay, let's unload this shit," Jesse said as he returned to the kitchen. "She'll probably sleep for about an hour or less. If it's more, I'll have to wake her or bedtime tonight will be a bear."

"Let's keep items out if they're needed for the casseroles."

We fell into an easy conversation as we worked together to put away groceries, boil water, and build casseroles. Jesse was possibly the easiest guy in the world to talk to. I found myself less overtly flirty while we worked; it was just nice to have a friend to talk to. Didn't mean I wasn't still interested in doing all kinds of deliciously sexy things with him, just that there was more to it than sexual attraction. Which was pretty new for me. I had friends. I had hookups. I very seldomly ever felt more than sexual attraction with the hookups. And I wasn't normally sexually attracted to my friends. So, to have Jesse stirring up feelings on both sides of the coin was interesting.

As we finished the casseroles, Hadley came walking into the kitchen looking a bit more rested than before. "Can we get cheeseburgers and fries with ketchup?"

Jesse shook his head. "Not today. But I can make you some fries and ketchup with dinner. Would you like a snack until then?"

As Jesse fixed some carrots with ranch and apple slices for Hadley, I slid the casseroles into the freezer. "Want me to get started on building the pieces?"

Jesse gave a grateful nod. "Yeah, I'll be down in a bit."

I was about halfway through the first piece when Jesse came down the stairs. "Wow, you're quick.

Hadley's going to watch a movie and read some books. I think bedtime will be early for her tonight. She's still adjusting after the move."

I gulped, trying desperately not to choke on my tongue. Jesse had changed from jeans into gray sweatpants. "You changed."

He glanced down. "Oh, yeah. Spilled ranch all over my jeans. Pulled on the first pair of pants I could find."

Gray sweatpants were my kryptonite. Dear God, did he have any idea how amazing he looked in them? Broad chest and shoulders, somewhat narrower waist, the slightest hint of a belly gone slightly soft with years—truly the sexiest *dad bod* I'd ever seen. And when had I ever thought the dad bod look was sexy? Something about Jesse's physique just did it for me in a way no other ever had.

Below his waistband, as was the usual effect of gray sweatpants, shadows promised a good time and I let my mind wander for a moment. Dropping to my knees, hooking my thumbs in the elastic, revealing a treasure. I licked my lips at the image.

But, because I was attempting to be responsible —at least for that exact moment—I cleared my throat and took a deep breath. "You should model for the brand, they'd sell millions with you as their poster boy," I muttered. "This one is almost done.

These are super easy. Basically, just popping pieces into place. No real building involved." I gestured toward the project and tried to ignore the flush that crept up Jesse's neck to his cheeks.

About thirty minutes later, we carried the storage pieces upstairs and placed them in Hadley's room and play area.

She squealed in excitement and began putting toys into one of the bins.

"Hadley, how about you and me work on organizing your area someday soon?" I asked her. "We can make sure everything has a place and it's all ready for when you start school."

Hadley jumped up and down. "Yes! I want to be ready for school." She glanced at the little desk we'd brought up. "I need supplies for my desk."

"We'll get it all ready. Promise."

"Daddy, can I watch one more movie before dinner?" Hadley begged with puppy dog eyes.

Jesse glanced at his watch. "Yeah, you've got time. But after the movie, I want you to read some books or color for a bit. Or you can play with blocks."

Hadley jumped onto her beanbag chair and queued up the next video on her tablet.

I followed Jesse to the basement. "I like that you

make sure she does activities that use her brain and not just staring at the tablet."

"Yeah, the tablet is easy to rely on, but I want to be sure she can use her imagination and play, too." Jesse started breaking down boxes and I joined in. "Thanks so much for your help today. No way I could have gotten all of this done by myself. You want to stay for dinner?"

I checked the time. "Any chance you want to chill with a before-dinner beer? I should get home in a bit. Doing cards with Dalton and Spencer a little later. Wanna check on Bev and see if she needs anything."

"Sounds good. I could use a bit of a breather before dinner." He walked to the fridge and pulled out two beers. "Not sure if Spinks forgot about these or if it was his version of a housewarming gift, but the dates show they're fresh."

"This basement is great. Not super fancy, but it's totally usable." I took the beer and popped it open.

Jesse did the same and flopped down on the couch. "Yeah, Spinks left a lot down here. There's more I'd like to add and fix up, but I think I'll spend a lot of time down here. Definitely need a TV."

Since there was nowhere else to sit, and I wasn't one to skip out on a perfect opportunity, I took a seat on the couch. Close enough to Jesse that our legs brushed together.

Jesse tensed, but only took a long swallow of his beer.

We chatted easily about which day would be best to do school shopping, the customers he had coming to the shop within the next week, my classes, and what my plans were for the preschool I wanted to open.

"Remington will be perfect for a school like the one you want to open. Aside from the tiny daycare that one church runs, and the few in-home daycares, this place is a mecca for families needing childcare and education." Jesse took another long drink. "And it sounds like you've got the perfect plan for setup and curriculum."

"From your lips to God's ears," I joked, but truly had a hard time tearing my eyes from Jesse's mouth.

I sighed.

My beer was gone and I had a feeling one beer would be the limit since Jesse still had dinner, bath, and bedtime to take care of. Shifting on the couch, pulling a knee up under my body, and stretching my arm across the back of the couch, I smiled at Jesse. "Thanks for letting me bulldoze my way into your day, I had fun. Hadley is a great kid, you've done an amazing job raising her." Heat radiated from Jesse's body and my skin savored it, begging for more.

Jesse cleared his throat and took the final drink of his beer. "I adore that kid and would never want her anywhere but with me." He worried his lip. "But I have to admit that adult conversation and support is something I miss. Today was great, thank you for your help. I know Hadley is going to love having you as her nanny."

"What about you?" I asked a bit breathlessly.

He swallowed, once, twice, his eyes never leaving my lips. "I feel really lucky to have found you. For Hadley. To help us."

"Nothing more?" I pressed, despite my mind doing a face palm at how forward I was being.

Jesse's breathing had increased and I swore we'd inched closer together. "Not sure what else there is," he answered, but I knew in my heart he was playing dumb. Had Jesse ever explored his attraction to the same sex?

I brazenly stroked my fingers against the skin of his neck. "Could have some fun. Easy, no expectations, no requirements, no timeline. Ride it out until it's over."

"I can't," Jesse choked out, tension rippling from him in waves. "We can't."

"We're grown-ups," I whispered, leaning in to close the gap between us, "we can do what we want." Pressing gently against his neck, I pulled him closer, my lips skating over his.

Jesse froze. He closed his eyes for the briefest of moments and I worried his next words would be to tell me to get out and never come back. Instead, he shifted, leaning closer, his lips connecting with mine in a searing kiss.

When I gasped, Jesse groaned, his hand coming up to grip the back of my neck as if to hold me exactly where he wanted me. With a slight movement on his part, I was pressed back against the arm of the couch as his broad chest came down to meet mine.

With very little thought as to how the situation was going to end—simply taking what I could get in the moment before Jesse inevitably made his way through the fog of lust and pent-up desires—I spread my legs, loving the way his hips settled perfectly between mine.

Another thing about gray sweatpants and similar attire, they did nothing to hide the quickly thickening evidence of how much Jesse was enjoying the kiss. As his tongue teased against my lips, as if begging for entrance, my hands skimmed down his back, stopping only when they found purchase on his firm, round ass.

When I urged him forward, my own hips thrusting up to meet his, Jesse moaned and deepened the kiss.

"Daddy, my movie's over," a little voice came over the monitor. "I'm going to color a monster."

Jesse sprang away from me as if he'd been burned. Standing up quickly, he ran a hand over his face and turned away from me. "Fuck," he mumbled. When he turned back around, his face was a conglomerate of lust, fear, and anger. "Cooper, I'm sorry. That was completely unacceptable. It will *never* happen again, but I'll understand if you aren't comfortable accepting the job."

I stood from the couch and moved right into Jesse's space. "The only *unacceptable* part of that was we didn't get to see where it might have ended." I wrapped my arms around his waist and nuzzled my nose against his jawline—more comfortable with him than any man I'd ever been involved with. "That had nothing to do with the job. My job as Hadley's nanny is a completely separate situation." I nibbled at his neck and ran my tongue over the spot, trying to commit his taste and scent to memory. "I'm crazy attracted to you—and please know I don't make it a habit to make out with employers—and I'm very much down with seeing how this could play out." I held back from rolling my hips against him since he seemed ready to bolt at any moment.

Jesse took a step backwards, not pulling away from me, simply sagging against the wall behind him. "This can't happen," he mumbled, more as if to try to convince himself than turn me away.

"It *can*. We clearly both want it to," I said with a slight pressure of my hard cock against his.

"Wanting something isn't always enough." Jesse took a deep breath and knocked his head against the wall. "There are about a million reasons why this can. Not. Happen."

"Go ahead and give your spiel, I've got counter arguments." I didn't let go of his waist, but I leaned back to listen.

Jesse snorted. "Well, in no particular order. I'm not gay. I'm your employer. I'm twice your age. Your dad is my best friend." He blew out a long breath between clenched teeth. "Not to mention, I come with a shit-ton of baggage and have no interest or plans to ever get into another relationship."

"If you can look me in the eye and swear you aren't interested, feel nothing in this situation, I'll walk out and you'll never have to deal with me outside of nanny capacity again." I met his eyes and waited.

After a long moment, Jesse closed his eyes and sighed. The slightest shake of his head spurring me on.

SIX
JESSE

WHAT THE ACTUAL fuck was I doing?

I'd given in to an impulse. An impulse I'd been successfully burying for years.

And then all that control had gone out the damn window.

I'd kissed Cooper.

Fuck.

He'd given me the perfect opportunity to back out of the awkward situation and keep some semblance of normal between us.

So why the fuck hadn't I taken him up on it.

All I would have had to do was look him in the eye and say I wasn't interested. Say I felt nothing between us.

A few simple words were all it would have taken. I truly felt Cooper was the type who would have taken me at my word and left that kiss in the dust with no more questions asked.

Yet, I couldn't do it.

I'd spent years ignoring feelings, squashing longings, pushing away desires. Back in high school, it was because I didn't know myself well enough and I wasn't prepared for the fall-out of even entertaining the idea I was bisexual. When I was with Nicole, it was because I was happily married and even if I *was* bisexual, I wasn't going to act on it.

But Nicole had recognized something in me whether I'd liked it or not.

Our marriage hadn't been in trouble simply because I had repressed my bisexuality. Our marriage had started to dissolve slowly over the years as we grew apart, realized our high school friendship wasn't enough, and lost that connection we'd once had.

Did my hidden interest in men possibly feed into that?

Yes.

Could I have been a more open, honest, and engaged partner?

Yes.

But Nicole's infidelity played a part as well.

In the past, I'd had strong reasons for not wanting to delve into my sexuality.

But now?

I still had reasons—as I'd quickly rattled off to Cooper—but the fear of learning about the *real* me wasn't as overwhelming. Giving myself permission to learn and explore actually gave me a fluttery feeling of anticipation.

But that didn't mean my reasons weren't still very real and very valid. Cooper may have been the guy who finally broke through my steely resolve, but that didn't mean he could be the man who helped me explore.

Could he?

No.

No, there was way too much stacked against us.

With his arms still wrapped around my waist, his intoxicating taste still on my tongue, Cooper looked up at me with mesmerizing gray eyes and challenged me to give him my best reasons for why we couldn't let anything go any further between us. "Go ahead and give your spiel, I've got counter arguments."

"Well, in no particular order. I'm not gay. I'm your employer. I'm twice your age. Your dad is my best friend." I blew out a long breath between clenched teeth. "Not to mention, I come with a shit-ton of baggage and have no interest or plans to ever get into another relationship."

Cooper smiled softly. "I know you've got

responsibilities to tend to and hopefully things to think about, so I'll make this quick," he started. "*Not gay* isn't a good reason. Bisexual? Pansexual? Haven't figured out your label? Don't need or want a label? If you're attracted to me—*anyone*—it doesn't have to be this big issue. No matter how you identify, you have every right to find yourself attracted to someone." Cooper's hands teased under the hem of my shirt and I sighed shakily when his fingers skimmed over my skin. Had any touch ever lit me on fire like his?

"There's more than just my sexuality. I know I have a lot to figure out—may never figure it out completely, but there's a lot I need to just be honest with myself about." I leaned into his touch.

"And I won't push or rush you in that area. I *will* be here as a supportive friend—whether you and I take this to the next level or not."

I nodded. "Thanks. I'd like that."

"Okay, let's move on to flimsy excuse number two. You're my employer." Cooper shrugged. "Sure, technically, that's true. But it's not as if you're my boss through an organization with Human Resources and rules and such. We're consenting adults. If we agree to a relationship of some type—staying on the same page in regards to not letting it affect me watching Hadley—then there's no wrongdoing."

"Those are the easiest ones to explain away," I hedged. "My age? Robby?"

Cooper scoffed. "Age is just a number. You're taking care of a five-year-old at age fifty. Would it fit into a nicer, neater box if you were playing the role of grandfather? Sure. But that's not the hand were dealt. I'm sure there are moments when you feel you're too old for what's been placed on your shoulders. But there's nothing *wrong* with an older father." He snaked his hands all the way up my back and trailed his nails down slowly.

I shivered. "I'm still twice your age."

"So? Sure, at five and ten, nine and eighteen, even at…" he frowned, "damn numbers, what's twice seventeen?"

"Thirty-four," I answered softly.

"Thanks. I could have eventually gotten it with paper and pencil." Cooper shook his head. "Even at seventeen and thirty-four it could have been considered *wrong*. But I've been a legal, fully-functional adult for many years now. I may struggle with numbers and my mind sometimes feels like it's going a million miles a minute, but I'm not dumb—I know a relationship between us likely wouldn't be the very smartest idea, but that doesn't mean it's not okay to at least give it a shot." He continued to trail his fingers up and down my back. "I've never really found the silver fox *daddy* type sexy, until you. First day I saw you, I had to pick my jaw up off the floor. We can't help who we like."

I sighed. I was torn between being annoyed that he was poking holes in my arguments and excited that maybe he'd take away all my reasons for why we couldn't work. "Fine. Even ignoring my baggage, you can't argue away the fact that your dad is my best friend."

Cooper gave a brief nod. "You're right, there's no getting away from that. But here's the thing. We're not discussing a long-term relationship. We're not planning an engagement or wedding. What's wrong with two consenting adults enjoying their attraction to each other? Does Dad even need to know?"

I squished my eyes shut, trying to separate the heat and desire coursing through my veins from actual rational thought. "Let's play the what if game for a moment. What happens if we're not careful and he finds out? What happens if we decide we want more than a short-term thing? How do we tell him? *Plus*, then explain that we'd been together right under his nose?" I shook my head. "The whole thing has disaster written all over it."

"Look, I love my dad and I respect his opinions. He had no problem with me being gay. He may be surprised to find out you're bi or pan or whatever, but he's not going to disown you." Cooper's hand came around to cup my cheek.

I chuckled without humor. "I'm more concerned about him kicking my ass for fucking his little boy." I froze as soon as the words had cleared my lips.

Cooper's grin was pure evil temptation. "And oh, how I imagine you fucking me," he whispered and licked his lips. "But here's the thing. I haven't been his *little boy* for several years. I'm a grown man. Who I choose to be with isn't his business, just as who *you* choose to be with isn't up to his discretion."

"It wouldn't be easy. Things would be awkward and messy; my life is already full of enough of that." I sighed and leaned my head back against the wall. No matter my reasons for *knowing* why nothing—absolutely *nothing*—could happen between Cooper and me, I was loath to disengage from his touch, send him away, make my final decision.

"I think it's important to remember that we're talking about something light and easy—maybe more than *just sex* since we're friends and involved outside of the bedroom. No big announcements or decisions have to be made right now. Robby doesn't need to know; no one needs to know. If we both opt *yes*, then it's just us for however long we decide." Cooper wrapped his arms around my neck and hugged me close.

"And what if our final decisions aren't mutual?" I winced. "I'm still dealing with the after effects of infidelity, the loss of my marriage—which never even had the chance to play out—and the grieving process. My therapist says I'm actually grieving several different things. The loss of my marriage, the loss of Nicole and Lauren, and the loss of my role as grandfather. I've made *a lot* of progress these past five years, and I'll keep working at it for Hadley, but sometimes it crops up and knocks me to my knees." I pursed my lips. "I don't know that I *want* another relationship—hell, I don't even know if I can *do* one —I wasn't the best husband I could be and look where it got me."

"What happened to Nicole and Lauren wasn't a punishment for you not being your best in your marriage. What happened to them was a terrible accident, but it wasn't payback for you," Cooper said firmly, his gray eyes flashing.

"It's not fair of me to start something with you, even if I could ignore the other reasons this is a terrible idea, only to leave you wanting more when I'm not able to follow through." I absently ran a hand up and down Cooper's back. "I don't even know if that makes sense."

"It does," he answered. "We're both on the same page at this moment. I don't have any reason to want a long-term relationship. I have enough going on with school and work and my future. I'm not looking for a proposal. I'm happy with my life and have no need for the proverbial white picket fence. We can just have fun." Cooper ran his hand through my hair. "As much as I hate to say it, I need to leave. Hadley's going to need dinner and I've kinda given you a shit-ton to think about." He took a step back, leaving space between our bodies.

I snorted. "You think?" I immediately missed his heat.

He grinned. "Nothing changes between Hadley and me. Nothing changes, workwise, between you and me. You let me know if you'd like to take that leap with me." He dipped his head to catch my eyes. "And if you say no, nothing has to change between us. I like you, spending time with you, that can stay the same."

I pinched the bridge of my nose. "Fuck. Even if I go with option *Lose your damned fucking mind and say yes*, you deserve so much better than some guy who has no idea what I'd even do if I got my hands on you."

Cooper laughed—the sound going straight to my gut. "Based on that kiss, I assure you that your lack of experience with a man will *not* be a problem." He bit his lip and let his eyes trail down my torso to the area of my sweats that was still definitely interested in the conversation. "We'd have such a good time. No strings attached fun while you learn and feed your curiosities. When you're done with it, we say goodbye. Nothing messy."

"And you think things can truly be that easy?" I cocked a brow.

"Definitely. If we go into things with a plan, we can assure there are no issues."

I took a deep breath and nodded. "I'll think about it. I still think it's a terrible idea—and Hadley has to come first one hundred percent of the time no matter what's happening between us—but I'll at least think about it."

Cooper grinned and I knew without question I was done for. "Perfect. I'll see you for school shopping."

I HAD the whole next day to think about what Cooper was offering.

But I also had a massive amount of work to do and a little girl to take care of.

In between placing orders for household items that I simply didn't have the energy to go shopping for, setting up the sandbox that had been delivered for Hadley, hanging a swing from the large tree behind the shop, and arranging the garage for my first customers, I barely had time for anything else.

But that didn't mean Cooper ever left my mind.

I appreciated he was giving me a little space and I respected that he needed *Cooper time* as well.

So, as much as I wanted to see him, Hadley and I just waved to the residents of Remington Place as they came and went throughout the day. It truly felt good to be back home and have friendly neighbors.

Bev made sure we'd be over on Thursday for dinner. I told her that Hadley wouldn't let us miss it.

Cooper's wave and smile as he jaunted from the backdoor to his car maybe would have seemed nonchalant to anyone else, but it held questions and promises to my eyes.

Hadley begged for Cooper to come play, but I stood my ground. She'd see him when we went school shopping the next day. I needed Hadley to understand Cooper wasn't at her beck and call. I also needed a little space to think about Cooper's offer.

Despite every single reason I could think of for why Cooper and I should *not* start something, I couldn't get his scent, his touch, his taste out of my head. When his hand had touched mine in the grocery store, I'd wanted nothing more than to hold on tight and never let go. Wanted to protect him from the sneers and mumbled comments.

But who was I to protect Cooper?

He was strong and proud. He didn't need me fumbling through figuring myself out. Maybe I'd never be as strong and proud as him. And he didn't deserve that.

But I couldn't get him out of my head.

His lips on mine.

Our tongues dancing.

The way he spread his legs for me.

How perfectly I fit against him.

The little whimpers he made as our hips rocked together and our tongues mated.

I wanted all of those things and more.

Cooper was right. We weren't talking about getting engaged and living happily ever after. This was a chance for easy, fun sex.

I'd be crazy to turn it down.

And I'd be even crazier to take him up on the offer.

I pictured Robby's face. What would he think of all the deliciously dirty things I wanted to do to his son?

My head spun with indecision and anticipation.

Would my business suffer if clients learned I was...not straight? Would they need to know? If

Cooper and I were keeping this thing completely casual, I'd assume that meant keeping things at home and not flaunting it out on the town. How long would Cooper be okay with that? Would he want to end things so he could find someone who was able to be out for him? Could that person ever be me?

I'd likely never get such a perfect situation again. Cooper was ready and willing. He was offering to let me explore and learn with no strings attached.

A tiny part of my heart gave a pang of protest. Would I truly be able to get into something with Cooper and keep it completely casual without getting emotions involved?

You did a pretty damn good job keeping emotions out of your marriage.

I winced at the painful reminder.

Cooper was offering something completely different than my marriage.

I'd been so detached, just going through motions, not able to admit the problems those last few years before Nicole died. But, as I'd learned through therapy, it was okay to let her shoulder her part of the blame as well—even though she was gone.

And now, I was so damn lonely. Five years of grief and loneliness weighed heavily on me.

But was me being lonely a good enough reason to

pull Cooper into something that could crash and burn?

I wasn't sure I was strong enough to say no even though my head was screaming at me to avoid what would surely end in disaster and heartache.

If I agreed to a casual fling, could I walk away?

What if casual turned to something more—a thought my traitorous heart seemed to be very interested in, and why was that? Definitely something to examine—would I be able to give Cooper what he needed? Could I be in an out relationship with a man? It was something I'd told myself for decades that I couldn't do. Ever.

But could I do it for Cooper?

I growled and wiped a hand over my face. "He's offering easy sex, nothing more. Stop making it into something that it's not."

Catching up on work and taking care of Hadley kept me busy throughout the day and I was exhausted by the time dinner rolled around. We enjoyed carrots and ranch along with a frozen pizza. Maybe not the healthiest of options, but I felt good that veggies were involved.

I put Hadley to bed that evening with three stories, two drinks, and one extra trip to the bathroom. After checking to be sure she was fast asleep, I took a long, hot shower and didn't even try not to imagine Cooper's pretty pink lips wrapped around my shaft as I came all over the tile wall.

Only a slight twinge of disappointment traveled through me when I noticed Cooper's window was dark as I climbed into bed. Dread and anticipation mixed in my chest as I thought of school shopping with Cooper the next day.

You should tell him no. Keep things professional and friends-only.

Yeah, I knew what I *should* do.

But my heart and body were in cahoots, shouting and cheering for me to take a leap into something I never in a million years would have thought I'd be doing.

The smart thing would be to turn him down.

But I was pretty damned sure I'd cease to exist if I didn't get to taste his lips again. Every fucking image I'd deemed wrong and taboo and pushed to the farthest, darkest corners of my mind over the years was coming to light ever since Cooper's offer.

And every image I'd pushed away now starred Cooper as the main character.

I wanted everything with him. Wanted to touch, tease, taste, and take. Wanted to feel him on me and in me. Wanted everything I'd told myself for so long that I couldn't have.

And Cooper was right there, offering exactly what I wanted and needed.

Was I weak for accepting?

Was I a horrible person for allowing my desires to surface when I should have been mourning the loss of my wife and daughter?

My first therapy appointment couldn't come soon enough.

But I didn't think I could pass up what Cooper was offering.

Even if a large part of me was screaming that it had *potential disaster* written all over it.

A sliver was whispering that it had *potentially life changing* carved into it.

"GOOD MORNING," Cooper said brightly when I opened the door. "Is it too early? I saw your light on and thought I'd come on over." He bounced on the balls of his feet and flipped a keychain over and over in his hand.

"Hadley's still asleep. I have two oil changes bright and early. After that, I can fix her breakfast and take a shower, then we can go." I fought the urge to reach out and pull him close.

Cooper stepped into the house. "I'll take care of breakfast." He bit his lip and eyed me up and down. "The sexy daddy mechanic look suits you." He winked.

Knowing I'd hear Hadley on the monitor and that she'd likely sleep at least another thirty minutes—but knowing my first client would pull in at any moment—I reached for Cooper's hand and pulled him into the little alcove between the kitchen and the backdoor.

The little gasp that escaped him only fueled my need and I pushed him against the wall before gripping the back of his neck and pulling him forward. Our lips met, hot and frantic, as Cooper's arms came around my neck and pulled me close, deepening the contact. His tongue dipped between my lips and I groaned at the heady flavor of Cooper and coffee.

My hands made their way under his shirt, his smooth skin tempting me to do more, take more. Instead, I trailed my hands up his back to grip his shoulders, my tongue continuing to lick and savor every part of his mouth.

Cooper's hands roamed until he gripped my ass and encouraged me to rock into him, our thickening erections straining against zippers, begging to take things further.

We finally broke apart as the sound of an engine pulling up the drive filled the air.

Breathing heavily, I pressed my forehead against Cooper's. "Good morning." I brushed a final kiss against his lips. "Never changed oil with a boner, so this should be fun."

Cooper laughed. "Try not to think about me when you're dipping the stick and lubing the shaft," he teased.

"Do you have *any* idea what those terms mean?"

He shook his head with a devious grin. "Not in the slightest. But they sound dirty and fun." A shadow of something close to doubt crossed his face. "So, does this mean you're on board with us having some fun?"

My heart thumped heavily and my breathing increased. "Yeah. I'm in. Hadley comes first. We don't tell Robby. And we walk away as friends in the end."

Cooper's gorgeous gray eyes flickered with excitement and heat. "Perfect. I can't wait to show you what you've been missing."

Two oil changes later—with very kind people who assured me they'd be back—a shower, breakfast, and two hellish hours of school supply shopping found Cooper, Hadley, and I in the little girls' department of a clothing store.

"You can pick three outfits and a pair of shoes," I told Hadley.

Luckily, my granddaughter was about as interested in clothes as her mother had been—which was close to zero—so we were done with that task within thirty minutes.

"Can we get French fries and ketchup?" Hadley asked sleepily as I pulled the truck out of the parking lot.

"We could grab food and go to the park," Cooper suggested.

"Perfect. We need some sunshine after all that shopping." I pulled into a local fast food location. "Drive-thru always gets it wrong. I'm going to run in. What do you want?"

Cooper reached for his wallet.

"I've got it." I waved away his money.

"Thanks. I'll take fish with cheese, fries, and a large Coke."

Fifteen minutes later—I guess I should have been glad to know at least we got fresh fries—I handed a bag of food to Cooper and put the drink carrier on the floorboard in the back.

"Hurry, Daddy. My tummy is hungry," Hadley whined.

"We'll be there in a couple minutes."

"Let's look for words," Cooper suggested and I was grateful for his smooth ability to distract Hadley.

We pulled into the Remington public park and found an open table right next to the playground.

"Food first, then you can play." I spread Hadley's fries out, made a puddle of ketchup for dipping, and tore her cheeseburger into four pieces.

She scarfed down her burger and most of the fries before taking a drink of her milk. "Can I go play now?" She pushed hair from her face.

"Want your hair pulled back?" Cooper asked her and reached into his pocket.

"You're carrying rubber bands with you these days?" I asked with a smirk.

He shrugged. "Figured they might come in handy. I've also got a paperclip and a screw. Just in case."

I laughed. "I didn't know you'd been a Boy Scout. Always prepared."

He finished whipping Hadley's hair into a ponytail. "Nah, the rubber band was on purpose. The paperclip was from a school assignment. The screw I'm sure belongs to something in my room and I'm just waiting for it to fall apart so I knew where it goes," he said with a laugh.

We ate our food and watched Hadley play.

"I just love seeing dads at the park with their kids. Always helpful to give us moms a break," a voice from the table next to us said. "Which ones are yours?"

"The dark haired one with the pony tail." I pointed to Hadley on the swings.

"And yours?" the pushy lady asked.

"Oh, she's mine, too," Cooper said. "I'm her nanny."

The lady glanced back and forth between Cooper and me for several beats. Then she gave a forced smile. "Oh, how nice. So, you and the *nanny* gave your wife the day off?" she kept at it.

I shook my head. This type of situation would *never* not be annoying. "No wife. Just me and her. And her nanny."

As the woman continued to stare as if she just couldn't figure things out, Cooper gathered our trash.

"We promised a walk to the wishing well," he said to me with a pointed look. "Let's grab Hadley."

After assuring Hadley she could play for a bit longer at the other playground area across the park, we gave somewhat pleasant smiles to the nosy lady and headed toward the wishing well.

The Remington wishing well was smack dab in the middle of the park. With several fountains and burbling water that flowed from different levels, it was really quite beautiful.

"Did you bring any money?" Cooper teased Hadley.

She shook her head and glanced between Cooper and me like a sad puppy dog. "My piggy bank is in a box."

"No worries, I'll spot you." Cooper pulled out five coins from his pocket. "But we have to count them first."

Over the next few minutes, Cooper and Hadley named coins and how much they were worth. Then he placed them in her hands and told her to make her wishes.

"Are you and Daddy going to make wishes?" Hadley asked.

"Sure thing," Cooper answered and handed me a penny while keeping one for himself.

We laughed as Hadley studied the water and walked from one side to another as if finding the absolute perfect spot to make her wish.

When she finally reached the end of all the coins, she came running over. "Make your wishes, sillies! I want to go play."

Cooper's eyes caught mine and he bit his lip to hide a grin before tossing his coin into the water.

Please don't let this be a mistake; let me come out unscathed. I tossed my penny toward the fountain. It landed with a tinkling sound on one of the statues.

I wouldn't have been able to do that again if I'd tried.

Maybe it was a sign.

Good or bad?

Who knew.

"IT'S ONLY an hour appointment so I should be home before bedtime," I told Cooper.

"Don't sweat it. We'll unload some more of her boxes and get things organized in her room." Cooper patted me on the back as he ushered me toward the door.

When he'd found out that I planned to take Hadley—along with ear buds and her tablet—to my first therapy session, he'd insisted on watching her.

"There may be days when you *can't* find someone, and it's good to know she can go with you if needed, but you've got me for now. Let me help," he'd said in way of argument.

As I drove to the therapist's office, I recalled those haggard days of no sleep, long hours of work, strapping a baby to my chest, and sobbing on the soft brown couch in my old shrink's tiny office.

Hadley and I had come a very long way.

But I knew I still had a long way to go.

I doubted I'd get much accomplished at the first appointment, although the therapist had spent over thirty minutes with me during a phone consultation, so maybe we'd get some actual work done.

The office was in an old house on the other side of town. Not as old as Remington Place, but just as stunning. Alicia, my new therapist, welcomed me inside and got me settled with hot tea and a cookie.

"I always like to have a little comfort snack during sessions," she explained. "Sit where you're most comfortable and let's get started."

An hour later, I thanked Alicia and walked from the office in somewhat of a daze. I'd not been expecting a lot from the first session, but I left feeling refreshed. Not that anything Alicia and I talked about was new or different from my old sessions, but I definitely connected with her and felt it to my bones that she'd be the right person to help me continue on the path toward healing.

When I pulled up to the house, I smiled at the text from Robby saying he'd be over after bedtime with beer. Replying that I could have two beers with him before *my* bedtime, I turned off the truck and went inside to find Cooper and Hadley in the kitchen.

"Something smells good," I said as I gathered

Hadley up in a hug and kissed her while she screamed and giggled.

Was it strange that I wanted to pull Cooper close?

"We maked a cake!" Hadley announced.

"I wasn't sure what you'd been planning for dinner, but Hadley wanted to make something so we opted for a cake." He checked the timer. "It should be cool by the time you finish dinner. You can use this can of icing and smooth it all over with a spatula."

My eyes must have shown I didn't trust myself to do that because Cooper laughed. "It's easy, I promise. Even a butter knife or spoon will work. Just take a glob and spread it around."

When the timer went off, Cooper pulled the cake from the oven and sat it on a rack to cool before telling Hadley he'd see her on the first day of school if not before.

She scampered off to her room after begging to watch one video before dinner.

"Therapy go okay?" Cooper asked.

"It was actually really good. It's always hard to find a therapist, but I think this one is going to be great. Thanks so much for watching her while I was gone. She would have been fine at the appointment, but I know she enjoyed staying here even more." I let my arm brush against his.

"We'll hear her on the stairs, right?" Cooper asked softly.

I nodded.

He wrapped his arms around my waist and pressed me against the sink. "So, we're doing this?"

I swallowed thickly and nodded. "I want to. I want to experience it and I think you're the only guy I'd trust enough to be comfortable with. I feel like you'd never judge me."

"Never." Cooper brushed his lips against mine. "Have you given any thought to what you'd like to do? Just kissing? Just touching? Mouths? Penetration?"

My dick swelled behind my zipper. "Yes," I answered breathlessly. "All of it. But slowly. Like, I don't want to go zero to sixty. And there's so much I don't know. Hell, I don't even know what I don't know."

Cooper laughed and kissed my neck. "It's okay. We'll go slow and I'll teach you things as we go along. No worries."

I cupped his face and kissed him, loving the roughness of his stubble under my hands, the tickle of his slight scruff against my lips. "I think I could be happy with just kissing," I said. "But don't worry. I wouldn't ask you to do just that."

Cooper smiled against my lips. "I'd be fine with it. I love kissing you."

"Are you going to be seeing other people during this time?" I blurted.

His eyes went wide. "No, not at all. Can I ask the same of you?"

"Who would I be seeing?" I scoffed, but the look on his face told me he needed to hear my answer. "No, when we're together—doing whatever this is for however long—I'm only with you. Promise."

Cooper smiled. "Perfect. Okay, you need to fix dinner and I have work to do. Maybe we'll meet at the window later?" He winked.

I growled before kissing him deeply. "God, I hope so."

"THERAPY GO OKAY?" Robby asked as we worked on the basement and sipped our beers. He'd brought a slip cover for the couch, a really nice chaise lounge, and a wall-mounted television. All three of which he insisted Celeste had in a closet or found at a thrift store, and would *not* take any money for them. I made him promise he wouldn't bring over any more furniture for a while. But, thanks to the gifts, I only needed to pop some soap and hand towels into the little bathroom, and the basement would be the perfect mancave.

"Yeah, I really liked her."

Robby waggled his brows. "Like, *liked* her?"

I punched him in the arm and we both laughed.

"No, asshole. I don't think having the hots for my therapist would be wise." *But having a fling with your best friend's son is so much better?* "Plus, after she gets all the lowdown on me, she'd never be interested even if I was."

"You know it's okay to be interested. In someone. Right?"

I nodded and shoved a corner of the slip cover between the cushion and arm of the couch. "I know. Both therapists have said the same thing." I shrugged.

"You have anyone you might be interested in?" Robby pressed.

Taking a deep breath—I knew he wasn't trying to push or piss me off—I blew it out slowly. "I don't know. Until this move, I hadn't even had a moment to breathe let alone think about dating. Things with Nicole had been so bad for so long, I just got used to taking care of things on my own. Then she was gone and I had Hadley and absolutely no time or business to be dating."

Robby kept busy with attaching the TV mount to the wall, but he kept on. "You ever going to talk to me about the whole sexuality thing Nicole made such a big deal of?"

"Rather not," I snipped.

"Man, I love you. I don't care who you like, I just want you to be happy. But it hurts that you can't talk to me about it." Robby stayed busy with the electric drill.

"I'm not purposely hiding anything from you." I ran a hand over my face. "I just don't really understand things enough myself. Honestly, I *did* hide things back in high school and later because I didn't have the courage to explore, didn't have the energy to take that step and see where it led."

"But after? Now?"

"I think I'm bisexual. Maybe pansexual. Hell, maybe gay. I know I've been attracted to women. Sex with Nicole was nice, but not spectacular. Was that because we just weren't right for each other? Or because I wasn't as into girls as I thought I needed to be?" I flopped down on the couch and took a long pull from my beer before flinging an arm over my eyes.

Robby stopped what he was doing. "I'll be

honest, the older I get, the more I realize I'm very likely not one hundred percent straight. Like, do I love Celeste? Find myself incredibly attracted to her? Still get off on sex with her? Of course. Can I appreciate a hot guy and how sex with him could be amazing? Definitely." Robby shrugged, never concerned about shocking me. "Now, in my case—happily married and not looking for an open relationship or anything else—finding guys hot isn't going to change things for me at this stage in my life. Never saying never, but it's not something I'm concerned about right now."

I waited, knowing Robby would get to his point.

"But in *your* situation, single and definitely at a point where dating could be very doable, I think you owe it to yourself to explore." He ran a hand over his short hair. "If I asked you right now to close your eyes and think about who you want to be with, do you see a female or a male?"

I groaned. *I see your damned son.*

"Or, you know what, maybe you don't even see someone sexually. Maybe you're in the asexual area?" Robby moved to sit on the couch. "My point is that you don't have to hide who you are. You're home. You have support. You can feel safe to explore. If you find a woman you want to date, great. If you find a man, perfect. Find someone non-binary, that works. If you want to do the whole serial dating thing, it's your deal. Want to settle down? No worries." Robby slapped a hand on my back. "I just need you to know that all I want is for you to be happy. If that's by yourself, fine. If that's with someone, that's fine too. But don't ever think you have to keep the real you from me. I love you and accept you no matter what."

I gave some sort of grumbled answer and we fell into silence.

"I hate that Nicole died blaming my sexuality for her infidelity. I may have been confused, but I didn't cheat. I didn't even *think* about cheating. My issues were my issues. Yes, they might have been part of why I was detached—but that likely would have happened even if I wasn't confused about who I was. I was faithful—detached and not as open as I could have been—but I would never have cheated. I probably should have trusted Nicole enough to tell her how I was feeling; we were always great as friends." I pinched the bridge of my nose. "It just hurts that she opted to cheat while I sat around trying to figure myself out but never once contemplated cheating."

"I know, man. I hate the whole situation for

everyone involved. The cheating was wrong. What led to the cheating was multi-fold. The fact that Nicole was still hooking up with guys *after* you'd agreed to therapy is fucked up. Whether you're bi, pan, gay, ace, *whatever*, you didn't deserve to be cheated on." Robby held up his hand when I started to protest. "I know you like to shoulder the majority of the blame, but I'm not here for that. Your sexuality didn't ruin your marriage. Your lack of communication, Nicole's infidelity, and perhaps two kids who really never should have gotten married had a lot more to do with it than your sexuality. I agree, you're not blameless. I know it's hard to work through issues when one of the parties isn't available. But you don't get to take all of the blame." He squeezed my shoulder. "Main thing right now, I need you to know that who you are—no matter who or what you like, whether you figure out a label, or just need time to explore—you're always going to be my best friend and brother. I've got your back now just like I did back then. And I know you've got mine; there's no one on the face of this planet I trust more than you."

I squished my eyes shut and let threatening tears sting my sinuses. Robby was the best friend a guy could ask for.

And I'd agreed to fuck around with his son.

He's telling you he loves you no matter what. He's encouraging you to find yourself.

I cleared my throat. Pretty sure he didn't mean to find myself by burying my cock in his son's ass. *Fuck.*

I stood up and swung my arms in a long stretch. "Thanks, man. That means a lot. Better get this TV hung before I turn into a pumpkin. Lots to do tomorrow."

Robby studied me for a moment before giving a nod. "Still feels like you're hiding something from me, but I can be patient…"

I snorted. "You've never been patient a day in your life."

He shoved me with a laugh. "So, maybe you start telling me *everything*." Robby sobered a bit. "Seriously, though. Just know I'm here when you're ready."

"Thanks. Now help me with this. I think it's the damned heaviest television I've ever seen."

We finished mounting the TV, cleaned up the basement, and headed upstairs. I gave Robby a hug and another thanks. "Really do appreciate your help and you just being here."

And how did I repay my best friend's kindness?

After a shower, I waited by my dimly lit window for several moments until a scantily-clad Cooper showed up and watched like a fucking perv while he swayed and swished, his lean body putting on a show and lighting me on fire. After a few minutes of Cooper's little show, he palmed his junk and blew me a kiss.

In a complete daze, I closed the blinds, dropped my towel, and climbed into bed. My brain and body were on complete overload as I tried to think of all the things I wanted to do with Cooper. Hell, I wasn't even sure what all was available to do with him. I knew I wanted to touch him, kiss him, just have my hands everywhere on him. Would he be willing to suck me? Would I want to do that to him? My mouth watered at the thought. Okay, that was a definite yes.

Forcing my head to stop there, I imagined what it would be like to watch as Cooper's lips stretched around my cock and he took me deep into his mouth. I stroked myself as my imaginary Cooper sucked me, his eyes never leaving mine. When I fondled my balls, picturing Cooper's fingers against my skin, I groaned. With a few more long strokes, I shot my load over my chest and belly.

As I came down from my high, I couldn't help but smile.

I wanted a lot more kissing and touching with Cooper.

I wanted oral if he was okay with it.

There was *a lot* more, but I knew we needed to go

slowly. Maybe Cooper could talk me through our next steps.

All I knew was that I needed my mouth and hands on Cooper again.

Soon.

SEVEN

COOPER

"You going to listen to anything Dalton and I talked about the other night?" Spencer asked as I attempted to calm myself with a cup of coffee on Hadley's first day of school. I knew Jesse would be nervous so I wanted to be as cool and collected as possible.

"I heard what you said," I answered with very little commitment.

The night I'd kissed Jesse for the first time, I'd come home to find Dalton and Spencer playing video games in the den. I must have been giving off major vibes or something because the moment I'd joined them, they'd pounced.

"What's up with you? Why do you look all messed up? You've got a wild look in your eyes." Dalton paused the game to study me.

"Nothing's up," I answered and my voice sounded breathless even to my ears.

"No, he's right. I've seen this look." Spencer's eyes trailed me from head to toe. "You've been getting some action. Who is it?"

Dalton cocked his head to the side. "I thought you were at the neighbor's house helping."

Luckily, we weren't playing poker or I would have lost every penny.

"Fuck, Coop." Spencer chuckled and ran a hand over his face.

He must have seen something on my face just a bit before Dalton caught on, because my brother was still looking at me as if he couldn't quite grasp what was going on.

Spencer smacked him on the chest. "He's fucking around with the neighbor guy."

I winced for a split second before jutting my chin in challenge. "It's no big deal."

Dalton's eyes went wide. "No big deal?" He pinched the bridge of his nose and blew out a slow breath. "You want us to believe that there won't be major fall-out from you fucking your boss? Your much older boss who happens to be our dad's straight best friend?" He leaned forward, resting his elbows on his knees and his head in his hands.

Jesse's sexuality wasn't mine to discuss, so I let that one go. "It's not like a real boss and employee situation. Age isn't an issue when both people are consenting adults." My chin lifted a bit more. "And it's not long-term; Dad doesn't need to know."

Spencer lifted his hands in mock surrender. "Dude, you know I've got your back. Secret's safe and all that. I just think you need to remember that curious straight guys never turn out well. Like, at all." I got the feeling Spencer spoke from the experience of a curious straight guy.

"I know, I know." Truly, I'd been disappointed by a couple straight guys who just wanted to fuck around with a guy and then go home to their wives; I'd promised myself I wouldn't get involved in that mess again. But Jesse wasn't married. Jesse might not have completely understood what he wanted, but I felt a connection to him. It was like I was drawn to him and wanted to help him find his way.

Yeah, and have a little fun doing it.

"Man, you're walking a very fine line. In more ways than one," Dalton finally said. "I've got your back and I won't say anything. But I want it noted that I think this is a terrible idea."

"Deal. When it all comes crashing down, I won't come crying to you," I offered.

"Nah, you will. And we'll be here," Spencer said with a wry smile.

I smiled back. "Thanks. I know it's absolutely insane to even contemplate getting involved with him, even for a short time." I shrugged. "But there's something about him that I just can't ignore. Figure we can both scratch an itch and move on, no harm, no foul as long as we go into the situation with eyes wide open."

Dalton studied me for a moment. "Just maybe guard your heart?"

I scoffed. "My heart isn't in danger. Neither of us is looking for anything real."

Spencer rolled his eyes and picked up his controller. "You know what they say about things finding you when you're least expecting them."

Dalton nodded in agreement.

"This isn't a damned Hallmark Christmas movie. We're not going to end up falling in love." I bounced on the balls of my feet and gestured wildly. "I plan to swallow his cock and let him thoroughly use my ass. Plain and simple. There's no falling in love in fucking around."

Spencer and Dalton both snorted.

"Seriously, though. Just be careful. And try to make sure things don't get awkward and messy; we do have to live next door. Bev will be pissed if you mess things up with her neighbor." Dalton started the game again.

"I'm an adult. I want to fuck him. Period. Once we get it out of our systems, we can go back to being just friends. I'm working for the guy, I can't let it get awkward." I waved off their concerns.

"And when Dad accidentally finds out his best friend is boning his son?" Dalton quirked a brow, but didn't take his eyes from the screen.

"He won't find out. And if he does, it's really none of his business," I assured, although I felt a little less confident about that part. Dad finding out could get all kinds of sticky, especially for Jesse. I didn't want him to have trouble because of me. *"That's a bridge we can cross if we ever get to it. But I don't plan on that happening."*

"You keep living in your fantasy world," Dalton grumbled.

"Hope the cock is worth it," Spencer said with a wink.

I bit my lip and grinned. "I'm sure it will be."

Now I just needed Jesse to get on board.

Spencer knocked on the table to get my attention. "You okay? You zoned out for a minute there."

I shook my head and took a final swig of coffee as Bev came into the kitchen. "Yeah, I'm fine. And yes, I heard you. It's all good."

Spencer gave a nod, grabbed one thermos of coffee and one thermos of soup, stuffed two large sandwiches, an apple, and a cookie into a lunch box, and gave Bev a kiss on the cheek. "I'll probably eat at the diner tonight. Don't save me any dinner."

When it was just Bev and me she put both hands on her hips and stared at me until I squirmed.

"What?" I blurted.

"You and Jesse Thompson have something going on?" she asked.

My cheeks heated and I nodded. "Yeah, something. Totally casual."

Bev huffed. "Child, how do you manage to get yourself into situations like this?"

"It's no big deal. He's lonely and curious. I'm horny and available. We'll enjoy a mutually satisfying fling for as long as it works out and then we'll walk away." I shrugged and stood to wash my coffee cup.

"Walk away? Just going to walk away from the fact that you're his nanny? He's your dad's best friend? You live right next door?" Bev tsked and opened the oven to turn the casserole she'd had cooking for nearly an hour already—she always said a nice slow cook was the key to breakfast casseroles.

"I'll still be his nanny. He'll still be Dad's best friend—Dad doesn't need to know any of this by the way." I laughed when she rolled her eyes. "And living next door won't change."

"Pretty sure the things you're hoping to get up to with that man are intimate enough that things most definitely *will* change. You may like to think that sex can be casual and meaningless, but when a friendship is involved from the beginning, feelings get tangled up; things get messy." Bev patted my cheek. "I just don't want to see either of you hurt."

I sighed. "No one is going to get hurt. He's not looking for a relationship. I'm not looking for a relationship. We'll do the whole friends-with-benefits thing for as long as we mutually deem necessary. Then it's just back to normal." I tapped my hands on the counter.

Bev shook her head and smiled. "Love is what happens when no one is *looking*. Do you even know what *normal* is between the two of you? For a bright boy, you're sure being pretty daft right now." She pointed a finger my way. "Mark my words, this will get messy. Maybe not end in disaster, but it will definitely get messy." She cocked her head. "It feels very ill-advised and I'd tell you to call it off if it were up to me, but I'm going to push aside my worries and choose to believe this may be a good thing for you. A learning experience. Heaven knows you're not going to take my advice anyway, might as well just let you enjoy yourself."

"Thanks," I said with a kiss to her cheek. "I'm a big boy, I can handle a little mess."

"It's more your heart I'm worried about," Bev muttered. "But we'll be here when you need us."

I gave her a hug and grabbed my backpack.

"Here, this is ready. Let me send some for you and Jesse." Bev pulled the casserole from the oven. "I'll just make a big plate, give me a second. Now, you make sure they know we're expecting them for dinner this evening."

I had a feeling Hadley wouldn't want the egg concoction, but Jesse and I could enjoy a nice breakfast. Maybe good food and a cup of coffee would help calm his jitters.

I took the plate, careful not to burn my fingers, and bounded out the door and down the stairs. Not only was today a first day for Hadley, I was hoping it was the first of many great days for Jesse and me.

Jesse opened the door with a steaming mug of coffee and a nervous smile.

"Good morning," I said. "Bev sent breakfast and wanted to be sure you remember about dinner."

He held the door open for me with a smile. "We'll be there."

"Hadley still asleep?"

"Yeah, I'll let her sleep about thirty more minutes unless her excitement wakes her up." Jesse pointed toward the coffee pot, but I shook my head. "Usually, I'll go out to the shop as soon as you get here, but I made sure to keep the morning open today since I want to be here for the first day and all that."

I stepped into his space and reached around to place the plate on the counter. Jesse's scent—soap, mint, and coffee—teased my nose and I closed my eyes, breathing him in deep.

When Jesse turned away, I bit back a brief sting of disappointment. But the clunk of his mug on the counter and his arm coming around my waist a moment later sent a shiver of anticipation through me. "I don't have any idea how to do this," Jesse mumbled as he pulled me close and brought his mouth to my ear. "But I know I *want* to do it."

I wrapped my arms around his neck and tipped my head back, offering him my neck. "Just do what feels good," I whispered.

Jesse's warm lips against my skin sent shockwaves through my body. He teased and tongued my neck before making his way to my ear, my jawline, and finally my mouth. When his lips hovered over mine, I had to force myself to be patient. It felt as if Jesse needed time to explore.

"My head is all sorts of messed up this morning. My baby is going to school, my business *needs* to do well, and a large part of me is stuck in a loop thinking of nothing but getting my hands on you. There's this tangled mess of *something* inside me, longing for things I don't even know I want—how can I want things I don't even know about?" He sighed, pressing his forehead against mine. "I'm hoping this will get easier as we go along, but I need you to know that I want everything."

"Everything?" I smiled and raised a brow. "Like kinky shit?"

Jesse snorted. "Okay, let's start with *everything* on

the tamer side. I'm not sure I'm ready to skip the primer lessons and go straight into the advanced shit."

"Can I suggest your first assignment?" I licked my lips, my eyes drawing straight to his mouth.

Jesse nodded.

"Kiss me."

He grunted, cupping the back of my head and pressing our lips together. The sweet, warm kiss quickly morphed into hot and hungry. I whimpered when Jesse's tongue swept along my bottom lip, teasing my mouth open, and dipping inside to lick and savor.

The taste of Jesse on my tongue would be something I remembered for the rest of my life. Long after this little thing was over, I'd dream of tasting him, feeling his lips against mine, his hands on my body.

Footsteps creaked upstairs and Jesse groaned. "Later," he whispered and brushed a final kiss against my lips.

Hadley came bounding down the stairs. "I go to school today!"

"Good morning," Jesse said as he grabbed her up in a hug. "Are you a little excited?"

"I'm *very* excited," Hadley answered seriously.

"I'm going to ride the bus and make friends and learn to read."

"Let's get you some breakfast then," I said.

"Cooper!" she scrambled from Jesse's arms and leaped into mine. "You're going to be here every morning?"

I nodded. "Yep. We'll spend mornings and afternoons together. When you're in school, I'll be at school, too."

"And Daddy will be working in his new shop." Hadley let me put her down in a chair at the kitchen table. "Can I have bananas on my Cheerios? And juice, please?"

We fell into what seemed would be an easy daily routine of breakfast and chatter. Jesse had a small television turned on to a local news channel and a story about a freak snowstorm causing travel issues in a mountain state flashed across the screen.

"You know, that's something we'll need to think about. If weather gets bad and both of our schools are closed, no worries. I can just be here all day. But if Hadley's home and I'm still in school, we'll need to have a contingency plan." I scooped part of the casserole onto a paper plate. "Bev can likely help out."

Jesse savored a bite of his breakfast. "And I can

set her up in the shop when I'm working. I was thinking of making her a little corner for reading and coloring and watching videos."

"Sounds perfect. Hopefully, we won't have an issue, but you never know with weather around here. Good thing is, a lot of the schools are equipped for virtual learning these days, so at least we won't have to worry about make-up days." I took another bite of the savory breakfast casserole. "Sorry to say I won't be bringing breakfast like this every day."

"It's so good," Jesse said around a big bite. "I'll get by with cereal and toast I guess."

"Daddy, can I watch a video?" Hadley asked as she took a final bite of her Cheerios.

"Let's do teeth, clothes, and hair first," I said, then winced. "Sorry," I mouthed to Jesse.

He shook his head. "Cooper's right. Teeth, clothes, and hair. As long as he's taking care of the hair part."

When Hadley had washed her face, brushed her teeth, picked out the outfit she wanted to wear, and sat still long enough for me to braid her hair, she skipped off to find her tablet.

When Jesse offered me coffee, I nodded.

"You nervous?" I asked as we sat down at the kitchen table.

"Yeah, can you tell? I'm trying to keep it together so she doesn't see it. But damn, this is hard. I remember Lauren going to school for the first time. I wished her luck and went off to work. God, I didn't even stay to watch her get on the bus—just left it to Nicole." Jesse ran a hand over his face. "I don't know if it's losing a child or just getting older that makes me realize how important it is to *be there* for the moments—big and small."

I reached over and put my hand on his. "Probably a little bit of both. She's going to do great."

"Yeah, I'm not worried about her. It's just hard watching her grow up. I've been so haggard during these first five years, I worry that I've taken things for granted or missed out. Like I was so busy grieving and surviving that I didn't take time to appreciate the little things. And now, boom, she's five and going to school." Jesse's eyes shone with tears.

"You've done an amazing job with her. She's well-adjusted, smart, creative—she's a good kid. I can't speak from experience, but I know my parents always talked about loving parts of each stage with us. Like they mourned the passing of time, but looked forward to seeing what was next." I cocked my head to the side. "I think it's probably one of the hardest things in the world to see your baby grow up, but also one of the most rewarding. Like, how can you be so proud of something but want to stop time completely all at once?"

"Exactly," Jesse said with a sigh. "It's like I'm preparing to put my heart on that bus this morning. I'll smile and wave, but inside, I'll be dying."

"You know, this is helpful. As someone who isn't a parent, knowing what you're going through will help me when I'm dealing with nervous, emotional parents as they bring their babies to my school." I took a sip of coffee.

"Glad I could be of service," Jesse teased. "Thanks for listening to me blather on. Just talking about it helps."

"I'm glad. I'm thinking it would maybe help other parents, too. Maybe when I open my school, I can arrange for those who might be interested to meet at a local coffee shop for a chat. Maybe talking after dropping their kids off would be good for them."

"I bet a lot would really like that." Jesse squeezed my hand. "I know your school is going to be a huge success."

"I've got a long way to go, but it's getting closer and closer to coming true and that's both scary and so damned exciting." I glanced down at our hands. Since when had a fling brought hand holding?

I pushed the thought away. Jesse was nervous. I was being a supportive friend.

"I'm really glad I've got a full schedule today, keep me busy so I can't miss her too much." Jesse took our empty mugs to the sink. "What time is dinner?"

"We'll plan on six. That give you time to get cleaned up?"

"Yeah, that works. I'll just try to keep Thursdays earlier days so I can be done in time."

"Oh! I was thinking, when you get all the emergency contact paperwork and whatnot from the school," I paused to smile at Jesse's frown, "yeah, you'll have homework," I teased, "be sure to put me and Bev down as emergency numbers after you. And maybe my dad? He'd be a last resort, but I'm sure he wouldn't mind."

"Good idea, thanks." He ran fingers through his hair and suddenly I was jealous of his hand. *I* wanted to be that hand sifting through his caramel brown and silver locks. "Damn, I hadn't thought about the fact I'd have homework."

"I'll help with Hadley's homework and I can help with yours, too. But I want to be sure you look at her work so you know all about what she's doing in school. I don't want you missing out on that."

Jesse smiled softly. "Thanks. You're really great, you know that?"

I shrugged and gave a wink. "You have no idea just how great I am. You just wait until I get you alone and naked," I whispered.

Jesse closed his eyes and groaned.

I stood by a bit later while Jesse helped Hadley load her backpack with school supplies, zip it, and heft it onto her back. The emotions warring on Jesse's face tugged at my heart strings. He was so in love with that little girl, so proud of her, so excited to let her go off on this new adventure. But his heart was breaking to watch her go. I flashed forward to all the firsts Hadley would experience. High school, prom, driving, college. How would Jesse handle those milestones? Something pinched deep inside as I realized I wanted to be there for those milestones as well.

No.

Nope.

Not a good idea.

That train of thought was a recipe for disaster.

I was sure I could still be part of Hadley's life for all of those stages.

As a friend.

Only a friend.

Jesse would be nearing seventy and I'd be just over forty by the time Hadley went off to college. Trying to fathom that was almost impossible.

Holy shit.

Either way, I needed to stop thinking about *Jesse and me* in the future. We'd hopefully still be friendly, but there was really no way to think we'd be anything more.

We'd barely done anything yet. And we'd agreed to casual and easy, no strings, no mess. The thought of anything beyond friendship two decades down the road was ludicrous.

So, why was I even entertaining the fantasy of Jesse with his arm around me, both of us holding back tears, as we watched Hadley drive off to college for the first time?

Fuck.

No. I was *not* letting my head and heart play dirty tricks on me.

Jesse was going to be the perfect pastime for fun, sweaty sex. He didn't want anything more. *I* didn't want anything more.

He'd probably be married to a nice woman his age by that time.

Maybe a guy.

And why did the thought of Jesse with *anyone* else take hold of my chest like an icy claw and refuse to let go?

I'd be married, running a successful preschool—hell, by that time, maybe I'd own a few around the state—and the memory of what Jesse and I shared would be tucked nice and neat in the back of my mind. Something I'd bring out to smile about when I was feeling nostalgic.

Period.

I needed to get Jesse naked and fuck all the weirdness from my head. Stat.

Emotions had no place in what we were doing.

You think it's a bit strange that you're already feeling so connected to this guy and you've not done anything more than kiss?

I sighed and flashed Jesse a smile when he threw a concerned glance my way.

Yes. Yes, I did think it was insane that I felt so much pull toward Jesse.

But when he smiled back, my chest warmed and I couldn't argue that there was *definitely* something—a spark, a connection, *something*—between us. More than physical, more than just sex.

Fuck.

What would these crazy thoughts and feelings do when we added sex to the equation?

The thought both thrilled and terrified me.

I *had* to keep myself together. I'd promised Jesse a

good time with no messiness. I was going to give him a good time with no messiness.

If my heart got more involved than I'd planned, I'd deal.

On my own.

I didn't need to pull Jesse into whatever mess I decided to fall into.

About ten minutes before Hadley's bus was scheduled to arrive, I cleared my throat and pushed the craziness from my head. "Let's get some pictures," I announced.

Hadley smiled and posed with her backpack and with Jesse. He picked her up and blew a raspberry on her cheek while she laughed. They made silly faces at the camera. He popped her down next to the front steps and knelt beside her for another shot.

"You should do a couple shots in front of things that will likely always be here. That way, you can take pics in the same spot every year." I gritted my teeth at the bittersweet feel of the morning. And, to be honest, I hated the thought that I'd likely not be around for many more first days of school.

Jesse had Hadley stand by a tree, the mailbox, and the front door.

"Hadley, you want a picture with Cooper?" Jesse asked as he pulled out his phone.

"Yes!" Hadley ran over to me and I hoisted her onto my hip.

Jesse took a couple shots, his eyes suspiciously shiny and his smile watery, before Hadley's excitement forced her from my arms and closer to the sidewalk.

The loud squeak of bus breaks split through the air. "Sounds like it's one stop away, we should go to the corner." I gestured toward the corner.

Hadley skipped down the sidewalk to the bus stop. It was on the opposite side of Remington Place, right where Remington Way and Pleasure Boulevard intersected. I was already thinking that I'd likely warm up the car and have Hadley sit with me until the bus pulled up once the weather turned cold.

"I'm guessing some of the future photo shoots won't have such an excited and willing subject," I teased as Hadley squealed and bounced up and down when she saw the bus pull around the final corner before her stop.

"It's hard to imagine her as a sullen teen." Jesse frowned. "Don't know how I'll get through those years. I'm not sure I was the greatest dad to Lauren during that time, I worry I'll screw up with Hadley."

"Hey." I nudged him with my elbow. "Don't go borrowing trouble and worry. Stay focused on the now. You've got an amazing kid who is nearly bursting with excitement about school. That's all that matters for today."

The bus driver suggested a picture with Jesse and Hadley by the bus and I took one of Hadley climbing aboard. One final shot of her waving through the window, huge smile on her face, and then the bus lurched away from the corner, growling and belching as it moved to its next stop.

Jesse's audible intake of air had me reaching for his hand and giving it a squeeze. "She's going to do great," I assured.

He absently returned the gesture before dropping my hand and shoving his hands in his pockets. "It's not her I'm worried about."

We walked back to his place making small talk regarding school lunch or packed lunch and what was available for a snack when Hadley got home that afternoon.

Once inside the house, Jesse crowded me to the corner of the kitchen counter and pressed his lips against mine in a burning kiss. "Do you have to go to school?" he asked between licks and nips.

I groaned, knowing it was a bad idea to hop up onto the counter and spread my legs for this man, but I did it anyway. "Yeah, need to leave soon." But instead giving any indication of leaving, I wrapped my legs around his waist and pulled him close as I deepened the kiss.

Jesse grunted as our thickening bulges connected. "Fuck, I wanna skip work and take you to bed, spend all day touching you and kissing you. I want—*need*— to learn every inch of your body." His hands caressed from my shoulders to my back before settling on my ass and pulling me hard against him. "I know it's going to sound pathetic and maybe even cliché, but kissing and touching has *never* felt like this before."

I kissed him again, rocking my hips into his, before breaking free. "Yeah? What's different?"

"Everything. Before was nice. Enjoyable. But simple. Nothing spectacular." Jesse sucked my bottom lip between his teeth, biting and then soothing the sting with his tongue. "This? This has me on fire. Like electric currents are shooting through my veins. I never understood the hot, passionate, *I saw stars* type making out and sex. But touching you, tasting you, having your body respond to mine, I'm thinking I was just missing out on what others had."

I had no words for his admission, so I pulled him into a searing kiss, my tongue exploring and savoring as I committed his taste to memory. I broke the kiss, panting. "As much as I'd love nothing more than to play hooky and spend the day in bed, we can't. One, it's not good for business. Two, we said we'd go slow. If we had *all* day in bed, we'd end up rounding allll the bases and sliding into home before dinner if I had my way." I nibbled at his ear.

Jesse groaned. "That sounds so good. Yes, let's do that."

I laughed. "No can do. You've got customers to impress and I've got a full day of preschool."

"After dinner?" Jesse asked hopefully.

I smiled. "Perfect. Dinner first. Then you and Hadley do your evening routine. You let me know when she's in bed and you're nice and comfy in the basement."

"Oh, that reminds me. You need a key." Jesse gave me one last lingering glance and then moved to the drawer he'd deemed *the everything drawer*. He rummaged around and came up with a silver key. "Here, this way you can get in if I'm ever not here."

I knew he was only giving me the key because of my nanny position. It wasn't like he was asking me to move in or be more than his fun fling. But the piece of metal burned against my skin as I slid it into my pocket. With a quick kiss, I squeezed his ass. "Be thinking of what you want to do tonight. I can't stay super late, but we can probably get about two hours before I need to head home."

Jesse growled. "Gonna be hard all day thinking about you."

"Just don't show up to dinner with a boner. Bev will give you shit," I teased.

I followed him out the backdoor and gave a little wave as I crossed to Remington Place and climbed into my car. I watched Jesse's perfect ass walk into his shop and I smiled. Basement time couldn't come soon enough.

DINNER AT REMINGTON Place turned out to be a really nice time.

Hadley chattered on and on about her first day at school and kept the entire crew entertained. It felt good to see her so happy and at ease with people I hoped would become our friends.

Cooper kept Hadley talking as he knew the best questions to ask a brand-new Kindergarten student.

Gabby, Dalton's girlfriend, seemed really comfortable with kids with the easy way she talked to Hadley. Dalton seemed a bit less at ease, but he was kind.

Spencer seemed a mixture of terrified and amazed by Hadley. He listened to her stories and smiled, but definitely didn't ask her any questions.

Bev was the quintessential grandmotherly type

and I got the feeling she'd be more than willing to have Hadley around. When Hadley mentioned she wanted to make a cake again, Bev beamed and said they'd have to make a baking day soon.

"You always been a mechanic?" Spencer asked me when Hadley joined Bev in the living room to read some books.

"Yeah, I worked on cars a lot with my grandpa so it was all I wanted to do when we were picking careers back in high school. I went to trade school and started working at a shop near Chicago. Worked there my whole career until I moved here. Hoping to be able to build this business up." I wiped my mouth and placed my napkin on my plate; the meal had been absolutely delicious.

"You have to keep up with licensing and certifications?" Dalton asked as he took a drink of his tea.

I wasn't sure if he was truly interested, but it was nice that he made a point to take part in the conversation. I nodded. "Yeah, I take a few certification classes and trainings each year to keep my license current."

"You taking new customers?" Spencer asked.

"Always," I said with a smile.

"Good, I'm not in love with the place I've been

getting my oil changed," Gabby said. "I'll definitely be making an appointment."

"Same. I can do some of the work myself, but finding the time to do it gets to be too much sometimes. I'd be happy to give you business instead." Spencer carried his plate to the sink and began to scrape it into the disposal.

"Totally," Dalton said. "Consider yourself at least three customers fuller."

"Love it, thanks. I've got references from my old shop if you need them."

"Nah, Dad vouches for you and Cooper said your shop looks as professional as any chain place he's been in." Dalton took his and Gabby's plates to the sink.

We visited for a bit longer before Bev and Hadley returned.

"Daddy, I read a book! Ms. Bev helped me and I read the whole thing!" Hadley scrambled up onto my lap.

"That's awesome! Did you tell Ms. Bev thank you for her help?"

Cooper gave Hadley a high five.

"Thank you," Hadley said to Bev. "She said we can have ice cream. Can we stay for ice cream?"

"We can do ice cream, then we need to head home for bath time and bed." I smiled at Cooper as he coughed and stood to take my plate. Was he looking forward to the night as much as I was?

"But I'm not tired," Hadley insisted even as she gave a huge yawn.

"Not at all," Cooper teased. "You have to get a good night's sleep so you can be ready for another day at school."

Hadley launched into a story about what she wanted to learn the next day.

Bev pulled a pan from the oven. "Cherry crisp. Who wants theirs with ice cream and who wants it plain?"

Hadley opted for just ice cream, Cooper for just cherry crisp, and the rest of us took our crisp with ice cream.

"This is so good," I said around a bite of tart cherries, sweet, crunchy crisp, and cold ice cream. "Coop, you should make this for an afterschool snack," I teased.

Cooper's eyes shot to mine and he quirked a smile. Too late, I realized I'd shortened his name as if we were closer than just nanny and employer. Damn. He was just so easy to be around—I truly felt like I'd known him forever—that it had been an easy slip. Did the others notice? Would they pick up on whatever was going on between Cooper and me?

"Something tells me that only one of the

Thompson family would be partaking and enjoying that particular snack." Cooper smiled easily and took another bite. "Plus, Bev always makes it better than I can. You'll just have to hope she makes it for a Thursday dinner again."

"The issue with Bev's cooking is that everything is so dang good, you feel torn between wanting a repeat of something you love but also wanting her to make something new so you can love it, too," Gabby said as she scraped her bowl to gather the last bite of dessert.

Hadley and Bev talked about what they'd make on their baking day.

Dalton, Gabby, and Spencer helped with clean-up and said goodbye.

Cooper gave Hadley a big hug and told her he'd see her tomorrow.

I thanked Bev for dinner and made sure Hadley did the same thing.

Then I watched Hadley skip down the back steps while Cooper walked with me to the gate between our houses.

"Goodnight, Hadley. Sleep tight. See you in the morning," he called out as she balanced on a crack in the sidewalk. Turning to me, he spoke softly, "Really want to kiss you right now, but Bev's likely watching and little eyes are near. You still want me to come over?"

"Hell, yes. I'll text you once she's in bed." I licked my lips and fought the urge to pull him close.

"Enjoy your time with her, don't rush. I'll just be doing homework." Cooper gave me a wink and bit his bottom lip before smiling seductively and turning back toward Remington Place.

Hadley and I spent the next hour doing bath and bed routine—I was glad Cooper had walked me through her folder and the paperwork before dinner —and she was yawning before the end of the second book. By the third, which she insisted she wanted to read, my big Kindergartener was out like a light. I closed the book—we'd start with it next time—and kissed the top of her head. Pulling the cover up to her shoulder, I clicked off the bedside lamp and made sure the baby monitor was on.

Hadley almost never woke in the middle of the night, unless she was sick, but she knew that I could always hear her on the monitor so it was a safety net for both of us.

I left her door open halfway, just the way she liked it so the hallway nightlight could shine in but not too brightly, and made my way down the stairs.

Once in my room, I took the fastest shower ever and texted Cooper on my way to the basement.

. . .

ME: *I'm in the basement. Backdoor is unlocked, can you lock it behind you?*

COOPER: *On my way.*

I GLANCED around the basement while my heart threatened to pound out of my chest. In some ways, I felt like some damned sneaky kid getting ready to make out for the first time. In other ways, I felt like a damned pathetic man who was hiding in my basement planning to make out with a guy for the first time.

Either way, I couldn't help the excitement and nerves.

I knew Cooper and I both couldn't stay up super late, so I figured we'd skip any drinking. I turned the television to a music channel and hoped it wasn't too cheesy to turn off the lights. The glow from the screen cast shadows in the room, but it was bright enough that I could see the pattern on the couch slip-cover. I wanted to be able to see Cooper and everything we did.

I heard the basement door open and close and

then I saw Cooper's socked feet coming down the steps and my heart tried to claw its way to my throat.

"Killing me with the gray sweats," Cooper teased as he walked toward me with a crooked grin. When he got close enough, I reached out and pulled him into a long, searing kiss and my whole body warmed as he sighed into me. "As much as I love the pants, I think I'm going to love getting them off of you more." He smiled and waggled his brows.

"Yeah, I want that. Want to see you naked. Want to be naked with you." I knew I sounded like a babbling idiot, but I couldn't stop the words.

"Let's set some boundaries before this goes too far," Cooper suggested, his hands rubbing up and down my back under my shirt. "As much as I'd like to think we could take all night, we know we can't. Let's talk about what we want."

"I want to touch you and feel you against me," I answered honestly.

"Start with mutual hand jobs and see if we're up for blow jobs before our time is up?" Cooper suggested. "You don't have to blow me. I understand if you're not ready for that."

I tried to breathe, but I couldn't, so I just nodded and squeaked out something that sounded like *yes*.

"Can I take off your shirt?" Cooper asked.

"Yeah. Can I?" I gripped the bottom of his shirt.

"Oh yeah." He grinned as he pulled my shirt over my head.

Once I had his shirt off and tossed to the floor, I couldn't help the growl that rumbled from my chest when our bare skin came together. The heat between our bodies, the slight prickle as our chest hair rubbed, and the electric shock that traveled through me when my nipples brushed against Cooper's chest was almost too much to take.

In a blur of movement, Cooper and I shucked our pants and fell to the couch in a tangle of arms and legs. My arms fit under his and I pulled his chest to mine as our mouths met in a hot, sloppy kiss. Cooper's legs fell open and I grunted when our heavy, thick cocks—separated only by thin cotton—rubbed together.

"Oh, fuck. I'm going to embarrass myself for sure," I muttered.

Cooper laughed. "We'll embarrass ourselves together then. Have a feeling the moment we're skin-to-skin, I'm going to blow." His hands roamed my chest, tweaking my nipples. He grinned when I gasped. "Anyone ever play with your nipples?"

I shook my head. "No. Didn't realize that would feel so good."

Cooper lifted his head and flicked his tongue

against first one nipple and then the other and I moaned. When his lips suckled a tight nub, I nearly came right then.

"Fuck," I gasped. "That feels like it goes straight to my balls."

"Good to know," Cooper said.

"Are yours like that?"

"They aren't super sensitive. I'm more sensitive on my neck and back. And a few other places that we won't get to tonight," he said with a wink.

My face went hot as I wondered just where those other places were. I vowed to find out where he liked to be touched and do my best to make my way there as often as possible.

"Can I touch you?" Cooper asked as his hand played at the waistband of my underwear.

"God, yes. Can I?"

Cooper nodded and we somehow shimmied from our underwear in record time.

And then his hand was on me and I nearly shot my load right then and there. "Fuck," I gritted out. His touch was so different than anything I'd ever experienced and I loved it.

I brought my hand between us and rubbed my knuckles over Cooper's long, heavy cock. When he whimpered, I stroked him up and down again. Nervous that I'd do something wrong, I trailed my fingers along his shaft, dipped gently to his balls, and ran a thumb over his slit.

"Jess, I'm not going to break," Cooper said breathlessly.

Loving the sound of my nickname on his lips, I took his length in my fist and groaned at the warmth and heft of his cock. The first time I'd ever touched another man's dick and I suddenly wanted everything. Wanted to see him come, wanted to feel him unload in my hand, wanted to run my tongue through his leaking slit, take him between my lips.

Cooper shifted under me, panting as I stroked him. "Here, rub against me."

I moved so our erections pressed together. The heat and friction took my breath away. When Cooper took both our lengths in his hand, I knew I wouldn't last long as my balls drew up and a tingle traveled through my lower back. "Gonna go quick," I warned.

"Put your hand around mine. We'll get off together." Cooper waited until my hand came around his and then started stroking in the most perfect rhythm. "Look at us," he urged.

I looked at our leaking heads, rock-solid shafts, and grasped hands. It was too much. "Go faster."

Cooper increased the speed.

I ran my thumb through Cooper's pre-cum and mixed it with mine.

"Let me taste," Cooper said, licking his lips.

I brought my wet, sticky thumb to his mouth and groaned when he licked it clean. When he gripped the back of my head and pulled me in for a kiss, I lost it. With our combined flavors on my tongue, my body tensed and I shot my release between us, my cock throbbing as it pulsed rope after rope onto Cooper's stomach.

He followed me right over and I shuddered as I watched his cum mix with mine on his pale skin.

We collapsed into a heap of heavy breathing and aftershocks.

"The good thing about that being over so fast is that we should have time for round two," Cooper said with a laugh. "Any idea what you want to do?"

"I want to taste you. I'll probably suck at it, but I want to try," I said.

"Mmm, I *hope* you suck at it," he teased. "Sucking is kinda the point."

I chuckled. "You know what I mean."

"Your mouth on my dick will never be *bad*. Even without experience, I'm going to guess you can get me off. Just do what you know feels good."

I heaved a sigh. "Will do. But I'm going to need at least thirty minutes." I rolled from the couch and ambled to the bathroom, feeling as if I was floating from the high I'd just experienced, and grabbed a towel.

Once we were cleaned up, I let Cooper take the lead as he arranged us on the couch like big and little spoons.

We spent the next thirty minutes just chatting and semi-dozing.

"The calendar that Hadley brought home today mentions a back-to-school night. You wanna come with? I mean, I don't expect you to, I know she's still my responsibility and it's not a part of your job. Just thought you'd maybe like to meet the teacher and stuff." I ran my hand up and down his thigh. I knew I had to make sure I didn't get *too* reliant on Cooper, but having him there so the teacher knew he was part of Hadley's life was important to me.

And part of your life?

"Sure thing. You okay with being seen as a couple? No matter what we tell people, they're going to assume. My mom will be there; I'm torn between wishing she was Hadley's teacher and being glad she's not. She loved preschool, but really loves Kindergarten these days." Cooper's hand rubbed gently along the arm I held across his chest.

"Honestly? It gives me a little bit of anxiety. But for the most part, I'm not terribly worried. You're the nanny, no one needs to know anything more than that. Like you said, this is just for fun and it will be over before anyone important needs to find out. After everything I've been through, it feels ridiculous to be concerned about what people might think about me." I sighed and nuzzled my nose against his hair. "And if I ever decide to date a man, I might as well get used to it, right?"

A weird feeling fluttered in my chest. I really didn't want to think about being with any man but Cooper.

And that thinking needed to stop right there.

What we were doing wasn't long-term.

For several reasons.

And I couldn't allow myself to forget that.

"I mean, you don't *have* to do anything. It's nobody's business." Cooper tapped his fingers against my arm.

"Would *you* want to date a man who couldn't be out and honest about who he loved?" I asked.

Cooper tensed for a split second before resuming the tapping. "No. But that's just me and you're not trying to date me. Just don't think you have to out yourself just to date someone." He shifted in my arms. "Sorry, fidgets are starting."

"What helps them?"

"Well, my medicine is really helpful. Caffeine can help relax me—hypes others up, can calm people with ADHD. That orgasm was a nice little relaxer," he said and I could hear the smile in his words. "I'll take a pill before bed that will help me sleep. Medicine in the morning is always a relief from the constant fidgets. My medication is time-released so it lasts pretty much all day, but by morning, I can definitely tell it's time for another dose."

"What does ADHD feel like?"

Cooper chuckled. "Like a three-ring circus in my brain and body times ten. When I was a kid, I was impulsive, couldn't stay in my seat, blurted out answers, interrupted, couldn't wait my turn, and had a hard time staying focused on assignments. Throw in the dyscalculia and I was a mess most of the time."

I pulled him closer, wanting to comfort him. "And now?"

He sighed. "Now, it's more in my head and the fidgets. I'm not as impulsive," he paused with a snort, "although, I guess offering a fling with my new boss could be considered pretty impulsive."

I kissed his neck, loving the way he moaned. "Not going to complain."

"I can sit for longer periods of time, but often have to stand or move when it gets to be too much. My head seems to constantly be going a million miles a minute. I have to put everything in my phone and write it down or I'll forget. I've learned how to stay pretty organized—which was a huge issue in school—and I work really hard to avoid distractions. I'll put on headphones and use ambient music when I'm working on assignments." He stretched his legs, still tapping his fingers on my arm—I wondered if he even realized he was doing it. "Dancing, moving, getting enough sleep, all those things help. I've learned how to use my strengths and work around my weaknesses. I feel anxiety a lot of the time, like I want to excel in what I do, but people expect me to fail—or maybe *I* expect me to fail; I always feel mediocre." He shrugged. "Not sure if that makes sense."

I nodded, brushing my lips against his neck again. "It does. I know it's hard to tell your brain things sometimes, but I want you to know that you are *not* mediocre in my eyes. You're amazing with Hadley, you do great in school, you have this fabulous plan, and you're focused on reaching your goals."

"My constant movement and lack of filter don't bother you?" he asked softly.

"Not at all. Maybe because I grew up with Robby, but I barely notice your fidgets. And I love your words; I never know what to expect, but talking to you is refreshing."

"So, when I'm fidgeting, I remind you of my dad?" Cooper teased. "Gross. I hope nothing we're doing tonight reminds you of him."

I laughed. "Not at all. No more talk of Robby, you're killing my vibe."

When he turned in my arms to face me, my chest tightened. I'd *just* gotten off and yet all I wanted to do was kiss him, touch him, taste him, and find that shared release again. I'd *never* felt this way about sex —it was exciting and scary.

"Not tonight, but tell me some of the things you might like to do," Cooper suggested as his leg rested over mine, our reawakening dicks nestled together.

"Oh God," I muttered.

"No, none of that. If we're going to do this, we have to be able to talk."

"I don't even know what I like or what I might like." But I knew I loved my hand trailing down Cooper's back to cup his ass.

"Have you ever watched gay porn?"

I coughed. "Um, no. Haven't watched much porn at all. The stuff guys in school watched never really did much for me."

"Assignment before next time, watch some gay porn. See if there's anything that looks like something you might like to try."

I nodded and swallowed thickly. "I want to taste you."

"That can definitely be arranged. Like, very soon." Cooper rocked his hips against mine.

"I want to try anal, but I want to do it first. So I know what it feels like."

Cooper's eyes shot up to mine. "Like, you want to bottom? Have a dick in your ass?"

My cheeks flamed hot, but I nodded. "Seems like I should know what it's like before I try doing it to someone else. Is that weird?"

Cooper smiled and shook his head. "No, not at all. I just don't get many men asking me to top."

I winced. "Shit, is that something you don't like to do?"

"Oh, I like it just fine and the thought of fucking you has me about to nut right here. Just wasn't expecting it."

"I have no clue what all getting fucked entails," I admitted.

"No worries, we'll get there." Cooper pressed a kiss against my chest before moving to take a nipple between his teeth, making me hiss. "And you want to top? Be the one doing the fucking?"

"Oh, hell yes. So much." I thrust my hips, loving the way our hard lengths rubbed together. "Can I suck you?"

"Fuck, yes. How were you picturing it?" Cooper asked breathlessly.

"Can you just lay on the couch? I'll get on my knees."

Cooper shifted to let me roll off the couch before he stretched out, his hard cock bobbing against his stomach. "You don't *have* to do this. Anything, everything, or nothing, it's all up to you."

I licked my lips. "I want to." My mouth watered at the image of my lips stretched around his cock. "Just be patient, I have no clue what I'm doing."

"No worries, just do what feels good."

I leaned forward and pressed a kiss alongside Cooper's navel before moving to nuzzle my nose into his dark blond, trimmed pubic hair. I gripped his cock and stroked as I placed a kiss against his lower abdomen. When he gasped, I glanced up. "Like that?"

Cooper nodded. "You found one of my most sensitive spots."

Smiling as if I'd uncovered hidden treasure, I kissed the pale skin again and sucked it between my lips.

Cooper whimpered. "Fuck, love that. Mark me, wanna see it tomorrow."

I growled, loving the idea of *my* mark being on

Cooper where only he could see it and remember what we'd done. I sucked harder and thrilled at the way his cock jerked in my hand. Once I'd left my mark, I moved my attention to his dick. All of the fear and worry I'd had over the years, the purposely pushing away any kind of fantasies, all of it went away and it was like I knew exactly what I wanted to do with this gorgeous man. I flicked my tongue across his slit and smiled when Cooper's hips bucked. "You taste so good," I murmured before swirling my tongue around his head. Parting my lips, I took him into my mouth and moaned at how perfectly right it felt.

"Oh fuck," Cooper panted. "When you moan like that, I feel it all the way to my balls."

I smiled around the mouthful of cock and took him deeper. Gagging, I popped off. "Sorry. Can't go super deep. What do you like?"

"Play with my balls. Not for now, but I like to be fingered, too."

I moved his leg, spreading him wide for me, and took his dick back into my mouth as I fondled his balls. Cooper gasped and rocked his hips as I stroked and sucked him.

"If you don't want me coming in your mouth this time, let me suck you," Cooper suggested.

"But I want you to get off," I protested,

continuing to stroke his cock while I played with his balls.

"I will. Wanna suck you while I jack myself."

My cock jumped at the idea. "Where do you want me?"

Cooper stood from the couch. "Sit there with your legs spread."

I felt like a kid scrambling to get a reward. Settling in on the couch, I spread my legs, my cock leaking against my stomach.

I groaned as Cooper knelt between my legs and those gorgeous gray eyes caught mine. He smiled and licked the head of my cock like a damned lollipop.

"Don't close your eyes. Wanna know you're watching me," Cooper demanded.

I grunted in agreement. "Wanna watch you come."

"You will. I'll get you off and then I'll jack myself on your stomach," Cooper assured me.

He set to work giving me the best blow job I'd ever had in my life. Maybe it was because it was a guy, maybe it was because it was *Cooper*, but I felt as if I was living in a fantasy as I watched his lips stretch around my cock, his eyes locked on mine, spit and pre-cum dribbling from his mouth.

Cooper teased my balls and I thrust up. His

answering moan vibrated all the way to my nuts and I knew I'd blow quickly. "Sorry, didn't mean to go so hard," I said, panting.

Cooper stopped sucking me long enough to speak. "I like it hard. Love having my face fucked. Wanna feel your cum all the way down my throat."

I groaned and thrust up, not as hard as I could, but enough to bring more moans from Cooper as he fondled my balls and jacked himself. The image playing through my head of him jerking off on my stomach was enough to have my balls drawing up tight. "Gonna come, Coop," I warned, not sure if he wanted me to unload in his mouth.

He just moaned and sucked harder, his cheeks hollowing out as he tugged at my balls and pressed a finger against my taint. As if he found a magic button, my body tensed as an orgasm washed over me. Pulsing jet after jet between Cooper's lips, I grunted as he milked every last drop from my throbbing dick.

Letting my spent cock fall from his mouth, Cooper stood and straddled my legs as he stroked his cock. "Fuck, gonna come," he said between gritted teeth.

"Can I jack you?" I asked.

Cooper whimpered and let go of his shaft so I could take hold.

"Come for me. Want you all over me, wanna feel you throb in my hand," I ordered.

"Fuuuck," Cooper groaned when I reached for his balls and teased my finger against his taint the way he'd done to me. He fell forward, catching himself on the back of the couch, and shot his release over my fingers and onto my stomach. "Holy shit," he gasped as he collapsed against me.

I wiped my hand against my chest before pulling him in for a kiss. Hot and sensual, savoring his mouth and the last little bit of our time together, our tongues tangled slow and easy.

"That was fucking amazing," I whispered against his mouth. "I wish we could have all night."

And wasn't that scary as hell? Were you supposed to want all night with a fling in your arms? Supposed to want to take your fling to your bed and cuddle with him?

Very fucking likely not.

I was so screwed.

Cooper would get this little affair out of his system and be ready to move on.

I needed to remember that and *not* let myself get attached.

Don't rely on him too much.

Don't look forward to your time together.

Don't fall for him.

What if…

No, just fucking *don't*.

"Me too, but we need to sleep. We'll maybe get an all-nighter soon." Cooper gave me a lingering kiss. "I'm going to go wipe off in the bathroom, but I'll shower at home."

I sighed as the cool air washed over my body when he left to go to the bathroom. Grabbing my shirt, I wiped myself as clean as possible and set the television to a five-minute timer before pulling my sweatpants on. I'd take a shower in my room.

Cooper came out looking thoroughly sated and I wanted to be responsible for that look on his face for the rest of my life. "Thank you, that was so good. I'll see you tomorrow morning. Don't forget your assignment." He gave a wink and started up the stairs. "We'll figure out our next meetup as long as you're onboard."

"Definitely. Maybe this weekend?" Following him, I paused with a terrible thought. "Unless you've got plans?"

"No plans. And I'm not going out with other people while we do this, no worries. You text me and let me know what you want to do next. I'll make it happen. Saturday night?" Cooper cupped my cheek and kissed me softly.

Was I supposed to feel this close to a fling?

Because, if not, my heart hadn't gotten the memo. I wanted to hold Cooper close and promise him forever.

Maybe it was the high from the sex? Yeah, that had to be it.

One thing was for sure, Cooper had shown me that soul-searing, electric type of heat and attraction I'd always thought was just in fictional stories.

And my heart hurt to watch him leave.

Could I really walk away from this man?

You won't have a choice. He was very clear that this was temporary and just for fun.

NINE

COOPER

THE BACK-TO-SCHOOL EVENT fell on a Thursday night a week later which actually worked out well because that meant Jesse didn't have to work around his bouncer job at the Wishing Well. But it also meant we missed out on dinner with Bev and the Remington crew.

So, Bev made alternate plans for Jesse and Hadley to come to dinner on Friday and for Hadley to sleep over and spend Saturday baking with Bev.

Between the anticipation of going to the school event with Jesse and the possibility of an entire night with him, I was about to burst at the seams.

Hadley got off the bus on Thursday super excited about showing us her table and cubby and book basket at school. She and I had a snack, went for a walk, played on the swing, said hi to Jesse, and then worked on her homework—which I was grateful to see was just reading that evening.

Jesse had texted earlier and said not to start dinner—we'd fallen into a pretty good routine of making casseroles on the weekend so they'd be ready for the week. I wasn't sure what he had in mind, but I wasn't upset to move the frozen dish to next week's dinner rotation.

He came in a little after five and I fought the urge to go to him and hug him. How damn easy would it be to fall into something with Jesse? We functioned as a family and I realized a little bit more every day that I wanted *more* with him.

Swallowing thickly, I pushed that thought away and smiled over Hadley's head as she wrapped her arms around his legs. I'd set this whole thing up by promising casual and easy and no-strings. I couldn't go back on that.

Jesse seemed to be enjoying himself. We'd gotten a couple more make out sessions in, but our big plans for that past weekend had gone up in smoke when Hadley ended up with a fever and ear infection.

Luckily, an antibiotic had kicked the slight illness quickly, but Jesse and I had agreed that trying to fuck around—whether our first or one hundredth time—with a sick kid was just tempting fate.

"Let me grab a quick shower then we can stop and get dinner before the school," Jesse said. "That okay?"

His words pulled me from my thoughts and I smiled with a nod. "Yeah, sounds good. I think someone might like fries with ketchup."

Hadley squealed. "Me! I like fries with ketchup."

Jesse and I laughed.

"You have time for one video," Jesse told the little girl.

She widened her eyes at the little treat and scampered off to her room.

"Well, you just made her day," I teased.

Jesse grabbed my hand and took me to the little alcove between the kitchen and backdoor. "Needed a few minutes," he mumbled before gripping the back of my head and pulling me close for a kiss that melted me all the way to my toes. His tongue swept into my mouth, seeking and tasting, feverishly exploring until I whimpered.

"You're supposed to take a shower," I panted. "Don't get me wrong, in an alternate universe, I'd say skip the shower, skip dinner, skip school and I'd drop to my knees and suck you off right here." I kissed him when he groaned. "But I think we have to be responsible right now."

Jesse chuckled. "Yeah, being an adult sucks

sometimes. No skipping anything. Just needed a moment with my guy." He froze. "Sorry, didn't mean it like that. You're not like *my* guy. Casual and easy. Walk away at the end."

My heart skittered to a stop. *No, don't take it back.* Those two little words had rocked my world and I wanted to hear them again. Wanted to believe they were real.

My guy.

I wanted to be his guy.

But no, he was right. We'd said casual and easy. Walk away in the end. I couldn't go back on that now. It wouldn't be fair to him. Like I'd roped him in with promises and then changed the details. No, that wasn't the way things worked.

I'd walk away when this was over.

Even if it meant leaving my heart at Jesse's feet.

I smiled. "I didn't mind that moment," I said, trying to sound as casual and easy as this whole thing was supposed to be. "But you do need to shower."

"Can we plan on our own sleepover tomorrow night? I want you in my bed. Wanna wake up with you in my arms." Jesse teased his lips over the shell of my ear.

"Definitely. You still want to bottom?"

Jesse grunted. "Yeah, for sure." He rocked his

hips against mine and I felt just how much he wanted it. "Since last weekend's *preparations* didn't end up being used, I figure I can use that as the practice run. I've got more supplies, so I'll take care of that. Everything from last weekend is still ready and waiting—prep, condoms, lube—we just need the time and privacy."

"And thanks to Bev and healthy ears, we've got it." I ran kisses along his jawline. "I think you should let me play a little bit before dinner tomorrow."

Jesse growled. "What did you have in mind?"

I ran my hands over his nipples, loving the way he moaned and leaned into my touch. "Bottoming takes some practice and prep—stretching is important. I'm thinking you let me slide a little toy into that sexy ass of yours so it can work it's stretching magic throughout dinner. Make things easier once we're in your bed."

"Holy fuck," Jesse muttered. "Never in a million years would I have *ever* thought hearing someone say *let me stick this in your ass* would turn me on so much."

I smiled. "So, that's a yes?"

"It's a hell yes." Jesse kissed me again, hot and searching. "Is it tomorrow yet?"

I laughed and pushed at his chest. "Nope, we've got shit to do. Let's go."

Jesse went to shower and I checked on Hadley.

And I purposely pushed away the thought of how easy it would be to make this a permanent situation.

Jesse had clearly stated he wasn't looking for that.

I had clearly stated I wasn't looking for that.

So, why were my head and heart so adamant about imagining Jesse, Hadley, and me as a perfect little family of three?

DINNER WENT WELL. If people around town had thoughts or suspicions about Jesse and me being more than employer and nanny, they kept them to themselves. It probably helped that Dad had told a lot of people about our little set-up and the vast majority of folks in town likely didn't automatically think about two guys in a relationship and probably couldn't even fathom a fifty-year-old being with a twenty-five-year-old.

We got a couple looks, but mostly the people were looking at Hadley or commenting to Jesse about setting up appointments for their vehicles. Remington wasn't the most liberal town around, but most people were pretty openminded. Okay, a lot of them were pretty oblivious, but at least the majority weren't hateful or out to hurt with their words or actions.

"You should carry business cards," I suggested as Hadley finished her fries.

"I really should. I need to order some." Jesse ran a hand over his face. "I love that I'm busy, but sometimes I get frustrated not having time to take care of little things like that."

I fought the urge to squeeze his leg. "How about I build some and get your approval before ordering?"

"Yeah?"

"Sure. I like doing that type of thing. I'll find something easy and cheap, they don't have to be fancy. I'll make it look nice and see what you think." I gathered the trash.

"You're pretty perfect, you know that?" Jesse leaned over as if to pick up a straw wrapper and lowered his voice. "Really want to kiss you right now."

My breath caught and I choked out a laugh. "Okay, we ready to head to the school?"

The school parking lot was packed, so we ended up parking by the fountain and walking to the school.

"Can we throw pennies in the wishing well when we come back?" Hadley asked. "I have wishes to make."

You and me both, girlie I thought with a wry smile. "I've got some coins, we can probably stop for a few wishes." I grimaced. I knew I had a way of taking over and I didn't want Jesse to think I was trying to parent his kid. "If Daddy's okay with it."

Jesse laughed. "Can't say no to wishes." He caught my eye. "My grandma used to say *every dream begins with a wish.*"

Holy shit.

"Look at you being all poetic and romantic," I teased, if only to help me swallow the lump I had in my throat.

Jesse scoffed. "Yeah, that's me. The poetic mechanic." He seemed grateful for the levity after the deepness of his comment.

"I want to throw *all* the coins in the water so I can make *all* the wishes. I want a pony and a four-wheeler and a doll that pees and a laptop and a cat and ten dollars and crayons and a basketball," Hadley chattered on and on about all the things she wanted to wish for.

"Well, I can maybe make at least a couple of those come true," Jesse mumbled.

"No room for a pony?" I bumped my arm against his.

We were greeted kindly as we entered the school and directed toward the Kindergarten hallway.

Hadley spotted her teacher, Ms. Nicholas, and went running toward her, waving excitedly.

Her teacher gave us warm hellos and spoke to us in a way that let me know she really *knew* Hadley and had taken time to learn of her likes and dislikes, her learning styles, strengths, and weaknesses.

While Hadley and a couple other children played with some of the toys, Ms. Nicholas dropped a few hints that Hadley perhaps struggled a bit with cleaning up, waiting her turn, and giving others a chance to speak. I felt Jesse tense next to me, but he kept his tone cordial as he let the teacher know we'd be working on those things at home.

At home. The words both warmed my heart and chilled me to the bone.

"Hadley speaks very highly of both of her fathers; she's very lucky to have you. Excuse me, I should mingle with other parents." Ms. Nicholas said her goodbyes.

I turned wide eyes toward Jesse.

"Hadley's telling people I'm her dad?" I asked under my breath.

"I'm so sorry, I'll speak to her. I know you don't want people thinking that." Jesse's face was drawn tight.

"No, it's not that. I just don't want you in an

awkward position. And we maybe should talk to Hadley about why she's telling people that."

Jesse ran a hand over his face. "Sounds like I also need to fix a lot. I was worried about this; knew I'd probably screwed up."

"Hey, don't. She's an only child. She's not really had to wait her turn or give others a chance to speak." I elbowed him. "Does she maybe need to work on those clean-up skills? Sure. But we'll work on it. Promise. She's a great kid."

Jesse sighed as if not convinced, but plastered on a happy face when Hadley waved us over to see her table, cubby, and book basket.

By the time we had cookies and juice in the cafeteria and headed back toward Jesse's truck, it was nearing bath and bed time.

"We only have time for a few coins, so make your wishes count." Jesse handed Hadley a couple pennies and I gave her three more.

When she'd scampered off to toss her coins and make her wishes, I placed a quarter in Jesse's hand. "Make a wish."

He glanced down at the quarter and smiled softly. "Big spender, huh? The bigger the coin the better the chance my wish comes true?"

"Guess you better make it and see." I closed my eyes and made my wish, tossing my own quarter into the fountain. Was I messing with fate? Kidding myself? Being unfair to Jesse? It was foolish to count on wishes, but I wanted more time with him. Wanted what we had to mean something and be real.

Every dream begins with a wish Jesse's grandma used to say. Well, I'd made my wish and I guessed I'd have to see if my dream would come true.

"HADLEY, Ms. Bev wants to know if you'd like to go over to Remington Place and help her make dinner." I placed apple slices, grapes, and a cup of milk in front of her as she settled in for an afterschool snack.

"Yes! What are we making? I can help. Ms. Bev said I can learn to cook just like her." Hadley crunched happily on an apple slice.

"I'm not sure what she's got planned for dinner, but she'll be happy to have your help." And I was going to be happy to have some time with Jesse before dinner.

"And I get to spend the night at your house," Hadley said.

"Yep. You and Ms. Bev will have all sorts of fun." I felt a bit guilty about having Hadley at my house and sneaking out to spend the night with Jesse, but not guilty enough to cancel our plans.

"She said we'll read books and watch movies and she'll do my hair. Tomorrow, we're making pancakes and she said we can bake all day. I'll have treats to bring to Daddy." Hadley chugged her milk. "Can I go over now?"

I chuckled at her excitement. I wondered if Bev was filling that motherly spot left vacant in Hadley's life. "Not just yet. We're going to pack for your sleepover, take a walk, and stop in the shop to say hi to Daddy. Then you can go over. Ms. Bev is napping right now."

"Napping? Why?"

"You won't always think naps are a punishment. A lot of grownups like naps; resting makes them feel better." I rinsed her plate and cup. "Let's go pack first."

After we packed her overnight bag and took a walk—Jesse and I both agreed that Hadley needed to exert energy *and* get fresh air and sunshine as much as possible—we popped into the shop to visit with Jesse.

Hadley sat on a stool she pulled next to the car Jesse was elbow deep in and chattered away about her day at school—the game she played at recess, the funny book her teacher read after lunch, the kid who blew milk out his nose when he laughed—and filled him in on how excited she was to go to Ms. Bev's.

"Hadley gets to go over to Ms. Bev's early to help her cook," I mentioned to Jesse and hoped the gleam in his eyes meant he was as excited as I was about the evening. "You should come in early if you're able. Give you plenty of time to shower and get ready." I gave a wink, knowing Jesse would catch on to what I meant by *ready*.

Jesse's nostrils flared and he cleared his throat. "Yeah, I'll be in as soon as I can." He placed a kiss on top of Hadley's head and told her he'd see her at dinner.

A little while later, I deposited Hadley with Bev— they were going to make roasted pork, herbed potatoes, green beans, homemade yeast rolls, and a dessert of some sort. Hadley nearly vibrated across the kitchen with excitement.

"You make sure you and Jesse are back here in time for dinner. No shenanigans better mess up my family meal." Bev gave me a stern look along with her warning.

"We'll be here. Shenanigans are mostly planned for tonight." I winked.

She pursed her lips. "You guarding that heart of yours?"

I must have gotten a look because she huffed.

"Cooper James, I told you that messing around with your boss was going to cause problems," she started in quietly while Hadley played with the measuring cups.

I held up a hand. "There are no problems. I maybe like him a little bit more than the *casual* I first suggested." And Jesse was *so* much more than a boss to me.

Her brow quirked as if to say *Mmhm*.

"But," I emphasized, "I told him from the beginning that this would be casual, easy, no-strings attached. We'll walk away as friends just like we planned."

"I can see it in your eyes, Cooper. You're falling. And walking away is going to tear you up inside."

Falling? Yeah, that was accurate. But I shook my head. "Maybe so. But I'm a big boy. I knew what I was getting into. And I'm not going to change the rules on him. He agreed to what we're doing because it was easy and temporary. This is new to him, he has a lot going on with his grief and healing, and I'm not pulling the rug out from under him." I shifted my weight from foot to foot while clicking the key ring I held in my hand. "Like how shitty to go into this telling him we can just have fun and move on when it's done, but then switch to *Oh, I really like you and you should totally just come out as bisexual and date me while you deal with grief, building a business, and being a single parent. By the way, can you let my dad know you're boning his son?"* I shook my head with a huff. "Yeah, not exactly fair. So, it's not going to happen."

Bev studied me for a moment. "Well, this won't be solved here and now, so go on with your plans. We'll have dinner ready. I'm feeling torn in this whole situation and kinda wish I knew nothing. Be safe and I love you." She patted my face and shooed me out the door.

I'm feeling torn in this situation and kinda wish I knew nothing.

Yeah, you and me both. I sighed. But that wasn't one hundred percent true. While I *was* torn, maybe I didn't really wish I knew nothing. Because that would mean not knowing Jesse.

And no matter how badly it hurt to walk away from him when this was over, I would never wish that I didn't know him. Jesse Thompson had brought an excitement, a happiness, and a fulfillment to my life that I'd never had, that I'd never known I was missing. Even if he couldn't be my *more*, my person, my forever, I'd be grateful to call him a friend.

You're an idiot if you think you can walk away from this and still be friends.

I pushed the thought away. I still had time with Jesse and I was going to make it count.

He was in the shower when I walked into his place. I closed my eyes and breathed deeply as the scent of his soap floated through the air. I knocked lightly on his bathroom door. "Come out here when you're done. I've got plans before we head to dinner."

I heard Jesse groan on the other side of the door and I smiled.

While I waited, I rustled in the backpack I'd brought with me and came up with a brand-new toy I'd bought specifically for the occasion. Nothing fancy, not huge—I wasn't trying to prep him to take a porn cock—just smooth and light, enough to stretch him so he could take me later.

Jesse came out of the bathroom just as I was tossing the lube onto the bed.

"You get everything taken care of that you wanted to?" I knew he'd wanted to do a thorough prep before his first time bottoming.

His face flamed, but he nodded. "Yeah, all good." His eyes flew to my hands and the small plug I gently stroked. "Is that it?"

I held it up. "Yep. It's functional *and* fun, but you don't have to wear it."

He shook his head. "No, I love being with you. I love everything we've been doing, but I want to do more. I trust you."

Smiling, I turned off the overhead light and turned on the side table lamp. "We don't have a ton of time. Bev threatened no dessert if we're late. Come over here and lay down on your back. I've got plans."

Jesse dropped his towel, his cock already half-hard, and climbed onto the bed. "Can you give me a few details?"

I sat on the bed and leaned over to kiss him, long and slow, my tongue dipping deep, loving the way he moaned for me. "First, I need you to know that, while I know this isn't super kinky as far as kinky goes, this is probably the kinkiest I've ever gotten. I'm not used to being the one running the show and making decisions. I kinda like it, but I'm not an expert and pretty much don't have any idea what I'm doing."

Jesse cupped my face. "I trust you. Now, tell me what you're planning to do."

I ran my hand over his nipples, teasing them and loving the way he gasped. "I'm going to rim you, work you open with my fingers, get you off, and slide the toy in. Then we'll go to dinner."

"Holy fuck," Jesse grunted, his cock now fully erect and leaking against his stomach. "Did Bev threaten you with no dessert if you give me a heart attack before we get there?"

I laughed and reached down to stroke his shaft. "No dying. We've got after-dinner plans."

"Are you getting naked?" Jesse asked. "I'm feeling a bit under dressed here."

I shook my head. "No, just you. This is just preparation, remember. Tonight is the real show. Spread your legs." I pushed a pillow under his hips and moved between his spread thighs. "Are you okay with this?"

"I actually have no idea what rimming is, so I don't know," Jesse admitted.

"I'm going to lick your ass," I said softly as I stroked him and played with his heavy balls.

"Oh fuck, I saw that on the videos I watched. Yeah, I'm okay with it. Nervous and kinda weirded out by it, but I'm ready. Because it's you."

My heart clenched. I kinda loved the fact that maybe Jesse would only ever want *this* with me. It wasn't fair of me to hope that, but I was a selfish bastard. "No touching yourself, I don't want you coming yet." I positioned myself for best access and nuzzled my nose against his taint before licking his balls. When Jesse groaned, I moved to press open-mouthed kisses on his fleshy ass. Licking my finger, I trailed it along his crack, loving his grunt of surprised pleasure when I teased across his hole. With tiny, soft flicks of my tongue, I began to lick at Jesse's pucker as he writhed and panted.

"Cooper, I can't do this. It's too much. I'm gonna come," he protested.

"No, you're not. Just enjoy what I'm doing—take notes because you're fucking me next." I swirled my tongue into his softening hole, loving the way he was starting to relax for me. "Can I use a finger?" I hated that we didn't have enough time for me to make this *really* good, but we'd have all night after dinner.

Jesse grunted a yes and I reached for the lube.

With my finger slicked and plenty of lube smeared around Jesse's entrance, I slowly teased at his hole. "I'm going to go slow, but it might sting a little."

"Not gonna lie, this is a whole lot better than my first prostate exam—the doctor had no bedside manner." Jesse joked, but he tensed as the tip of my finger worked against his muscle. "Let you in on a little secret. I've maybe kinda been doing this to myself for a couple weeks in anticipation of having you inside me."

I closed my eyes and groaned at the image of Jesse fingering himself. "Fuck, that's hot." Knowing he was a bit more prepared, I slipped my finger all the way in and licked my lips at Jesse's tortured sigh. "So fucking tight. Gonna make me come the moment my dick slides inside." I slowly pumped my finger in and out while leaning in to lick Jesse's balls. Shifting my angle, I worked my way deeper in hopes of finding…

Jesse yelped and arched from the bed. "What the hell was that? Do it again," he begged.

"Jesse Thompson, meet your prostate," I teased and brushed against the bundle of nerves again, loving the way it made Jesse writhe and beg.

"Damn doctor was definitely doing it wrong," Jesse blathered. "Fuck, that's amazing."

"Can I add another finger?" I asked.

Jesse hissed out a *yes* and I gently worked a second finger into his ass. He grunted, maybe a little more pain than pleasure with the addition.

"You okay?" I paused my movements to give him time to adjust.

"Yeah, it burned for a minute, but it's good. So full."

"Just wait until it's my dick." I let my fingers slide slowly in and out of Jesse's tight ring. "Think you can come this way? Want you all soft and pliant so I can slip the toy in. Can't wait to watch you during dinner, know what you were getting up to earlier, know your hole is stretched around the silicone, know you're anticipating my cock filling you up later."

"Oh fuck, Coop. Your mouth is wicked. Yeah, I

can come." He reached for his cock, but I batted away his hand.

"Nope, that's mine," I said as I shifted so one hand could stroke his dick while the other finger-fucked his ass. "Tonight, I want your mouth on me. Then I'm going to press my hard cock into your tight ass and make you come. Wanna feel you come on me while I shoot my load deep in your ass."

Jesse grunted as his cock got impossibly harder and his balls drew up tight. "Fuck, Cooper, I'm gonna come."

I increased my strokes on his cock and pressed deeper with my fingers. With the slightest brush against his prostate, I dropped my head to suck his cock into my mouth. Jesse groaned my name as his dick pulsed his release, his ass clenching tightly around my fingers as I swallowed everything he gave me.

While he was still shuddering from his high, I slipped my fingers from his body and lubed up the plug. "Relax for me," I murmured as I pressed the toy gently against his entrance.

"My bones are mush, should slide right in," Jesse muttered with a satisfied smile on his face. He hummed softly as the silicone breached his muscle.

"That feel okay?"

He nodded. "Yeah. But I have no clue how I'm supposed to enjoy dinner with something in my ass."

"Just keep thinking about how much you'll enjoy later with my cock in your ass," I soothed against his ear.

Jesse growled and turned to capture my lips. "No one else I'd rather be doing this with. You make it fun and easy. Never in a million years would have thought I could have this."

My heart stuttered. I wanted to tell him we could have *this* forever. The Cooper who wasn't looking for a relationship and didn't want to settle down had suddenly left the building. The part of Cooper Scott was now being played by a man who wanted Jesse for real, in his bed, in his life— wanted to make a little family with Jesse and Hadley.

"You okay? Sorry, that was too much." Jesse winced. "Just really appreciate you giving me this experience. Years from now, I'll look back on it with fond memories."

And there was the pin to burst my hope-inflated heart. Fun and easy. Walk away. It's what Jesse expected because it's what I'd promised. "No worries. No one else I'd rather be doing this with either." I gave him a final kiss and rolled from the bed to wash up. "Let me wash real quick and then you can clean up. We'll head over in about fifteen minutes."

Jesse moaned as he walked toward the bathroom. When he came around the corner, I couldn't help but smile at how loose and sated he looked. "You worked some sort of magic on me. I feel like I'm floating." He came up behind me at the sink and wrapped his arms around me. "I don't want to miss dinner, but I'd *really* love to cuddle back into bed with you in my arms."

"Later," I quipped, attempting to keep things light and easy. "Got any ideas for things you want to try?"

"I did my homework assignment and watched some videos." He shrugged as he used a cloth to wipe himself clean. "Maybe I'm too vanilla, but I honestly just want to feel you in me, wanna see your face and watch as you fill me up."

I groaned. "That can totally be arranged. Maybe you start on top? That way you can see my face, but you'll be in control of things. We can move to a different position later."

Jesse bit his lip.

"What? Something else on your mind?"

"I know we can't—and I get it, we have to be responsible since this isn't a permanent thing—but I really liked watching the videos where they don't wear condoms." Jesse's face went a gorgeous shade of red.

I took a deep breath. "Yeah, so fucking hot." *God, yes, I want that with you.* "But you're right, it wouldn't be a good idea. That gets way too far away from fun, easy, walk away territory." I swallowed thickly as my hands grazed over his nipples. "I've never had sex without a condom." *And I want to with you.*

"Really? That's good. I don't like thinking of you putting yourself at risk." Jesse nodded, but seemed like he still had something on his mind.

"What else are you thinking about?"

He wrinkled his brow. "Kinda liked watching the guys who took turns fucking each other."

"Flip fucking? We can play around with that, see if things work out. I'll likely come very quickly once I'm inside you, so maybe you can fuck me too." My cock, already irritated with me for not letting him have any action earlier, pressed hard against my zipper. "But for now, we need to head to dinner."

Jesse dressed and pulled me into a long, lingering kiss before we headed out the door and crossed over to Remington Place.

I sighed. I'd truly thought I could keep this fun and easy, walk away with no issues—I'd done it with several hookups in the past—but there was no way I'd be able to leave Jesse without some major heartache. He wasn't just a fun and easy fuck for me, not just a guy I was showing a good time. Jesse meant something to me, something so much more than just fun and easy.

I *had* to walk away—and probably sooner rather than later once he got his curiosities filled—but it definitely wasn't going to be *fun* or *easy*.

Dinner turned out to be a really fun time.

Hadley was so proud of the food she and Bev made, and she loved how everyone gushed about how good it was.

"I think she may just become a chef just for the compliments," Jesse said as he gathered her on his lap and kissed the top of her head before she ran off to sit at her own seat.

I doubted anyone else would have noticed, but I couldn't take my eyes off Jesse and the way he squirmed or caught his breath from time-to-time had me doing some squirming of my own. He'd shift in his chair, bite his lip, and then look at me as if he was ready to devour me.

Not gonna lie, dinner ended up being one *hell* of a good foreplay session.

"I've got news," Bev said as Dalton, Spencer, and I gathered the empty plates and scraped the scraps into the disposal. "My nephew, Andre—I call him Dre—is going to be moving in with us. He's going to take the open room. He's coming back this way from California. Not going to spill his whole history, but school wasn't for him and he became an EMT. He went home recently to help his parents—you've heard me talk about my estranged sister and her husband. They're older than me and Dre wanted to help. They had some," Bev pursed her lips, "*disagreements* regarding Dre's life and let him know his help wasn't needed."

I had a feeling there was a lot more to that story. Bev didn't talk much about her sister, but I knew from a few things she'd said that her sister was staunchly religious and extremely judgmental.

"I've not seen Dre since he was a little boy, but we've stayed in touch over the years. When I heard he needed a place to stay, of course I offered."

"Sounds good. Glad you've got a room for him. I'm sure being here with you will be helpful. Having an EMT around will be nice in case of emergencies," Gabby said.

"He's also been working to get involved in the fashion scene. I'll leave it up to him to tell you all about it, but he's always been interested in creating his own styles. I think some of that got suppressed the older he got, but now that he's on his own, he seems to be delving back into it." Bev pulled a pan of dessert from the refrigerator. "Banana bars with cream cheese icing. Hadley was a big help with these."

Dalton and Gabby made a big fuss over wanting some of Hadley's baking, and even Spencer—who always seemed scared to death of Hadley, yet strangely intrigued by her—pulled out all the stops going on about how good the banana bars were.

"You look at her like she holds the mysteries of the universe," I joked as Spencer watched Hadley scramble back onto Jesse's lap and take bites of the tasty dessert.

Spencer cleared his throat. "I've never been around kids very much. They're amazing. Like complete humans, but tiny. They're just these little bitty men and women—real people in miniature bodies."

I laughed. "Yeah, I guess they are. She's a great kid."

Spencer raised his brow. "Seems to be. How's her dad?" he asked quietly.

I choked on my cake. "Not here."

"Mmhm," he hummed and gave me a knowing look. "Still planning on just walking away?"

I pushed away from the table and took my plate to the sink as Spencer chuckled.

After a game of Go Fish—where Hadley and I played as a team so she could learn—Gabby, Dalton, and Spencer said their goodbyes and headed off to their rooms. I knew my brother and Gabby would likely shower and settle in to watch their shows—they only rarely went out to bars or movies. Spencer would probably put on his headphones and draw or play video games. Unless he decided he wanted a cup of coffee later and he'd head to his favorite little diner. I hadn't yet been able to pin down why he liked the diner so much when we had perfectly good coffee at Remington Place.

Jesse checked in with Hadley to be sure she was still okay with staying over at Bev's house. I had a moment of panic that she'd freak out and want to go home, but Hadley gave Jesse a hug and a kiss and all but pushed her dad out the door before running to talk to Bev about the movie they were going to watch and if they could have popcorn.

I followed Jesse down the back steps and pulled him to the far corner of the house into a dark little crook. Wrapping my arms around his neck and loving the soft sigh that came from him, I sifted my fingers through his hair before pulling him in for a long, slow kiss. "I'll hang for just a bit, take a shower, and then come over," I said when we finally broke apart.

"I'll be there."

"Maybe I'll put on a little show as I get dressed," I teased.

"Maybe I'll watch and try not to come in my pants," Jesse threw back.

We laughed and I gave him a final kiss with the promise to see him in under an hour.

I spent a bit watching the movie with Hadley and Bev, but then told Hadley I'd see her tomorrow when she was done baking.

"And we're making catteroles on Sunday," Hadley said absently as she continued to be absorbed in the movie.

I laughed at her mispronunciation of the word. "Yep. Lots of cooking to do." I kissed the top of her head and told her to sleep tight. Turning to Bev, I patted her shoulder and kissed her cheek. "Gonna shower and go out. I'll see you tomorrow."

The knowing look in her eye and smirk on her face told me she knew exactly what and who I was going to be doing. "You be safe. Guard that heart. It's all fun and games until someone ends up devastated."

I smiled softly and gave a little wave before heading to take a shower.

I didn't rush my shower and prep routine but I also didn't drag it out—I wanted to be ready for anything, but I was about to jump out of my skin wanting to get over to Jesse's place.

When I returned to my room, wrapped only in a towel around my waist, I went straight to the window and chuckled when I saw Jesse standing at his as if waiting for me. I gave a little wave and saw him smile as he waved back.

I reached for a simple pair of black cotton bikini briefs and dangled them in front of the window. Jesse gave a nod. Slowly, I dropped the towel. I'd been in a constant state of arousal since our time in Jesse's bedroom and my dick was beyond impatient to get the show on the road. I shimmied into the underwear and did my best to arrange myself in spite of my *predicament*. Cupping my hand over my bulge, I did a slow little turn to point my ass toward the window. Giving it a little shake and a hand caressing one of my cheeks, I gave Jesse a wave. Pulling on a shirt and pants, shoving my feet into shoes, and grabbing the bag I'd packed earlier, I rushed from my room.

Only to run smack into Dalton.

"Where you going in such a hurry? Was going to ask if you wanted to play a game with me and Spence." My brother eyed me suspiciously. "A bag? You spending the night somewhere?" He scowled.

I bristled as all the insecurities and doubt

throughout my life came tumbling over me. "I'm a grown-up. I can take care of myself. If I want to spend the night with someone I can. Despite what you might think, I'm actually smart enough to do most things on my own." Sure, I had to set alarms to make sure I took my meds and write everything down so I wouldn't space appointments and shit, but I wasn't dumb.

Dalton held up his hands. "Hey, that wasn't what I meant. You're one of the smartest people I know so don't go there. Just don't want you getting in too deep and ending up hurt. You're going to Jesse's, aren't you?"

I jutted my chin and stayed quiet.

"I saw the way you two looked at each other throughout dinner. I maybe don't get what you see in him—what you two could possibly have in common—but I can't argue with the attraction between you." Dalton reached out and gave my arm a little push. "Just be careful. You said this was going to be temporary and no-strings. Neither of you looked very temporary and all sorts of strings seem to be attaching themselves every which way."

"I'll walk away. It's what we agreed to."

"Even if it's not what he wants now?" Dalton cocked his head.

"Jesse has his own situations to deal with.

Therapy, Hadley, the shop, he doesn't need to heap on more issues with coming out, attempting a relationship with me, *telling Dad*." I waved my hand. "We'll be fine. I'll still be Hadley's nanny for at least this school year, they'll still come over for dinner, everything will be good."

"And when he starts dating? Brings a woman to dinner? Or a man?" I must have turned as green as the shot of jealously that raged through me because Dalton just chuckled and shook his head. "Yeah, that's what I thought."

He walked away but called over his shoulder as he headed up to the third floor. "Just be careful, man."

I gritted my teeth. Bev, Spencer, Dalton...they all saw right through me. They knew I'd gone and fallen for Jesse. But what they didn't know was that I was determined to see this through to the end and keep up my part of the agreement. And, no matter how much I dreamed of being with Jesse permanently, building a family with him and Hadley, I also had to admit to myself that I needed to stay focused on school and working to open my business. Did I have time for a serious relationship?

No.

What if Jesse told you right now that he wanted

something more, something more permanent? Would you tell
him you had to focus on school and your business?

Hell, no. If Jesse wanted more, I'd be all over
that.

But there was the dig.

Jesse didn't want more.

He wanted a man to safely explore with.

That's all I was to him and I needed to remember
that.

But for the time being, we'd have a lot of fun
exploring.

I opened the backdoor to Jesse's place and locked
it behind me. Kicking my shoes off, I made my way
to his bedroom and couldn't help the smile that
filled my face when I saw him stretched out on the
bed in just his underwear.

He'd drawn the blinds on his window and turned
off the overhead light. Two candles created dancing
shadows on the walls and I swore he'd put a dimmer
lightbulb in his bedside lamp.

Romantic, caring Jesse made it very hard to
remember this was just for fun. I'd *never* had
someone light candles for me.

I tossed my bag to the floor and stripped off my
shirt and pants. Crawling onto the bed, I moved
between his legs and thrilled at the heated touch of

our bodies pressing together. "Hi," I murmured against his lips.

"Hi," he said before devouring my mouth like he was starved for me.

We kissed for what seemed like an eternity, exploring and playing, no time limit to our evening. When Jesse finally broke the kiss, we were both panting. I licked my lips and ran my hand over his rock-hard cock. "I could seriously just spend the whole night kissing you," I murmured against his lips.

"If that's what you want, I'm game. I'd probably even get off on it. Love kissing you." He pressed open-mouth kisses against my neck and I couldn't help the whimper that escaped.

"I'd like to take things further if you're still interested." I continued to stroke his length through his underwear.

"Definitely interested."

I moved to tease a finger over his nipples, loving the way he groaned, and leaned in to flick my tongue against one and then the other. Locking my lips around one nipple, I sucked and reached down to snake my hand under his underwear. Gripping his shaft, I gave a gentle stroke. "Still want to bottom?"

Jesse ran a hand through my hair and grunted out a *yes*. "But I don't want to start on top like you suggested. Wanna be on my back, legs spread, so I can see you."

"You on top might give you a little bit more control over the penetration and depth."

"I get that, but on my back seems a lot more... *intimate*..." Jesse's cheeks flushed, "and after this is over," he gestured between us, "if I'm with someone else, I may not feel comfortable with being that open. I feel comfortable with you. If you're willing."

I swallowed hard. Jesse admitting he wanted something that intimate with me, while also mentioning *the end* and being with someone else, cut me to the bone. But I pushed on with a nod. "Yeah, I'm willing." I moved to remove his underwear. "You still want to try flip-fucking?" I slipped my own down my legs and kicked them to the floor.

"Thought about it some more, I think I'd rather just come with you inside. Next round, I want to top." Jesse's legs spread wider to allow me to nestle between them.

"A plan I can work with," I teased. I rolled from the bed and came back with a warm, wet cloth. "I plan to rim you again and would rather skip the lube flavor if possible," I explained.

When I knee-walked across the bed, Jesse grabbed a pillow and shoved it under his hips in a flurry. "This is going to be over so fast," he grumbled. "I'm about to come and you've barely touched me."

"You and me both. You're okay with me coming inside? Or do you want me to pull out and shoot on you?" I caressed his gorgeous ass and tapped on the end of the plug making him shiver.

"What I really want is to have you bare in me, but I know that's way too much for what we're doing. But yeah, I want to feel you unload in me." Jesse ran a hand over his face. "Can I just pause the action for a moment to say how fucking surreal this is?"

"What's surreal?"

"I've spent my entire life ignoring, avoiding, adamantly denying that I found guys attractive. If I did it enough, it would eventually be true, right?" He threw an arm over his eyes. "And now, I'm dying to have you touch me, taste me, and fuck me."

"And it's upsetting you to feel this way? You're mad that you gave in?" I was torn between wanting him to deny it and knowing that if he agreed, it would be easier for me to stay disconnected and just walk away.

Jesse uncovered his eyes and looked right at me. "No, not at all. I'm spread out here, thinking I *should* be ashamed or angry or trying to excuse my behavior away in some way, but I don't feel *any* of that. It feels like a damn dream, a fantasy world...like I'm about to get everything I've ever wanted."

I longed to believe that maybe, just maybe, Jesse meant *me*. But in keeping with the fun and easy theme, I opted for the lighter version and took hold of the plug to tug on it gently while stroking my shaft. "Well, my cock is pretty average, but I hope it fulfills all of your hopes and wishes," I teased. My heart hurt, wishing for more.

A flash of something crossed Jesse's face, but he offered a small smile. "I think average is the perfect place to start."

I set to work slowly and gently easing the silicone in and out of Jesse's body while he began to writhe and pant. "Gonna take this out, wipe you down, and then lick that pretty hole of yours."

He groaned. "Yeah, want that." He reached to stroke his cock, but I pushed his hand away. "You're mean," he grumbled.

I laughed and slipped the plug from his body.

Jesse sighed. "That was a weird sensation, but I kinda already miss it."

"No worries, I'll fill you again real soon," I murmured as I used the cloth to wipe up any lube from the toy. Satisfied with my work, I shifted positions so I could spread Jesse's ass and tongue his hole. He was already more open and soft than he'd been before, but I knew taking my dick would be a bigger stretch than the plug. I swiped my tongue along his taint and dipped in and around his pucker as Jesse whimpered and tried to buck his hips.

If things were different for us, I'd plan a day in bed, nothing but slow, leisurely sex. But I had to push that from my head. That wasn't what this was about.

And since when had I ever wanted slow and soft? Intimacy wasn't something I was about. Hard and fast had always served me just fine.

But then I went and fell for Jesse and all I could think about was taking my time with him, spending hours in his arms, sharing our bodies with each other.

I could have spent forever licking his hole, but Jesse was grunting, his cock leaking all over his stomach, and my own dick was begging for some action, so I rolled to the edge of the bed and grabbed the lube and a condom.

Slicking two fingers, I worked them past Jesse's tight ring. "Fuck, you're going to feel so good on my dick," I groaned.

Jesse panted, thrusting his hips. "Want that. Wanna feel you. Please, Coop. Fuck me. Please."

I ignored his pleas, pressing my fingers deeper and angling just enough to brush his sweet spot.

Jesse grunted and his cock jerked. "Damn it, Cooper. Stop teasing. I wanna feel you in me."

Taking mercy on him, I slid my fingers from his body, and opened the condom. Rolling the latex down my hard length, I kept chanting to myself *easy and fun, easy and fun*. That was all this was. I was just helping Jesse explore and find out who he really was.

What if...

No, I pushed any thoughts from my head and focused only on giving Jesse a good time. Moving between his legs, I slicked my cock with lube and smeared a good amount around his pucker. Holding the base of my dick, I pressed the head against Jesse's tight ring and pushed in slowly.

He groaned as I slipped in inch-by-inch. Tensing, he winced slightly, but blew out a breath and gave me nod. "I'm good. Just a little sting. Fuck, that's good. So full. So much more than the toy."

I pressed the rest of the way inside and stilled when my balls brushed against his warm skin. "Give me a second. Been a while since I've done this and I might blow if I don't get myself under control." The tight heat of Jesse's body was almost too much.

When I finally got a grip, I began slow thrusts in and out, loving the way Jesse grunted and groaned with each slide into his body. Giving in to temptation, even if just for a moment, I leaned down to bring our chests together. Wrapping my arms around him, I kissed Jesse for all I was worth as I pumped hard into his ass.

I'd never fucked a guy in this position.

Never even been fucked in this position.

I loved the closeness, the connection. But that was all Jesse. No one else would have made me want this.

When a warm tingle spread across my lower back, I knew there wasn't much time. I pulled back, changed my angle, and moved to a deeper thrusting to peg Jesse's prostate. "Jack yourself," I commanded. "I'm close and I want you to go first."

Jesse moaned as I finally allowed him to touch his cock. He took himself in his fist and stroked with a tight grip. His other hand lifted his balls, tugging and twisting.

Lifting his legs to my shoulders, I increased my speed and the force of my thrusts as I gripped his hips.

"Fuck, Coop, I'm close. Go hard."

I slammed into Jesse's ass over and over, my eyes splitting time between watching his face and watching him stroke himself. "Fuck, Jess. I need to come. Let me see you, wanna feel you on my dick."

Jesse groaned, his head thrown back, as he shot creamy, white ropes of cum onto his chest and stomach. "Fuuuck, Cooper," he panted, "fuck, so good."

I lost all semblance of control when Jesse's ass clenched around me. I gripped his hips and gave one last thrust before tensing and unloading into the condom as his muscles milked every drop from my pulsing cock.

With a breathy chuckle, I collapsed onto Jesse's chest and let him wrap me up in his arms. We both sighed when my softening cock slipped from his ass, but neither of us moved from the embrace for several breaths. Finally, I moved just enough to remove the condom and fall back onto Jesse.

A few moments later, my breath finally returning to normal, I nuzzled my nose against his jawline before whispering at his ear, "Was that okay?"

Jesse huffed out a laugh. "Okay? That was the most amazing orgasm I've ever had. For real. Is it always that good?"

I wasn't sure how to answer that. No sex had ever shaken me to the core like sex with Jesse, but I didn't want to let things get too serious. On the other hand, I was loath to tell him he could have what we had with someone else. I wanted his pleasure, I wanted every single one of his orgasms. Couldn't stand the thought of Jesse sharing what we'd just had with someone else.

"Sex is good. Period," I finally murmured.

Jesse tensed before seeming to shake off whatever had caused him an issue. "Not in my experience. Maybe Nicole and I just weren't right together—which is hard to think about because she was one of my best friends—but our sex life was nowhere near what you just showed me."

I wanted to promise him night after night—*forever*—of what we'd just shared. But I couldn't. It wasn't fair. "Maybe you're more gay than bi. Or maybe you and Nicole just didn't click sexually." I rolled to the side and grabbed the wet cloth to wipe us both clean. "Maybe you and another woman would burn up the sheets. Maybe you and a guy will go off like a firework. You've got plenty of time to explore and see what works for you."

Jesse turned to face me, his hand cupping my face before stroking down my arm to take my hand. He studied my face for several beats, a serious look in his eyes, before he smiled slightly. "Thank you for giving up your time to help me with this. Without you, I never would have had the courage to explore. You're a safe place and make me brave enough to try without fear of judgment or ridicule."

My heart tried to soar, but the pain Jesse's words had inflicted made it too hard. So, I just smiled softly and willed any tears that were threatening to just back the fuck off. "Never any judgment or ridicule. I just want you to find the real you and give yourself the chance to find happiness." I leaned in and kissed him. My words and the kiss were way too deep, but I couldn't help it. *Fuck.* I wanted this man with every fiber of my being. But we'd been doomed from the moment I first offered a fling. I took a deep breath and closed my eyes. "Let's sleep. I believe you suggested round two would be *me* getting fucked and I'm all about that idea."

Jesse chuckled and pulled me close, kissing the top of my head.

Several hours later, based on the time glowing red on Jesse's little alarm clock, I woke as Jesse rolled from the bed.

"Sorry, gotta pee," he mumbled as he ambled to the bathroom, his perfect ass jiggling just slightly in the candlelight.

I took my turn in the bathroom and returned to the bed with what I hoped was a seductive smile. "Hmmm," I drawled as I climbed onto the bed while Jesse checked the candles—which we likely shouldn't have left burning, "whatever should we do now that we're both awake?" My cock immediately had ideas.

From the look of Jesse's semi-erect dick, his was on the same wavelength. "I think I may have some ideas." He joined me on the bed and rolled me to my back as he settled between my legs. "I want to fuck you so damn bad. Having you inside me was fucking amazing and I want to give that to you."

"Then get inside me," I teased as I nipped at his bottom lip.

"Can I play around first?" Jesse's cheeks flushed adorably.

I nodded. "I'm game."

Jesse grabbed a pillow and helped me prop up my hips before he positioned himself at my ass and spread my cheeks. The hot puffs of breath against my most sensitive skin told me he was nervous and turned me on more than ever. "I may be terrible at this," he warned.

"Jess, your tongue on my hole couldn't be bad even if you tried. If you don't like it, just stop. It's not a requirement."

A warm, wet swipe against my entrance made me gasp and then Jesse set to work devouring my ass like it was his last meal. If I didn't know better, I would have sworn he ate ass for a living. "Fuck, Jesse, that's so good," I panted. When his tongue began to thrust into me, I lost the ability to speak and had to settle for little grunts and whimpers. "How much porn have you been watching?" I was kinda teasing and kinda not; he was *good* at rimming.

Jesse reached for the lube with a chuckle. The

snick of the lid filled the room and I bit my lip in anticipation. He smeared lube into my crack before working one finger inside.

I moaned, loving the way he slid in and out. "Do two," I begged.

He added a second finger and pressed kisses against my ass as he finger-fucked my hole. "Love watching you open for me," he growled. With a slight shift in his position, Jesse changed his angle and his strong, thick fingers brushed against that sweet spot, nearly sending me into orbit.

"Fuck, do that again," I pleaded. "So good."

Jesse spent a few more moments stretching me and playing with my prostate before pulling his fingers from my body and reaching for a condom and rolling it on. "What position do you like best?"

"Wanna try a few different ways so you can experience a variety," I pushed him to his back, "gonna ride you first." I straddled his waist.

"Wait, wanna suck you first," Jesse commanded, his eyes gleaming as he licked his lips and watched my cock bob. "Come here."

I moved up to his chest. Taking my cock in hand, I smeared the leaking head against his lips. "Open up."

Jesse's tongue flicked out to lick my slit before he opened around my head.

I groaned when he took my cock between his lips as I fed him a little bit more. When his hands gripped my ass and pulled me forward, my dick surged to the back of his throat and I gasped. "Fuck, Jesse. Don't gag yourself," I warned.

He allowed me to pull back a bit, but continued tonguing and sucking my shaft as his fingers spread my ass cheeks and he teased my lube-slick hole.

"Fuck, I need that dick," I panted.

Jesse groaned when I pulled my cock from his mouth, but his eyes lit on fire when I shifted to his waist and reached behind me to guide his rock-hard length to my hole. "Why do I feel like a virgin on my wedding night?" Jesse asked. "I'm excited and nervous and so scared I'll fuck this up."

I leaned down to kiss him. "Your dick in my ass will never be bad." I sat back up and lowered myself inch-by-glorious-inch onto Jesse's shaft, gasping and whimpering as his thick cock stretched me open. "Fuck, Jess. So good. Love the way you fill me." When I bottomed out, I took a few moments to catch my breath and regain some control before I began to ride him. I couldn't tear my eyes away from Jesse's eyes as he watched me, pure ecstasy filling his face. Before I let myself get too far gone, I slipped from his cock and moved to the mattress on my hands and knees. "This is a common position," I said. "Gives you a lot of the control and power."

I whimpered as Jesse guided his cock back into my eager hole and gripped my hips. Dropping to my elbows, I lost myself to the hard and fast and thrusting. "Wait, let me show you another way." I moved to lay down completely flat.

Jesse groaned and slid his dick between my cheeks, making me gasp as he pressed back into my body. He dropped his much larger body onto mine, covering every square inch of me as he fucked me into the mattress while kissing my neck. "You're so fucking amazing," he whispered, "so damn good. Never knew it could be like this." He thrust into me a few more times before pausing to pull out. "I'm not gonna last much longer. Can I have you on your back?"

I swallowed thickly, not sure I could take the intimacy of the position. But in the end, I just nodded. I wanted to give Jesse everything. I rolled to my back and spread my legs. Jesse took his place between my thighs and lined up his cock head before pushing his way into me with a moan.

I threw my head back, loving the stretch and fullness. "So fucking good, Jess. Fuck me, make me come."

Jesse leaned close, shifting so we were chest-to-chest, my legs burning as they stretched to adjust to the new position. "I wanna watch you jack yourself and come for me. Wanna feel your ass tighten around my cock when you shoot your load." He thrust hard and slow into me for several moments while exploring my mouth with his seeking tongue.

I felt his absence when he pulled away, but the new position allowed me to watch as he fucked into me.

"Jack yourself," he commanded and my balls immediately drew up tight.

Taking myself in my hand, I stroked my cock hard and fast while playing with my balls. "Fuck, Jesse. So close," I panted, running my thumb over my slit.

He took hold of my hips and slammed into me, his long, thick cock brushing at the bundle of nerves deep inside.

With his final thrust, I lost myself to the orgasm rolling through me as I shot hot, thick ropes of white onto my stomach. Jesse came at the same time, tensing and holding himself deep in my ass as his cock throbbed, his release pulsing into me as my muscles clenched around him, pulling every drop from him.

Jesse pulled from me, tossed the condom away, and gathered me in his arms. His heavy breathing and soft kisses against my ear made me want to tell him that I'd *never* had sex that good. Made me want to tell him how badly I'd lost my heart to him.

But I knew I couldn't do that.

So, I scratched my nails lightly up and down his back and whispered, "You're a natural; quick learner."

Jesse laughed. "It was okay?"

"Beyond okay," I said—I couldn't let him think he wasn't good, he needed to build his confidence if he was going to try dating at some point. "We should shower before we end up crusty and stuck together."

"Lead the way," Jesse said with a sleepy laugh. "Then I need sleep."

"You want me to leave?" It would be best if I just went home. Sleeping in Jesse's arms wouldn't help the situation at all.

"Only if you want to," Jesse said as he turned on the water. "I'd like to keep you here. We won't get many more nights like this."

I figured he probably meant because Hadley would be back home. But he also could have meant because our situation was temporary.

"I'll stay. Maybe we can play in the morning? Then breakfast before I go home?"

Our shower turned into sleepy, laughing fun as we washed and joked around, both of us in desperate need of some shuteye. By the time we were washed and dried, my sluggish body barely made it back to bed before I was heading to dreamland—sex was a better sleep-aid than any prescribed medication; too bad I couldn't have Jesse to help me sleep every single night. I was just awake enough to take notice of Jesse's big, strong arm wrapping around me and pulling me close as he kissed the top of my head.

We slept until the first rays of sunlight began to peek through the blinds. I woke feeling antsy and horny. I rolled from the bed and grabbed my medication. Swallowing it down with a handful of water from the sink and giving my teeth a quick brushing, I climbed back into bed knowing Jesse and I could have some fun while the pill kicked in. After a shower, I'd get some coffee in me and my day would be well on its way.

"You're up early, you okay?" Jesse asked as he rolled my way, his thick morning wood brushing against my thigh as he pulled me into his arms.

"Yeah, just needed to take my meds before I got too fidgety."

"You good? Need something else? Or want to work out the fidgets with me?" Jesse ran his hand down my back to cup my ass.

"Let's take care of my fidgets here. I bet you can help calm them," I teased.

Jesse smacked a kiss against my lips and rolled

from the bed. "Just gonna piss and brush my teeth," he said with a wince.

"You sore?" I felt bad, but I also loved that he could feel the remnants of me being inside him.

"Just tender, not painful," Jesse called from the bathroom while he peed. He popped his head around the doorway a few moments later with a toothbrush dangling from his mouth. "I kinda like that I can feel it, like it's a reminder of what we did." He disappeared to finish at the sink.

Fuck. Yeah, I got exactly what he was saying. Moving from the more serious side of things, I grinned at him as he walked toward the bed, his thick cock just begging for attention. "You have anything you're wanting to do from the videos you've been watching?"

Jesse hummed. "There are *a lot* of hot scenes, but most of them aren't for me. I think I'd like to see you bent over something. And then maybe have you on top of me, both of us on our backs? That position looks like it's really good."

Just hearing Jesse talk about sex was enough to have my cock leaking. "Perfect. Grab a condom and lube." I moved from the center of the bed to stand next to it.

When I would have bent over and spread my legs, Jesse tossed the foil packet and bottle of lube onto the mattress and wrapped an arm around my chest. Pulling my back against his warm chest, he used his other hand to move my head, maneuvering me so he could devour my mouth. He kissed me as if savoring every single second of our lips and tongues together.

"Bend over, let me see that pretty ass," he demanded.

Pulling myself from the heaviness of the kiss, I bent over the edge of the bed, spread my legs, and reached around to spread my cheeks.

Jesse groaned as he brushed a finger against my hole.

"Like what you see?" I teased.

He grunted and opened the condom.

"Get inside me and take advantage of it." I wiggled my ass and waited with breathless anticipation for the press of his cock against my entrance. "And don't think you have to be gentle. Wanna feel you the rest of the day, see your fingerprints on my hips."

Jesse smeared lube around my hole, slipped two fingers in to play for a moment, and lined up his cock with my hole before gripping my hips and sliding his thick length deep into my ass.

I sighed at the stretch and fullness. "Go hard," I demanded.

When Jesse began a punishing rhythm, his

fingers digging into my hips and his balls slapping against mine, I took hold of the sheets and whimpered with each hard, deep thrust.

"Shit," Jesse bit out, "gonna come. Get on the bed. Want it the other way."

I waited for Jesse to stretch out on the bed, his rock-hard cock begging to get on with it, before straddling him and laying back to bring my back to his chest. Getting into this position wasn't the easiest, but I knew it would allow me to stroke myself easily while Jesse pounded up into my ass, so I wasn't complaining.

Jesse reached to guide his cock back into my waiting ass and I groaned when he was right back where I needed him. As if he'd been taking tons of notes on how to make our position work, Jesse wrapped his left arm around my chest, his right arm pulled up my right leg, and he bent his knees for better thrusting.

"Hold your other leg," he instructed.

With both legs bent and pulled up high, my ass was spread wide open and stretched around Jesse's thick cock.

"Jack yourself," Jesse commanded. "Gonna fuck you hard, but it's not going to last. Wanna feel you come with me."

I took hold of my cock and began to stroke as

Jesse pistoned his hips, pumping his cock in and out of my ass as he held me tight against his chest.

"Fuck, Jesse, I'm gonna come," I warned just as my cock pulsed and shot my load over my fist onto my belly.

Jesse thrust over and over before pausing deep in my ass and growling against my ear as his release washed over him, his cock throbbing in my ass as we both panted and moaned.

"Holy fuck," Jesse said as he rolled slightly to the side, keeping me tight against his body, letting me rest against the mattress as little aftershocks traveled through both of us.

"I'll second that," I said breathlessly.

"Are the fidgets gone?" he whispered against my ear as he slipped from my body and got rid of the condom.

I chuckled. "I'll let you know when I can feel my body again."

We lay together, completely sated, for several moments.

"Probably better shower and get the day started," I suggested even though all I wanted to do was stay wrapped in Jesse's arms.

He sighed and kissed my neck. "Yeah, you're right. I've got cars to work on and groceries to buy."

"And I have homework. Hadley can stay with me

while you go grocery shopping. You want me over here tomorrow to help with casseroles?"

"Definitely. Can we still go grab breakfast before heading back to the real world?" Jesse asked.

"Yep, sounds like the perfect way to end a perfect weekend."

We shared a shower and got ready before climbing into Jesse's truck.

"Bev would gladly cook us breakfast, but this place is good. Spencer loves it here," I said as we walked into the little diner conveniently and aptly named Remington's Hometown Diner.

The waitress led us to a booth way in the back and we both ordered coffee while we perused the menu. After ordering—I got something sweet, Jesse got savory, and we planned to share—a familiar laugh caught my attention. I peered around Jesse toward the breakfast counter.

Sure enough, there was Spencer, a huge grin spread across his face as he chatted with a super-hot guy—dark hair, a fair, tawny complexion, and gorgeous dark eyes crinkled at the corners as he laughed at whatever he and Spencer were talking about.

"Very interesting," I murmured.

"What?" Jesse asked and started to turn around.

"No, don't look. Spencer, is at the counter. He

eats here a lot; I've never understood why he comes here when we have perfectly good coffee at home." I glanced toward the spot where Spencer was sipping a cup of coffee and eating what looked like a breakfast sandwich. He was dressed for work which meant he skipped Bev's food and came to the diner.

"And you've figured it out?"

I shook my head and frowned. "Not in the slightest. Spencer isn't gay. Well, I can't say that for sure. We're close and I love him dearly, but we don't talk a lot about super personal things. He knows a lot more about me than I know about him. I know he's had a rough life and he doesn't believe in himself the way he should. He doesn't really date from what I can tell, but I don't really know anything about his sexuality."

"And now?" Jesse pushed.

"I don't think I've ever seen him laugh like that. He's talking to a very hot waitperson and laughing. He looks happier than I think I've ever seen him."

"That's good, right?"

I continued to watch my friend. "Yeah, it's great. I guess I'm just wondering—is that guy the reason he's here all the time? Is he the one making Spencer happy? Why is he laughing and happy here, but stoic and reserved at home with us?"

"Maybe it's easier here with strangers," Jesse suggested.

I nodded. "Yeah, could be."

"So, *very hot*, huh?"

My brows shot up. "Um, yeah. Like model hot. But he doesn't look like the conceited type. Actually, he looks kinda quiet and nerdy if I'm being honest. But he's *hot*."

"Can I see?"

I slid toward the corner of the booth so I was out of Spencer's line of sight in case he caught Jesse looking. "Yeah, but make it quick and be sneaky. He can't see you."

Jesse slowly turned his head to glance over his shoulder to where Spencer was finishing up his meal and pulling his wallet from his work jeans. "Oh, yeah, he's definitely hot. I mean, Spencer isn't hard on the eyes either," he said as he turned back around.

"Right, but he's my best friend so I don't see him like that." I peered around again to watch Spencer pay his bill and give the waitperson a little wave. The cutest damn thing in the world was seeing the guy behind the counter watch Spencer leave the diner and then rushing to the door to watch Spencer walk to his truck. "Holy shit, I think Spencer has a secret admirer."

"Kinda looked like Spencer was admiring right back," Jesse said.

I nodded, deep in wonder about this new development. I wouldn't push Spencer, but it was definitely a plot twist I hadn't seen coming.

Our breakfast arrived and we split our sweet and savory dishes while chatting comfortably and drinking second cups of coffee.

When we got back to Jesse's place, he opted to head to the grocery store first. "Once I'm back, I'll come get Hadley. She can hang with me for the rest of the day while I work in the shop. Come over tomorrow. We'll do lunch and food prep."

I wanted to throw my arms around his neck and kiss him senseless, but I figured it was better to keep things as unattached as possible. Goodbye kisses seemed a lot more serious than what we'd both agreed to, so I gave a little wave and walked through the gate to Remington Place even though it felt as if I was leaving my heart in a puddle at Jesse's feet.

TEN
JESSE

COOPER FIT into my life like the final piece to a five-thousand-piece puzzle. Relief, satisfaction, joy, and the feeling of everything being just right filled me as I thought about the man.

We'd fallen into the perfect routine over the first few months of school and I was grateful to have him on my side to help with Hadley. That little girl was wild about Cooper and it hurt to think about a day when he wouldn't be available to be her nanny. I wasn't naïve enough to think this set-up could last past this year; I'd never expect Cooper to give up on his dreams and stick around as my babysitter.

Business was booming and I couldn't help but feel proud that I'd not only kept all of Spinks's old customers, but I'd pulled in new ones as well. I was busy all day, every day, and my earlier worries about the mortgage and saving for Hadley's college had quietly taken a place on the back burner for a while.

My evening shifts at the Wishing Well were a life-saver, although, if I were being honest, I would have opted to spend them with Cooper had it been offered. But I loved the place. I'd been there enough now to recognize the regulars and have people I enjoyed chatting with. Most of the patrons were there just for socializing and easy drinks, but I'd been able to keep a few people from driving when they'd imbibed a bit too much and that was a complete win in my mind.

Hadley had taken to school like a fish takes to water. She loved every moment of it and was doing wonderfully. She was learning responsibility, started taking initiative on clean-up time—because of Cooper mainly, but also because she learned it at school—and even had some friends she enjoyed hanging out with. The first day Cooper took Hadley to a friend's house for a playdate, I nearly cried in the shop while elbow deep in an engine. The little girl I'd been so concerned about—would she make friends? Was I getting her enough socialization? Did she need more than I could give?—was thriving and I couldn't help but feel happy, relieved, and proud.

And a little sad watching her grow up. She had to take those steps. She had to spread her wings. And I had to let her go. Sure, it would be a slow progression in the grand scheme of life, but it still stabbed at my heart to know I was already having to learn to let go a bit at a time.

The stab at my heart was just as bad when I thought about having to let Cooper go. I knew our time was limited, but we'd not set a firm date for ending things, so it was like waiting on the other shoe to drop.

Sometimes, I caught Cooper seeming *almost* coupley, like he wanted more than just a fling with me. But just when I'd think maybe he'd agree to something more, he'd pull back as if reminded the whole thing was supposed to be fun and easy with no strings attached.

The biggest problem with that was I'd gone and attached all sorts of strings.

Heart strings.

And they were tangled up tight.

I'd gone and fallen in love with Cooper Scott.

It didn't matter that he was my nanny.

Didn't matter that he was half my age.

As much as it scared the shit out of me, it didn't matter that he was my best friend's son.

All that mattered was I loved him.

The type of love I'd always thought just existed in movies and romance stories.

The type of love I'd accepted I'd never have.

The all-consuming, fireworks, easy and comfortable, want-you-in-my-life-forever type of love and it was eating me up inside.

I was in love with a man who showed me how to explore. A man who gave me the courage to find the real me. A man who offered me a fling and nothing more.

And I was helpless against it.

With each passing day, I wondered if Cooper was getting antsy to move on. Was I keeping him from finding a new guy to have fun with? Were we pushing our luck with each day we kept our little affair going—Robby wasn't going to stay oblivious forever.

Sex with Cooper was amazing and we'd taken advantage of every single little moment of privacy we got over the past few months since our first night together. The basement after Hadley's bedtime was our own private oasis—to the point I wondered how I'd ever be able to be in the space without longing for Cooper when he was no longer in my life in that way.

But there was so much more between us than just sex.

How someone who was so much younger could be the perfect yin to my yang was beyond me, but we fit together as if we'd been made for each other. Physically, emotionally, everything between us was just *right*.

Cooper and I had what Nicole and I had never found. To be fair, Nicole and I were likely never meant to be more than friends and we were much too young. Forcing ourselves into building a relationship on such shaky ground was a recipe for disaster neither of us had been prepared for.

Maybe Cooper and I worked so well because we'd gone into it with zero expectations? I didn't have answers. I just knew that I was in love with him. I wanted him in my life permanently. I wanted to build something with him. I wanted to call him *mine* for the rest of time.

Which meant I had to let him go.

I'd agreed to a fling. Nothing more.

Flipping the arrangements now would be completely unfair and I wouldn't do that to Cooper.

So, I'd work to keep things sex only and not be surprised when Cooper said it was time to walk away.

All of these thoughts were a jumbled mess as I walked into Alicia's office for a therapy session. She'd been a Godsend and I felt as if I was making progress working through my grief for the first time in five years.

I took the hot tea and cookies she offered and settled onto the comfy couch.

After some pleasantries, Alicia dove right in.

"We've not done a recap for a few sessions. Let's start there. How are you feeling about Lauren?"

I sighed and rubbed my chest as if the ache there would ever go away. "I miss her every single day. I hate that she isn't here to see Hadley grow up. Hate that I may be doing things differently than she would have. Even though she was young, she loved that baby with all her heart and it hurts that Hadley never got the chance to know her mother." I wiped a tear from my eye. "But I'm starting to have other feelings. I feel proud of the way Hadley's adjusting to school; she's so damn smart and she's doing so well. I talk to Lauren in my head a lot and I know she's so proud of her little girl. Even though I wish it was different, I feel like Lauren is happy with the way I'm raising her baby. It's like I'm still nervous, but the crippling fear and doubt I had about being able to do the dad thing a second time around is a little less with each milestone and success Hadley has."

Alicia nodded and wrote some notes. "That's good. Progress for sure. What about Nicole?"

I took a deep breath. "That one's a little more complex."

She smiled knowingly and waited.

"I lost someone who used to be my best friend, the mother of my child. But we weren't in a good place at the time, so it's hard to separate those feelings. It's easier these days, but not *easy*. I miss my friend and I mourn the loss of Lauren's mother, Hadley's grandmother." I sipped my tea and blew out a breath. "I'm still angry that she cheated. Angry that she wasn't willing to communicate with me and try to save things." I paused for a long time and stared out the little circle window above Alicia's chair. "But I'm also accepting that she was right about a lot of things. I wasn't one-hundred percent in the relationship, probably never had been and probably never would have been. And that wasn't her fault. Do I wish we could have been open and honest about it and figured out something that worked for both of us? Yeah, for sure. But at the time, I wasn't willing to admit to who I really was so that wasn't going to happen. I hate that, by not being honest with myself about the real me, I put her in a position where she felt unloved and alone. But I also hate that I kept myself hidden and feeling guilty for so many years."

Alicia scribbled on her notepad. "Sounds like you've made a lot of progress in your journey through grief, but also maybe found out some things about yourself?"

I smiled and nodded. "Yeah. A friend has helped me finally embrace the fact that I'm bisexual." I frowned. "At least, I think I'm bi. Hell, I might be gay. I don't know." Alicia was the first person other than myself and Cooper I'd officially said the words to.

"Is the label important to you at this point in time?" I loved that she didn't seem shocked, just her normal, professional self.

I shook my head. "Not really. Maybe someday. I'm not really interested in dating right now, but at least I've been honest with myself. I like men. Maybe the same as I like women? Maybe more?" I sighed. "I don't really know. But I was so tired of ignoring it, pushing it away, lying to myself."

Alicia cocked her head to the side. "And this friend?"

My heart clenched at the thought of Cooper. "He gave me the freedom to explore. Gave me the courage to admit to myself who I really am."

"Sounds like a special person," Alicia hedged.

"He's amazing. The best."

Alicia just waited.

"And I'm pretty sure I've gone and done the stupidest thing imaginable."

"Oh?"

"I fell in love with him." I threw my head back against the couch.

"And he doesn't feel the same?"

"I don't know. Sometimes it feels like he does, but we got into this whole thing with the agreement that it was just for fun. Easy. Walk away at the end."

"And it's the end?" Alicia watched me intently.

"We didn't set a time. For me, it's just the beginning. I feel for him what I've never felt for anyone else. He makes me feel alive."

"You've told him this?" Alicia asked.

I ran a hand over my face. "No. He's *a lot* younger than me. He offered a no-strings-attached fling. It feels wrong to take what he gave me and turn it around like I'm trying to trap him into something he doesn't want."

"And you know he doesn't want it?"

"Things are…complicated. He's my nanny. He's also my best friend's son," I explained.

Alicia nodded, but I didn't feel judged. "That may be difficult in the no-strings-attached arena."

I laughed. "Yeah. Definitely didn't think that one through."

"Your relationship with Nicole crumbled in part due to lack of communication, yes?" Alicia asked.

I nodded.

"Maybe communication is the best in this situation? Talk to him about how you're feeling? Instead of assuming he doesn't feel the same, give him the chance to hear your side. Instead of deciding what's fair or not fair, let him know what's going on in your heart." Alicia glanced at the clock. "We're out of time for today. We'll revisit this next time."

I set up my next appointment and headed toward my truck.

Usually, after a session, I felt untangled and relieved. This time, I felt more jumbled and anxious than ever.

I pulled out my phone and texted Robby to see if he wanted to come over that night. I needed my best friend.

"She seems to have no issues going to bed," Robby commented as he handed me a beer when I returned to the basement. "Dalton and Cooper used to fight bedtime tooth and nail."

"We've got a pretty good routine going." *Thanks to Cooper* I thought, but kept that part to myself. "And she's usually pretty tired from school. Cooper keeps her busy in the afternoons, so by bedtime, she's ready to conk out."

Thinking of Cooper had me recalling our brief time together before Robby had come over.

Coop had pulled me into the bathroom while Hadley watched one of her two allowed videos after dinner. "I'm glad Dad is coming over; you guys need to hang out more," he'd whispered against my jawline before nibbling up to my ear. "And I've got a school project to work on, so I was going to have to bail early anyway."

I'd felt bad telling him Robby was coming over—truth be told, I wanted Cooper there more than anything—but I knew learning to function without each other was something we both needed to do. Okay, *I* needed to learn how to function without Cooper. He'd be fine without me.

And damn, if that didn't hurt.

Did he really have a school project? Or was that an excuse? The first of many he'd start to give as he pulled away from me?

We'd taken full advantage of the video Hadley was engrossed in upstairs. Cooper on his knees for me, sucking me deep, licking and teasing, swallowing every drop of my release was something I'd dream about forever. I couldn't imagine dropping to my knees for another man. Nuzzling my nose against Cooper's trimmed thatch of hair, savoring the scent I'd come to adore, thumbing through the drop of precum on his slit before licking his head and parting my lips for him to feed me his cock...I couldn't picture that scene with anyone but Cooper.

And I didn't want to.

Maybe Cooper had helped me to figure out the real me, but that didn't mean I'd be able to move on after him. I'd been alone for years and I'd rather be alone after Cooper than deal with the heartache of even trying to replace him.

"Dude, where'd you go?" Robby nudged me and I quickly came back to the present.

"Sorry, man. Long day. Therapy session has my head all fucked." I took a seat on the couch and didn't even bat an eye when Robby stayed standing, movements constant.

"But it's going well? The therapy?" Robby asked as he paced.

"It is. Alicia is really good. She says it's more that I was finally ready to move through the grief, but I think a lot of it is having a good therapist." *And maybe Cooper too?*

"Well, you seem different." Robby held up his hand. "In a good way. I wouldn't ever expect you to stop missing them or being sad, but you seem to have found some happiness and it shows."

"Being back in town has helped. Having friends

around is great. I'd *known* I was pretty much alone before, but being here and having so much support has really opened my eyes to *how* alone I was." I took a drink to wash away the threatening tears. "Helps a lot to see Hadley doing so well and the business taking off. I owe a lot of that to you and your family."

"Bullshit," Robby said as he did squats—like father like son. "Celeste and me have watched Hadley *once*. We brought a few items over for the house. It's not like you couldn't have done all of this without us."

"Cooper has been a Godsend," I admitted even though I often tried to steer the conversation away from anything regarding my best friend's son.

"I'll give you that. Probably could have found the same success with someone else, but I know CJ— Cooper—is good at what he does. I'm really glad you two found each other." Robby did a few quick jumps and finally flopped down on the couch.

I'm really glad you two found each other.

I swallowed thickly.

So was I.

Damn. So was I.

Would Robby feel the same if he knew his kid had been deep-throating my dick in the bathroom less than an hour before he arrived? Would it make a difference to him if I told him I was in love with Cooper?

"Yeah, he and Hadley have bonded and he's a huge help. Gonna hate to lose him."

"Start planning ahead. I think there are at least a few teens on this street who could likely be at the house when Hadley gets off the bus—get her a snack and play with her. May not be the most convenient thing, but you're lucky your shop is on-site; you could walk her to the corner in the morning for the bus." Robby drained the last of his beer and placed it on the side table.

"Yeah, we'll get something worked out. Just feel really lucky that Cooper was available and willing for this first school year." *Oh, how available and willing he was* I thought to myself as I remembered the wicked gleam in his eye as I'd swallowed his cock earlier.

"You been thinking about dating? Getting yourself out there?" Robby asked with a waggle of his brow. "Celeste and I both work with some single people we'd love to set you up with. And you know we'd be happy to watch Hadley."

I laughed. "I can't say for certain that I'm ready to date, but I'm a lot more open to it now than I would have been at any time in the past five years."

Robby beamed. "Great to hear. Should Celeste

and I keep our eyes and ears open for possible dates of a certain gender?"

I took a deep breath and bit the inside of my jaw. "Either, both. Hell, I really don't know. And I said I'm more open to it, not that I'm completely ready for it."

My best friend's eyes shimmered brightly. "That's all I need to know, man. All I need to know." Robby reached over and placed a hand on my shoulder. "I want you to know you're loved and accepted, no matter what. I just want you happy."

Wonder if that sentiment would change if he knew what you and Cooper had been getting up to.

I gave a brief nod and finished my beer in hopes of not crying. "Thanks. Means a lot."

ELEVEN
COOPER

"DADDY, DANCE WITH US," Hadley called out as she and I bebopped around the kitchen while waiting for the casserole to bake.

"Oh, I think you two are doing just great without me," Jesse said with a smile as he watched us from the doorway.

"Nope, come on. It's a dance party," I insisted and reached for Jesse's hand.

With a reluctant smile, he let himself be pulled into the middle of the kitchen.

"Hold me up," Hadley said, her arms stretched up to me.

I picked up the little girl, my heart constricting as it always did these days as I thought about our limited time together and how much I'd miss her and Jesse.

Hadley wrapped her arms and legs around me and reached for her dad. "Dance with me," she instructed Jesse.

No movie script could have planned it better, but somehow a little girl giggling about a dance party maneuvered our little trio and held on so that Jesse was plastered against my back as the three of us swayed to whatever song played from my phone.

In a split second, I pictured this little family of three. Jesse, Hadley, and me. We worked so well together, fit so perfectly. God, I wanted that. Wanted Jesse and Hadley to call my own. Wanted Jesse as *mine*. I loved him in a way I'd never known possible and my heart dreaded the day I had to let him go. I knew the heartache was coming—looming over me like a damn sword swinging from the ceiling—and I was helpless to stop it. But I also had no power over the way I'd stupidly gone and fallen for Jesse.

The warm press of his chest against my back, the brush of his breath against my ear as he laughed at something Hadley said, it was all a bit too much. I broke away, handing Hadley to Jesse. "You two finish the song, I've got to get the casserole out before it burns," I explained lamely. The dish could have baked for at least twenty more minutes without burning, but the rush of emotions that had washed over me when I thought about what I was losing when Jesse and I called it quits was just too much.

Sure, I'd still see him and Hadley. And I was grateful I wasn't losing Hadley. But even though I'd still have Jesse as a friend, I'd miss our connection, the closeness, everything we had that was so much more than just friendship. Even if sex was taken out of the equation, Jesse and I had something special. We'd fallen into such an easy give and take without even trying and I knew that wasn't the norm.

I thought back to the wishes I'd made at the fountain. I'd wished for Jesse to feel about me the way I felt about him. Wished for our circumstances to be different. Wished for a redo on our arrangement where I hadn't promised just fun and easy, so I could tell him I wanted more than he'd agreed to give. Wished I didn't have to walk away.

As I pulled the casserole from the oven, I tossed another coin into the fountain of my imagination. I wished I'd never have to feel the pain of seeing Jesse with someone else even as I wished for nothing but his happiness. Tears stung my eyes and I left the casserole to cool.

"You can eat in about fifteen minutes," I explained as I quickly wiped tears from my eyes. "Green beans are in the microwave." I gave Hadley a kiss on the cheek and rushed to the door to pull on my shoes.

"Hadley, can you go wash your hands, please?" I heard Jesse say.

"Can I wash my baby's hands too?"

"Yep, don't forget her feet," Jesse teased and I knew he was buying time.

I needed to get out of there.

Hadley's footsteps scampered through the house as I stood.

"Hey, what's wrong. Talk to me," Jesse said, concern etched across his face.

I fell in love with you and I never want to give you up. I want forever in your arms, forever in your life, forever with you and Hadley. I'm so damn sorry that I promised fun and easy, but I don't think I can actually walk away. I love you, damn it.

All of the words begged to pour from my mouth, but instead, I shook my head and sniffed while clicking the keychain in my hand. "Nothing. All good. I'm having dinner with Mom and Dad tonight, so I can't stay."

Jesse tipped my chin up and studied my eyes. "Are you sure that's all?"

I nodded. "Yeah, no worries. Enjoy your dinner. I left the homework folder on the table for you to look through and sign. We got her worksheet done and did more on her scavenger hunt. You'll need to do the reading."

My breath caught as Jesse brushed a soft kiss over my lips. "Thank you. I wish..."

"Daddy, we washed our hands and feet!" Hadley announced as she rushed back into the room with her baby doll. "We're hungry!"

Jesse took a step back and I immediately felt the loss of his warmth, his strength.

I gave a quick nod and rushed out of the house.

Dinner with my parents would be good. Something to take my mind off the inevitable heartache headed my way.

A couple hours later, I helped Mom and Dad clean up the kitchen as we chatted about school. Being in a family of educators meant that school was almost always a topic.

"Hadley seems to be doing wonderfully," Mom gushed. "The teachers just love her."

I smiled, feeling warm and proud of Hadley. "She's a great kid."

"Talked to Jesse, he seems to be doing great. Settling in, business is good, he's thrilled with your work with Hadley, and the therapy sessions are really helping," Dad said as he unloaded the dishwasher. "I know it's only been a few months since school started, but it's so good to see him healing and learning to accept himself."

"That's so good. He's got so much time ahead of him, I'd hate to think of him being alone," Mom said as she rinsed a glass. "I know he has to heal and everyone's journey is different, but I'm glad he's on his way."

Dad nodded as he took the silverware to the drawer. "I asked him about dating. For the first time ever, he actually came out and said that he might be bi or gay. I suggested that maybe we could set him up with some singles from work."

My heart clawed at my throat, but I was powerless to do anything but listen as they talked. My nose burned and I wasn't sure if the movement in my hands was from nerves or fidgets, but I hated every word and every second.

"And?" Mom asked. "I have the perfect friend in mind. He's about our age, recently divorced, amazing with kids. They'd be so good together."

"I was thinking of the Language Arts teacher on my team. Her husband died and she's just getting into the dating scene." Dad waved a fork around. "*But* we can't move too fast. He said he's more open to dating now than he would have been in the past, but I'm not sure he's completely ready. Probably needs time to work his way toward being comfortable with it. I was just thrilled to hear him finally admit to himself that he's not straight. I think that will be a huge weight from his shoulders."

"You knew he wasn't straight?" I blurted.

Dad shrugged. "He's my best friend. I've known him since forever. I maybe didn't *know* he wasn't straight, but I always suspected. All I want is for him to be happy being his true self. I think he's well on his way."

I swallowed thickly. I was so damn proud of Jesse for having the courage to come out—even if he wasn't set on labels or if he even wanted them—and accept the real him. Dad was right, Jesse was on his way to happiness and contentment within himself.

And maybe ready to date?

Bile rose to burn my throat.

If Jesse was indicating he was more open to dating now than in the past, my work was done. I'd done what I set out to do.

We'd had our easy fun.

Jesse knew himself much better now.

It was time for me to walk away.

"You want dessert?" Mom asked. "Coffee?"

"Huh?" I pulled myself from the despairing thoughts. "Oh, um. No. I've got a project to work on. Need to head out."

I didn't catch much of what Mom and Dad said as

I left their house and I was back at Remington Place before the drive even registered with me.

"Dude, you look like shit. What's up?" Dalton asked me when I wandered into the room where he and Spencer were playing games.

I plopped myself onto the sofa and ran my hands over my face.

"Is it Jesse?" Spencer asked gently.

I nodded.

"What's wrong?" Dalton asked, pausing the game.

"He told Dad he's maybe open to dating," I muttered.

Dalton frowned and Spencer winced.

"So?" Dalton said.

"But not dating you?" Spencer asked.

I shrugged. "*Dating* me was never an option. Fucking me was the agreement. Fun, easy, and walk away. That's what I offered him. That's what we agreed to. And now, it's time."

"Is that what *you* want?" Spencer asked.

I closed my eyes and willed the tears away.

"Shit, man. I told you to be careful. You went and fell for him?" Dalton sighed. "Does he know?"

"No," I bit out. "I wouldn't put him in that type of awkward situation."

"So, *you* don't want to end things and you have

no idea how he feels, but you're going to call it quits?" Spencer narrowed his eyes. "Don't you think talking things out may be better?"

I shook my head. "No. He was so reluctant to do this whole arrangement with me anyway. He had excuse after excuse. He wasn't gay, he was too old, he was my boss, he was Dad's best friend. The only way I got him to agree was assuring him it was temporary and we walked away with no-strings attached." I pinched the bridge of my nose while my legs bounced restlessly. "I can't turn it around and change the deal now. That's not fair."

"Then get it over with," Dalton said. "Don't drag it out. If you really think it's the only way, just end it now."

I hated his words and wanted to work out my fidgets by pummeling his face. I glanced toward Spencer.

He shrugged. "I still think talking it out is for the best, but what the hell do I know? I haven't been in a real relationship my entire life. A few fast fucks here and there don't make me an expert. I guess you gotta do what feels right."

I swallowed the lump in my throat with a nod. "Yeah." Standing, I gave a halfhearted wave and headed toward the kitchen. I texted Jesse a quick message.

. . .

ME: Hey, can we talk real quick?

JESSE: Sure. Meet you by the gate?

I SENT a thumbs up and walked out the backdoor.

I was gonna cry.

I was gonna puke.

But I was gonna make things right with Jesse before it got any harder.

"Hey, what's up?" Jesse asked as he reached to cup my face.

I wanted to fall into his arms, beg him to hold me, to love me, to never let me go. Instead, I summoned every bit of strength I had and delivered what had to be an Oscar-worthy performance.

"I think it's probably time we call it quits," I said, proud of the barely-there quiver in my words.

"What? Why? Did I do something?" Jesse's face paled even in the darkness.

I shook my head. "We agreed to fun and easy. Said we'd walk away. Didn't feel right setting an actual deadline, but I think it's time. You're doing great; I don't want to be what holds you back. I've got a lot going on with school. Just seems like a good time to push the sex side of things away."

Jesse looked as if I'd just punched him in the gut *and* kicked his puppy.

"I'll still be here morning and afternoon for Hadley. I can still watch her when you're at the Wishing Well or need to get groceries," I assured him. I figured he was panicking a bit about that part. "You're good with making the casseroles now and Thursday dinners are still required." I tried to smile. "But we'd agreed to this from day one, so it's only fair to stick to the details. No strings, right? Clean break. Walk away as friends."

"What if I..." Jesse started, but snapped his mouth shut.

"What if you what?" *Please. Please, tell me you don't want out.* I wanted to beg him, fall at his feet and plead. *Tell me you feel the same about me. Please. Tell me you're willing to deal with all the reasons we shouldn't be together and fight for all the reasons we're so damn perfect together.*

Jesse just shook his head and blinked a few times. "Nothing. Doesn't matter. You're right. Sticking to the original arrangement is for the best. As long as Hadley is cared for, that's all that matters." He stuck out his hand.

I nearly lost it, nearly expired into a puddle of

gooey heartbreak right there at his feet as I took his hand.

"Thank you for all you've done for me. I wouldn't be where I am now without you and I'm forever grateful. You've taught me things I never would have learned on my own. You gave me the courage to be *me*. I'm glad to call you a friend." Jesse spoke gruffly as he shook my hand.

I nearly broke my molars as I bit back the tears, but I returned the handshake and nodded. "It was fun. I'll see you on Monday morning."

And with that, I turned and rushed into the house, up the stairs, and into my darkened room. Safe in my own space, with no one to watch me fall apart, I let go of the tears and sobbed at what I'd just walked away from.

My heart would never be the same.

TWELVE
JESSE

I'D KNOWN Cooper was pulling away.

Known he was likely looking for the right moment to end things. He'd never indicated *forever* or anything close to it.

Absolutely hated it, but I'd known he was probably getting antsy wanting to move on with someone else. We'd both known from the beginning that I was just a fun little project for him.

From the moment he texted me saying that he wanted to talk, I'd known where things were headed.

Hell, I'd known things were headed for disaster from the day he offered the fling. And yet, I'd stupidly gone along with it. Let my desires and curiosities get the best of me.

Which was how I'd ended up with a broken heart, swollen eyes, and a headache from clenching my teeth trying to fight off the tears every damn moment I was around Cooper after he ended things.

I hadn't slept well since that night.

I wasn't eating well. At all.

Luckily, I could do a lot of my shop work on autopilot because my head was a fucked-up mess.

I did my best to keep on a happy face for Hadley and keep up her routine.

But my heart hurt and I wasn't sure how I'd ever get over loving and losing Cooper.

Can you lose something that was never really yours *in the first place?*

To his credit, he stuck to his job requirements and took care of Hadley without missing a beat. If I thought I saw red-rimmed eyes, evidence of sleepless nights, and a bit more lack of focus in Cooper, it was probably wishful thinking. And what kind of ass did that make me? I didn't want him to feel as miserable as I did.

Cooper was friendly, but more reserved and professional with me. His behavior with Hadley didn't change in the least and I appreciated that he could move on so easily and not let her be affected.

I wondered what it would be like to so easily walk away from what we'd had. To be honest, underneath the hurt and heartache, I was pissed.

Whether fair or not, I was pissed at Cooper. Yeah,

he'd done exactly what he'd promised from the very beginning and I could acknowledge that. But the fact he could touch me the way he did, share with me what we shared, introduce me to something I never thought I'd have, and then just walk away as if nothing had happened? That shit hurt, but it was a little easier to be pissed about it than wallow in the pain.

And I was pissed at myself. If I just would have said no from the beginning. If I would have just used him for sex. If I would have been smarter.

But no.

I didn't do any of those damn things.

I went and fell in love with him.

There were so many reasons we shouldn't have worked.

But the one overwhelming reason in our favor— the one that made no sense and kept me awake at night—that I couldn't let go of?

We *did* work. We fit. As friends, as partners, as a couple. Cooper slotted into my life as easily as my next breath. And I needed him just as badly.

Without even realizing I needed him, I'd gone and opened my heart to Cooper and we connected on a level I wasn't even sure I believed existed.

Sure, I could take care of Hadley without him—it would involve some inconvenience, but I could do it.

But I *needed* Cooper in my life. Needed everything about him.

Because I loved everything about him.

His lack of a filter.

His enthusiasm.

His fidgets.

I didn't mind the skills he'd honed to keep himself organized. Alarms? Notes? Calendars? Bring them on; those things were as much a part of who Cooper was as his mussed-up hair and gorgeous gray eyes.

I loved his smile, his touch, his laugh. Loved the way he loved Hadley.

In the grand scheme of things, I barely knew him, but my heart yearned for him as if we'd spent several lifetimes together. I was so damn proud of him and I wanted to be by his side when he graduated and built his business.

And yet, I was left faking smiles, coordinating schedules, and handing over a paycheck as if Cooper was nothing more than a half-my-age employee.

It sucked.

I absolutely hated every minute of it.

By the middle of the week, I knew I had to do something. My raw, aching heart needed professional help. I called Alicia and begged for a slot, grateful when she said she'd make room for me. Feeling thankful that I'd had a light load in the shop that day, I made my way to Alicia's place.

Over cookies and tea, I poured out what had happened with Cooper. Going into more detail than the previous session, I explained the intricacies of our relationship—or lack thereof—and how broken and adrift, lost and alone, I felt.

Alicia skimmed her notes. "At our last session, I suggested that you let Cooper know how you were feeling. Be honest about wanting more than just the agreed-upon fling."

My cheeks pinked and I ducked my head.

"Did you do those things, Jesse?" Alicia cocked her head. She knew the answer, but she'd stare me down until I replied.

I shook my head. "No. I'd hoped I would have more time. And it seemed wrong of me to turn the tables like that."

"Tell me more about that."

"He offered something fun and easy. Offered to help me find myself. I never would have taken that step—can't imagine myself comfortable enough with any other man—without Cooper. But what he offered was temporary from day one; he made that very clear. He's twenty-five, he's got his whole life ahead of him. He gave me a chance to explore and it gave him a chance for fun. That's it." I ran a hand over my face. "I'm not even getting into the fact that his dad is my best friend—none of that was supposed to matter because the whole thing was planned out to be short-lived. Easy. No-strings." I let my head drop back against the couch. "So, how was I supposed to go to Cooper and tell him I was changing the parameters? Sorry, kid, I know I agreed to walk away, but I've gone and fallen in love with you so let's spend the rest of our lives together." I huffed out a humorless laugh. "I can't expect Cooper to give up his life for me, be tied down to me, all because I decided I like dick, especially his."

Alicia blinked a few times and scribbled something on her notepad. "I have two things to offer before our session ends for today. One—and keep in mind, there's no way to know this for sure without having an honest conversation—there's always a possibility that Cooper offered the no-strings option just to get you to say yes. I doubt he suggested a fling with thoughts of forever in mind, but he also probably knew *easy* was the best way to get you to agree." She held up a hand. "Again, that's speculation on my part. But I have a feeling if he'd offered committed dating at the beginning, you would have balked."

I pursed my lips. "Yeah, probably. But that

doesn't change the fact that me going and falling in love with him wasn't part of the plan."

Alicia cocked a brow. "Which leads me to part two. Without talking to him, you'll never know how he's feeling. I'm not trying to be a romantic here, but there's always a possibility that Cooper feels the same as you and is just as conflicted about the deal as you are." She smirked. "As an aside, this is where I highly recommend—in case it comes up in the future—never agreeing to a fling with your best friend's son who happens to work for you and be half your age."

I snorted. "So, I'm supposed to believe that all I have to do is talk to Cooper and things will fall right into place and we'll live happily ever after?"

She rolled her eyes. "Not at all. I'd say it's a fifty-fifty chance. You may spill your heart to Cooper and find out that he's not at all interested."

"Gee, thanks," I muttered.

"My *point*," Alicia continued, "is that being honest is the key. You're going to see Cooper a lot, be in his life, right?"

I shrugged. "Yeah, he's still Hadley's nanny and Robby's son, there's no way around it. Plus, he's my neighbor for now."

"Do you want to live day after day, week after week, month after month regretting that you weren't honest, didn't tell him how you really feel?"

I closed my eyes.

"Telling him the truth very likely won't change your circumstances." She smiled softly. "But not talking, not being honest, those are things in your past you've admitted you regret. Do you want to have those regrets with Cooper?"

I shook my head and sighed. "So, I just tell him I'm in love with him? *Hey, Coop, I know it was just supposed to be fabulous sex, but I went and fell in love with you. Just thought you should know. Can you watch Hadley on Wednesday night?*"

Alicia bit back a laugh and made notes. "I think you approach that in the way that feels the most comfortable for you and Cooper. But yes, I think you'll feel relieved when you've opened up."

"Open up, pour my bloody heart out to him, and then just try to scoop it all up and move on when he tells me it was just a fling to him. Sounds lovely; can't wait."

"Would it be worse than what you're feeling now?" Alicia asked. She lifted a cardigan-covered shoulder and twisted her lips into an empathetic smile. "Again, I'm not saying being honest will change the direction of where you and Cooper are meant to be. Very likely, you'll still be hurt and healing after. But at least you'll know you were honest and there are no secrets between you and Cooper."

I groaned and glanced at the time. "Thanks for listening. Not sure I'll be able to do what you said, but thanks for the advice."

Alicia confirmed my next session and I left.

With the rare afternoon free, I drove around town, did some errands, grabbed some lunch, and enjoyed the sunshine at the park. Being on my own, nowhere to go, no one to keep an eye on, no deadlines to meet was nice, but it also made me realize how much I loved having Hadley with me. And Cooper.

As I savored a meal alone, no opening milk or ketchup packets, no reminding of a few more bites before playtime, my gaze traveled to the fountain where Hadley, Cooper, and I had made wishes.

I gathered my trash, tossed it in the can, and made my way to the water.

Every dream begins with a wish.

My grandma's words echoed in my head.

Fighting tears and the ache in my heart, I scoffed as I tossed a penny into the fountain. I didn't come to Remington wishing to fall in love. My dreams hadn't allowed for that; hell, my dreams just wanted a safe and stable life for Hadley and a reprieve from my own grief.

But now? If wishes came true, things with Cooper and me would be different. Better. *Something.* Instead, he was gone, moving on, and I was left alone, longing for a love I'd never dreamed of.

"Maybe wishes aren't always enough," I mumbled bitterly as the pain in my heart seared through me.

THIRTEEN
COOPER

By the middle of the week after ending things with Jesse, I wasn't sure which way was up. Without my medication and coping skills learned over the years, I likely would have been a complete mess. Or more of a complete mess than I already was.

As it was, I was barely holding it together.

My physical fidgets were amped up, but my mental twitches were driving me insane. Medication and routine kept me sane, but I was fighting daily against lack of focus, lack of organization, lack of confidence. Left to my own mental barrage of self-doubt, I had very little confidence in myself for getting through the heartache or moving on.

Thank God for alarms, lists, my calendar, and Hadley. Without those things, I probably would have been like a little vibrating toy bouncing around the living room floor until it finally ran out of batteries and gave up.

Not a moment went by where I didn't want to go to Jesse and tell him I'd made a mistake. But I kept telling myself I had to hold firm. Jesse hadn't asked for the baggage that came with what I felt for him. I wouldn't put him in that awkward position. I was a grown man; I'd gotten myself into the situation and I'd just have to deal with the repercussions.

Repercussions being a broken heart—flayed open, bleeding, barely beating.

It would get better, right?

It *had* to get better.

Once my heart eventually stopped its painful throbbing, I vowed I'd never put myself in this position again. Falling in love with Jesse had been the easiest thing I'd ever done—also the scariest and probably the stupidest—but it was the losing him that I vowed to never do again. Never again would I allow myself to be in a situation where this type of pain could be the outcome.

Losing him. Can you lose someone who was never really yours?

I sighed heavily, fighting back the ever-present tears, as I headed up the back steps to the kitchen door.

"Cooper, perfect timing, I wanted you to meet my

nephew Andre King," Bev said. "Dre, this is Cooper Scott, Dalton's younger brother and Spencer's best friend."

A gorgeous man with a wide, bright smile stepped forward and stuck out his hand. "Nice to meet you, Cooper. Call me Dre."

I shook his hand, noticing how his deep brown eyes and golden-umber complexion matched Bev's. A smidge shorter than me, Dre had a broad chest, wide shoulders, and looked as if he worked hard to keep his physique. With long, gorgeous braids pulled back from his face, I swore the guy could have easily been a fashion model. "Good to meet you. Glad you're here," I said. I meant the words, but my current state of emotional upheaval didn't allow for much enthusiasm.

Bev eyed me for a moment and then pointed to the table. "Sit down, we were just about to have tea and cookies."

I knew from the cocked brow on Dre's face that the information was new to him, but he seemed to sense there was no arguing with his aunt.

We both sat as Bev bustled around the kitchen preparing a plate of shortbread cookies and mugs of sweet, hot tea.

"Cooper, you look like the remnants of what the cat dragged in, left to rot in the sun and then shoveled from the stoop," Bev said, her hand resting lightly on my shoulder as she waited for the water to boil.

"Gee, thanks," I grunted.

"I've given you some time and space, but I think it's high time you fill me in on what's got you in such a mess."

I glanced at Dre.

He cleared his throat. "I can go unpack." He started to push back his chair.

"Nonsense. You're a part of Remington Place now and we're family," Bev said with a pointed look my way.

I shrugged. "She's right. We're family. You'll hear about everyone's sordid details sooner or later."

Dre blanched as if worried his own secrets would somehow seep out if he wasn't careful.

They will, buddy. They will. Your Aunt Bev has a way about her. No use fighting it.

I started to explain to Bev what was going on, but took a brief moment to fill Dre in on the who and what Jesse was to me. His eyes grew wide, but he nodded as I gave him the short history.

Then I launched into the explanation of ending things with Jesse.

"You broke up with him?" Bev asked in shock.

I wrinkled my brow. "Not even sure if what we

had was enough to deem it a *break-up*. I ended what we were doing. Just like I'd said we'd do from the very beginning."

Bev studied me as she placed steaming mugs of tea on the table. "I guess I don't understand the *why* of your decision."

I chomped on a cookie, barely tasting its buttery goodness while tapping my fingers on the table. "Jesse agreed to temporary. He indicated to my dad that he was maybe ready to date. I couldn't hold onto him forever; it seemed best to rip off the bandage and deal with the fall-out."

Dre silently ate his cookie and sipped his tea.

Bev cocked her head. "You *set him free* so to speak, even though you developed feelings for him you hadn't planned on?"

I snorted. "Understatement. But it doesn't matter. Just because I was stupid and let my heart get involved—yeah, I know you told me to *not* do that—doesn't mean that Jesse needs to deal with it. What we had allowed him to figure himself out. Now, he can find someone his own age, someone more appropriate." I winced and swallowed down the pain that came from those words. Trying to imagine Jesse with anyone else was a knife to my heart.

Bev frowned. "I don't know, Coop. I saw the way

the two of you looked at each other. I'm not completely sure it was one-sided."

I took a deep breath, weary of the constant threat of tears, and dropped my head to the table. "I wish things were different. I can't wish we'd never met because I value him and Hadley way too much for that. But I wish there wasn't so much against us. Wish he felt the same as me."

"Do you know that he doesn't?" Dre asked.

I lifted my head and stared at him.

He shrugged. "I spent *a lot* of years in denial and not being honest with myself and others. I'm just saying, maybe you should let him know how you feel. Maybe he doesn't feel the same, but you'll lift a weight off your shoulders by at least giving him your truth."

I flopped my head back onto the table and sighed, my fingers and toes both tapping out my fidgets. Dre's advice was logical, but the pain in my heart wasn't interested in logical. All I wanted was to stop hurting and have Jesse in my life for real. Not temporary, not just for fun. For real and for always.

Bev touched my elbow. "Sit up. Wallowing isn't pretty and it's not doing you any good."

I sat up with a frown and flashed a look of annoyance toward Dre who was chewing his cookie with a poorly-hidden smirk. "Wallowing is all I feel like doing."

"Wallowing isn't productive." Bev pushed the plate of cookies my way. "You said you wished things were different; do you want a relationship with Jesse? The good and the bad and everything in between?"

I nodded as I swallowed thickly. "Yeah, I do. For just a short time, I let myself pretend that what we had was real and it was the happiest I'd ever been."

"You're ready to deal with becoming an instant parent? The looks and whispers of people who see you with a man twice your age? The outcome of Robby finding out you're involved with his best friend?" Bev patted my hand as she spoke.

"Yeah, I am. I'm not saying any of it would be easy, but the end result—Jesse and me together— would be worth it." I pinched the bridge of my nose and bounced my knee. "I wish I could snap my fingers and make it happen."

Bev hummed, but stayed quiet for a moment. When she spoke, she took my hand. "You ever read a book called *Ways to Live Forever* by Sally Nicholls?"

I shook my head. "Not that I can remember."

"Well, it's good. You should read it. I'm hoping I don't regret this advice, but I feel like it's the right thing to do," Bev murmured. "There's a line in that book that's always stuck with me. *'There's no point in having wishes if you don't at least try to do them.'* Now, I'm not saying pouring your heart out to Jesse is going to get you exactly what you want with him. Maybe he truly doesn't feel the same. But I think you owe it to yourself and him to be honest. If the outcome stays the same, you can move on and start the healing process. But at least you'll know. Sitting around *wishing* things were different is pointless. You've gotta *try* if you're going to get anywhere with wishes." Bev squeezed my hand.

"So, you're both saying I should hand Jesse my heart, bloody, raw, and barely beating, tell him I went and fell in love with him, and just stand by *hoping* he feels the same?" Both knees were bouncing now and I wanted to slam my head against the table.

"Would it hurt any worse than what you're hurting now?" Dre asked.

I leaned back in my chair, feeling sullen as I patted my hands on my legs and said nothing.

"Now you listen here, child. You're not going to sit here and try to convince me that you can't talk to the man." Bev wagged a finger in my direction. "This whole thing started because you came right out and offered him sex with no strings. If you can tell a man you just met that you want to climb him like a damn tree, you can tell a man you fell in love with how you're feeling."

From the corner of my eye, I noticed Dre shoving a cookie in his mouth. Probably in hopes of hiding the smile he was fighting.

"It *is* different," I whined. "Back then, there were no feelings involved other than lust and sexual tension. *Now*, there's uncertainty and fear and love and stupid things like wanting to spend the rest of my life with him and Hadley." I groaned and fisted chunks of my hair as my knees bounced so hard I nearly fell from the chair.

Bev tsked as she stood to gather the mugs and empty plate. "I seem to remember you telling me you're a big boy and you can handle a little mess."

I huffed, but said nothing.

"Well, here's your mess, big boy. You need to handle it. You owe it to yourself and Jesse to at least clear the air. You'll both feel better in the end." She patted my shoulder. "And believe me, those of us around you will be glad when you stop your wallowing."

Heaving myself from the chair—and feeling a weird combination of wired beyond belief and weighted down by feelings I didn't want to be having —I trudged up to my room.

For the next thirty minutes, I did a frantic combination of dancing, push-ups, and yoga in hopes of calming my head and body. I broke a sweat and my muscles ached, but the pain in my heart and frenzied jumble in my head didn't ease in the least.

Slamming headphones onto my ears, I flopped onto my bed and flipped through playlists on my phone. My body and mind were screaming for loud and chaotic, but I knew soft, ambient sounds would be best. I chose a meditative list and attempted to focus on my breathing.

Twenty minutes later, I still felt buzzy and overwhelmed with heartache, but my head was clearing enough to replay the words Dre and Bev had said.

Were they right that talking to Jesse and being honest would help?

I didn't want to give myself false hope that a conversation would bring us back together, but I *did* realize that hiding away from the issue wasn't the most responsible thing to do.

My entire life, I'd been told—okay, maybe not *told*, but *expected*—to screw up. CJ was forgetful. CJ wouldn't follow through. CJ was a great kid, but he lacked discipline. CJ tried hard, but he just didn't have what it took, always fell short.

Well, fuck that.

Cooper wasn't like that.

Maybe a large part of the expectations of failure were in my own head, but I'd be damned if I was going to lower myself to that lack of confidence.

Sure, I'd started the thing with Jesse as a fun distraction. A way to get into his bed without spooking him so much that he hightailed it away from me.

I'd never expected it to turn into something more. Something *real*. So real I could feel it in every cell of my body.

So, was I going to be like CJ and let everything fall apart?

Or was I going to be Cooper and deal with my mess?

I took a deep breath.

The thought of pouring my heart out to Jesse was scary as fuck.

But Bev and Dre were right. I needed to be honest with him. Best case, he felt the same and we took the next steps together. Worst case, he didn't feel the same and I moved on to healing a broken heart. Either way, hiding the truth wasn't going to help the situation.

Taking a deep breath, I blew it out as slowly and evenly as possible.

I'd accepted what I needed to do.

The *how* and *when* of doing it were next on my to-do list.

FOURTEEN
JESSE

AFTER LUNCH AT THE PARK, I drove aimlessly around town until I ended up in the middle school parking lot. I parked next to Robby's car and sat staring off into space. I had no clue why I'd ended up at the school, and no clue why I was still sitting there, but I couldn't seem to make myself leave.

An hour later, a knock at my window scared the shit out of me and I jumped awake to find Robby standing at my truck door with narrowed eyes and pursed lips. I rolled down the window.

"Everything okay?" he asked as he shifted his school bag from one shoulder to the other.

"Yeah? No?" I ran a hand over my face. "I don't even know."

"Wanna grab a drink? Happy hour at the Wishing Well," Robby suggested.

"Sure," I mumbled. "Meet you there?"

A few minutes later, I walked into the bar and forced polite greetings and small talk with my colleagues and regulars. Seeing Robby at a far corner booth, I excused myself from the chit-chat and made my way toward my best friend.

What the hell are you doing?

I took a deep breath. I had absolutely no clue, but I knew it felt right to be talking to Robby. I slid into the seat across from him. We each ordered a beer. Robby ordered loaded fries.

"Sorry, I'm hungry. We can share." He shrugged and slipped the appetizer menu back into the holder as the waitperson walked away.

We spent the next bit of time talking about Robby's students, funny things that had happened in class, and Hadley's recent homework assignment where she'd had to create a scavenger hunt.

When our orders arrived, Robby dug into the fries with gusto. The man had *always* been able to eat a ton and never gained weight. Had to have the highest metabolism of anyone I'd ever met.

I drank half my beer in one swallow before halfheartedly picking at the fries.

"Okay, I've got some food in me and some beer to fortify me. You going to tell me what the fuck is up with you?" Robby cocked his head and studied me.

I sighed and took another long drink of my beer. Catching the attention of our waitperson, I indicated I'd take another—knowing I'd stop at two no question since I needed to drive *and* be functioning for Hadley after Cooper left. "I don't even know where to start," I hedged. I'd had absolutely no plan when I ended up at Robby's work. I didn't feel like I could out what Cooper and I'd been doing without Cooper's consent, so it wasn't like I could spill my guts.

Well, at least not completely.

"You wanna try?" Robby urged.

"I guess I wasn't completely honest with you last time we talked," I started.

Robby waited.

"When I said I was maybe a little more ready to start dating than I had been in the past, that wasn't completely accurate."

"Okay," Robby said patiently. "You're more ready than you let on? That's great."

"No, it's not that. I've been dating—well, sort of. I've been involved with someone for a while. It was something that was supposed to be just easy and fun, no strings, walk away at the end."

Robby raised his brow as he waited for me to continue.

"Well, it ended."

"And," Robby pushed.

I leaned forward, head in my hands. "And I'm fucking miserable."

"Wait," Robby's fingers tapped on the table as he shifted in his seat. "I need to make sure I'm following here. You started something with someone that was supposed to be temporary and casual. Now that it's over, you miss the dating? Miss the sex? Miss the person?"

I sighed and fisted my hands in my hair. "All of the above."

"So, you've got feelings for this person?"

I appreciated that Robby wasn't pressing the *who* of the story. "Yeah. Like major feelings. I never expected to feel this way about someone and it's turned into this all-consuming thing."

"Like lust? Or more than that?"

"More. So much more. Like—and fuck if this doesn't make me feel guilty as hell—I loved Nicole. But I realize now that what we had was always more friendship love than *love* love." I pinched the bridge of my nose. "This person? It's like finding everything I've ever wanted—hell, it's like finding things I didn't even know I wanted, didn't even know I was missing—and I'm a fucking mess."

"Why did it end?"

I laughed without humor. "That was the deal

from the beginning. Walk away. No attachments, no commitments, nothing serious."

"You ended it or they did?"

I took a deep breath. "They did. Said it was probably time to go our separate ways."

"Do they know how you feel?"

Shaking my head, I closed my eyes. "No. I never expected to fall for anyone. Ever. Definitely didn't expect that a fling would turn into something more. Not sure it's fair to unload all this shit on a person who only offered casual. But I'm also not sure how to deal with the pain of losing someone I never expected to fall in love with."

Robby's eyes went wide. "Wow, *love*? That's a lot."

"Tell me about it." I scrubbed my face. "Fuck. I have so much baggage. No one should be saddled with my shit. But I miss what we had so badly." I took a deep swallow of my beer. "How the hell do I tell someone that our fling has now become something I want for the rest of my life? It doesn't even make sense to me how this even happened, and now I want something I never in a million years thought I'd find or even want."

Robby whistled slowly. "Yeah, that's a lot."

We sat quietly for a few moments. Robby blatantly studying me—I didn't blame him, he'd known me for decades and had *never* seen me like this—and me just sitting, sadly stewing in my heartache.

"Okay. Yep, that's it," Robby muttered to himself as if he'd just come to a decision.

"Huh? What's it?"

"I think you need to go for it." Robby drained his beer.

"Go for what?" I wrinkled my brow.

"Go for love. Maybe it doesn't make sense. Maybe it seems like it's way too much. Maybe you never planned for it and never would have thought you wanted it." Robby gestured wildly. "But don't you think you owe it to yourself to at least give it a shot?"

I snorted. "Are you forgetting that he ended it? Maybe he's not interested in a shot."

To his credit, Robby's eyes only widened a fraction when I mentioned *he*. "Then he tells you it's not what he wants and you start the process of moving on. But if you don't at least take the chance and *try*, you'll forever wonder what if. You've got to let him know how you feel or you'll regret it for the rest of your life." Robby rapped the table with his knuckles. "We both know life is way too short to live with regrets."

My mind immediately flashed to Lauren and Nicole.

My wife—my friend of so many years—did she die with regrets? Did I play a part in them?

My daughter—so young, never getting to experience the best years of her life, never knowing what an amazing little human Hadley was. I recalled that conversation with Lauren so many years ago. Her telling me that I needed to let go and find the happiness I didn't have with Nicole. Telling me to find what I *needed*.

What did I need?

I swallowed thickly.

I *needed* Cooper.

Period. Full stop.

And what if he didn't need me?

I'd deal. But I wasn't going to live with what ifs and regrets.

I had to be honest with Cooper.

I'd deal with the fallout, but I needed him to know.

After paying my bill and saying a distracted goodbye to Robby—promising to see him at Bev's dinner the next evening—I rushed home as a seedling of a plan took root in my head.

By Thursday evening, I was a jumpy, jittery mess of nerves and emotions. I had a plan and I wanted more than anything for it to work, but I'd resigned myself to accepting whatever answer Cooper gave me. At least I'd be able to rest easy knowing I didn't go down without a fight and I gave myself the opportunity to be happy. Cooper had given me the courage to be myself and that was what gave me the strength to follow my heart and tell Cooper the truth. Even if it meant a second round of heartbreak.

Dinner was a lively affair with the addition of Robby, Celeste, and Bev's nephew, Dre. Laughter, conversation, and true friendship filled the dining room as we enjoyed Bev's delicious cooking. Hadley kept us all entertained as well, and by the time dessert arrived, I'd almost convinced myself that things were going to be okay. Even if Cooper and I didn't get a chance, I had friends to love and support Hadley and me.

But then I caught Cooper watching me and my chest squeezed painfully. It was now or never. I couldn't keep avoiding the situation; I was stalling and it was doing me no good. Gathering the courage to ask Cooper to step outside, I swallowed my nerves and made my way toward where he was standing by the sink.

Before I had a moment to speak, Cooper turned to me. His frantic eyes searching mine. "Hey, could we maybe talk outside for a minute? I promise it won't take long."

Blinking in surprise—not sure how to pivot from my loosely planned request to ask the same—I nodded and followed a relieved looking Cooper out the backdoor.

Patting my back pocket to assure myself the item was still there, I gestured toward the shop. "We can use my shop if you'd like."

Cooper nodded, cleared his throat, and made a beeline toward the building.

Throwing open the door and rushing inside, Cooper spun on his heel and faced me.

I knew it was my now-or-never moment.

"We need to talk," we both exclaimed in a rush of words.

Chuckling, we both sputtered, "You go ahead."

Cooper closed his eyes. "God, why is this so hard?"

"Go ahead. You go first," I urged as every single word I'd planned to say swirled anxiously in my head.

He looked a little green around the gills, but Cooper reached into his pocket and pulled out a handful of coins. "I had no plans for this, and I know it's not fair, but the very long and sordid story made short is that I went and fell in love with you. I'm sorry it wasn't what we agreed to. I'm sorry I changed the deal. I'll understand if you don't feel the same." He held out the coins. "But I need you to know I'm ready to throw them all in. Every single wish, they all lead to you. All of my wishes are for us taking a chance. I want more with you; I want you and Hadley. Forever and for real. Always." Cooper's eyes glistened with tears and his hand shook as he placed the coins in my hand.

I laughed through tears that threatened to spill from my eyes. Taking a deep breath, I blew it out slowly and tried to gather my words. "Well, I guess I'm glad I let you go first because you just made my part a whole lot easier." I held tight to the coins and kissed the knuckles of my hand before sliding them into my front jeans pocket. Reaching for my back pocket, I cleared my throat and pulled out a little booklet. "I made something for you."

Cooper took the paper with a trembling hand.

I swallowed thickly and willed my voice not to wobble. "I wasn't wishing—for you, for love, for anything. I didn't know what to wish for even if I'd wanted to make a wish. But my heart knew. It kept wishing for you and slowly but surely, a wish I didn't even know I wanted to come true found its way to me and brought me you." I nodded toward the booklet.

Cooper opened and began to read with quivering voice. "You are never given a wish without also being given the power to make it come true. You may have to work for it, however. Richard David Bach." He chuckled and let out a wavering breath before continuing. "Life is too short to be scared and not take risks. I'd rather be the person that's like 'I messed up,' than 'I wish I did that.' Justin Skye."

Tears started to pour down Cooper's face and my heart gave a lurch, hoping against hope that his tears and the coins in my pocket meant he was feeling the same as me.

Cooper cleared his throat and continued. "The most fantastic magical things can happen, and it all starts with a wish. Pinocchio." A laugh bubbled from him. "Stop wishing, start doing."

As he read those words, I stepped forward and took him in my arms. "Cooper, I know we agreed to easy and fun—that was likely all I was capable of agreeing to at the time. But things got very real, very fast for me. I didn't mean to, I tried to stop it, but I fell in love with you. *Every dream begins with a wish* and there's no one I'd rather see my dreams come true with than you," I whispered gruffly, tears burning my eyes.

Cooper nodded. "Oh my God," he murmured, "I want that, too. So damned bad."

With a slight nudge against his chin, I lifted his mouth to mine. There had never been a sweeter, hotter, more promise-filled kiss in the history of kisses. Our tongues danced, savoring and seeking, whispering of forever and always.

Just as I lifted Cooper to the workbench and his legs spread around my hips, a low clearing of a throat sounded from the doorway.

We both froze.

Taking a deep breath, I looked Cooper straight in the eye. "We're good. We've got this, yeah?"

Cooper nodded and slid from the bench. "Yeah. Together."

I turned toward the doorway to find Robby with his arms crossed over his chest, a scowl hooding his eyes, and Celeste, eyes wide and confusion marring her face, peeking over his shoulder.

"I think some explanations are in order," Robby bit out.

Tucking Cooper behind me, I nodded. "You're right. We should talk. But I need to know you're not going to punch me."

Robby's eyes went wide and he scoffed. "Fuck off, man. That's offensive. Of course, I'm not going to punch you." He glanced between Cooper and me.

"Just feeling waaay out of the loop and trying to wrap my head." He took a deep breath and blew it out.

We made our way to the little patio and took seats just as Bev, Dalton, and Spencer came out of Remington Place with concern etched on their faces.

"Everyone cool, calm, and collected?" Bev asked with a pointed look for the four of us. With nods all around, she smiled. "Good. I'll just go in and keep Hadley busy."

When I took Cooper's hand, Spencer smirked and Dalton snorted. "Shortest break-up in history," Cooper's brother teased.

"Make each other happy," Spencer advised before they both gave waves and headed back toward the house.

An hour later, Cooper and I had done our best to explain the situation to Robby and Celeste.

For her part, Celeste had taken everything in stride and reached for Robby's hand with a fond smile. "I get it. I never planned to fall in love with this one. But no matter how much I tried to deny it, there was no getting around it."

Robby kept scowling and opening his mouth as if to speak before closing it with a snap and a shake of his head. "I can't say I *understand* because all I keep thinking about is *that's my kid* and *eeww, that's Jesse,*" he muttered.

"Gee, thanks," I deadpanned.

Robby stood to pace. "I mean, I don't mean it in a bad way, I'm sure plenty of people would find you attractive." He shuddered. "Just not me. It's like thinking about my brother's dick or something."

We all laughed.

"Some people are into that," Cooper said with an innocent batting of his lashes.

"Stop," Robby winced.

"But not me," Cooper continued with a sly grin. "I'm just into sexy silver foxes who happen to be my dad's best friend."

Robby groaned. "Fuck my life." He spun on his heel and wagged a finger in our direction. "No talk of your sex life. I don't want to hear about dicks or lube or orgasms or *anything* to do with it. The more I can pretend you two are never naked together, the better."

Celeste laughed. "They'd probably appreciate the same in return. Pretty sure Jesse has no desire to hear about your dick and Cooper definitely doesn't want to hear about his parents' sex life."

Cooper and I both winced and shuddered.

"Okay, so it's agreed. No sex life discussions. I

really think that should be a given in most friend and family relationships," Cooper said.

I gave Cooper's hand a squeeze before standing to face Robby. "You're really okay with this? I haven't ruined our friendship?"

Robby's lips twisted. "I'm not going pretend that I *get it*, but I'm not against it. I've seen a change in both of you lately—didn't know what it was from at the time—and I can see that you're good for each other. If two people I love can find happiness with each other, I'd be a fucking ass to stand in the way of that." He wrapped me in his arms and held me tight. "We're good. Just don't hurt him; take care of him and make him happy."

I nodded and slapped him on the back.

"I've got the perfect idea. How about we take Hadley for the weekend. You guys can hole-up here or take a little getaway," Celeste said. "A little weekend celebration before back to real-life?"

I reached for Cooper's hand and pulled him to stand up. "Want to?"

He smiled and nodded, biting his lip.

That look went straight to my cock and I knew exactly what we'd be doing all weekend.

I woke on Saturday morning with Cooper in my arms, in my bed, and it took me a moment to realize I wasn't dreaming.

Finding out Cooper felt the same about me as I felt about him had been…well, it had been everything I needed in my life.

Hadley had jumped at the chance to spend the night with Bev on Thursday, and Celeste and Robby had taken her home with them after school on Friday.

Cooper and I had barely left my bed since Thursday night.

That night, we'd come together hard and fast, a furious coupling that had me worried for the health of my heart and lungs. We'd spent most of Friday luxuriating in each other's arms, talking about anything and everything, dozing and whispering our love to each other.

Cooper grumbled into my chest. "The only way I'm getting out of this bed is if I get to play out a sexual fantasy *and* you take me to the diner for French toast."

I laughed. "Not sure either of us are going to be able to walk, but I'm down for trying." Rolling him to his back, I kissed him long and deep. "Good morning. Have I told you recently how much I love you?"

Cooper smiled up at me and I knew without a shadow of a doubt he was the piece of me that had been missing for all these years. I had friends to love, I'd had my daughter to love, I had Hadley to love, but Cooper coming into my life completed me in a way I'd never known I needed.

"Mmmm, I think you might have said it once or twice as you slammed your cock into me last night, but I'm always up for hearing it again," he teased.

I laughed. "And I'm always up for slamming my cock into your pretty little ass again," I murmured against his mouth, "but for the record, I love you."

Cooper moaned into my mouth, his tongue sliding against mine as his body stretched, thighs opening to make room for me between his legs. "And I love you." He froze and held my face with his hands. "You don't think we're moving too fast? Maybe we're just all caught up in lust?"

I kissed his nose. "We'll keep things like they are for the rest of the school year at least. We can reassess in May. If we're ready, you can move in. If not, no worries. I don't want to push anything, but I want you in my life. Want people to see us as a partnership. Want Hadley to know she's got both of us loving, supporting, and caring for her."

Cooper's eyes softened and he kissed me slowly. "Okay, that's what I want too, I just don't want to feel like I'm pushing you into something too quickly."

We kissed for several more moments before I tore my mouth from his, panting. "If you get to play out a fantasy, can I suggest a little something additional?"

"You're not even going to ask what my fantasy is?" Cooper bit his lip.

"If it involves our cocks, I'm all for it."

"Very well," he teased. "What do you want?"

My cheeks heated as I leaned in to kiss his collarbone. "Remember how we used to talk about going bare, but decided we couldn't because it was just casual?"

Cooper's eyes caught fire and he nodded.

"Now that we're no longer just casual…" I trailed off.

"You want to take me bare?" His words were a breathy whisper.

Swallowing thickly, I gave a little nod. "If you're okay with it. We both know we're clear." I chewed on my lip as I rocked my hips against his. "And I want your bare cock in my ass, too."

"Fuck, yeah," Cooper murmured. "Fits perfectly with my fantasy."

"Tell me what you want," I said as I nuzzled against his neck.

"I was leaning toward flip-fucking already, but

the bareback is an added bonus." Cooper's nails trailed down my back before he gripped my ass. "Take turns, I'll suck you, finger you, and jack myself. Right when I'm ready to come and your hole is begging for me, I'll slide my bare cock inside and fill you with my cum."

I groaned and thrust my hips against him. "Holy shit, Coop. You're going to have me coming before we even start."

He chuckled and played with my nipples. "Then, you'll eat my ass, stretch me while you stroke your throbbing cock, and right before you blow, you'll slam into me and fill me, hot and deep."

"God, yeah," I growled. "Want it, now."

Cooper pushed me to my hands and knees and bent close to tongue my ass.

"Coop, I won't last long. If you want my cock in you, you can't tease for too long," I warned.

"No worries. I'm so close." He pressed his tongue against my hole before slipping two spit-slick fingers inside. "Plus, I'm hungry. I want French toast."

My laugh turned into a gasp as he worked me open. I heard the slick stroke of his fist on his cock and his breathy little moans as he jacked himself. "Want that dick, Coop. Wanna feel you unload in me."

He groaned, pressing his cock against me and

sliding in deep. With only a few strokes, his cock was pulsing in me, emptying his hot load deep inside as he cried out.

Gripping my dick to keep from coming, I savored the throbbing heat of his release for a few more moments. "God, so good. Feeling you so hot in me," I murmured.

"My turn," Cooper said as he moved to roll to his back.

I growled as he spread his legs for me. Maneuvering to the right angle for eating his ass, my tongue began a slow, teasing assault on his hole until Cooper was writhing under me. Moving to finger-fuck him while I stroked my rock-hard shaft, I took a moment to enjoy the way he thrust his hips and fucked himself on my fingers.

"Want your cock, Jess. Wanna feel your cum in me," Cooper begged.

Knowing I was seconds away from shooting, I pressed my cock head against his pucker and savored his whimper as I slid into him. The tight heat that opened for me did me in and my cock shot spurt after spurt of my release into him. As much as I loved watching where his body stretched and took me in, I couldn't pull my eyes from his face. As I unloaded into him, his body clenching and milking for me for every last drop, I swore I saw our future in his eyes. A future of love and family, true partnership, learning and growing together.

I reached to cup Cooper's face and leaned in to kiss him, my cock slipping from him as I rolled us to our sides. "I love you. No one I'd rather make wishes and build dreams with than you."

"Mmm, that's so sweet and I love you, too. So damn much." Cooper shifted to tongue my nipple and laughed when I gasped. "But right now, if every dream begins with a wish, you better be wishing for some damn diner-style French toast because your boy is hungry and dreaming of carb-loaded, battered, bready goodness."

I chuckled and slapped his ass. "I'll spend the rest of my life doing everything I can to make your dreams come true," I promised with a kiss.

"Even if it's for something as silly as breakfast?" Cooper asked.

"As silly as breakfast, and as big as dreams that seem impossible. I'm vowing here and now to stand by you and support all of your wishes and dreams," I said gruffly. "Forever."

One Year Later

"If you want this ass before a certain first-grader wakes up, you better get to it," I whispered against Jesse's ear as he grumbled awake on the first day of school.

"Mmm," he hummed. "A little more sleep or my boyfriend's ass? Decisions, decisions."

"Let me make it easy for you," I said as I rolled him to his back. Straddling his waist, I reached for the ever-present lube in the drawer and slicked myself and Jesse's wide-awake morning erection.

"Fuck, Coop," he groaned. "Never gonna get tired of waking up to this."

I smiled and reached to line up his dick with my ass. Working his thick length into my tight hole, I whimpered at the hot sting of the invasion. "Gotta keep it quiet," I warned. "She's not awake yet, but no telling how long we have."

Jesse gripped my hips and began long, hard thrusts as I stroked my cock. "Come for me, Coop. Wanna feel your ass clench around me when I shoot my load."

Jesse's dirty words and commands could always get me off and my balls drew up tight as he continued to pump into me. "Fuck, Jess. I'm close. Gonna come," I panted.

With a quick move I'd come to expect during our lovemaking, Jesse shifted and pinned me to the bed so he was nestled between my spread legs. Leaning in to kiss me long and deep, he slammed into me with long, sure strokes.

Throwing my head back, I slapped a hand over my mouth to keep quiet as an orgasm washed over me. The satisfied grunt and final slam of Jesse's hips were all the warning I got before his throbbing cock shot thick and hot into my ass.

After catching our breath, we cleaned up and pulled on pajama pants before collapsing into bed to wait for Hadley. She'd gotten into a habit over the summer of running to our room when she woke up —which was why the monitor was still a must so we weren't surprised by any of her spontaneous visits.

Hadley had been thrilled to have me take a more permanent role in their lives. She'd actually broached the subject with us before we'd brought it up with her.

"Can Cooper be my other daddy?" she'd asked one day toward the end of Kindergarten. "Samuel has two daddies and I told him I wanted Cooper to be my other daddy."

Without a plan for telling her we were together, Jesse and I had glanced at each other and shrugged. "You'd be okay with Cooper being here more? Us being a family?"

She was nearing six at the time, so we hadn't been exactly sure what to expect in terms of understanding or acceptance, but Hadley had just shrugged. "He's here a lot and we're already family. I just want to tell Samuel I have two daddies, too."

So, just like that, I'd moved from nanny and friend to daddy and partner.

The transition had been crazy easy. Honestly, sometimes it scared me *how* easy it had been, but Jesse convinced me to just accept it and be grateful.

LATER, when the whole crew gathered at the corner of Remington Way and Pleasure Boulevard to see

Hadley off on the bus, we chatted like life-long friends.

"So, the girl down the street is going to be here every day after school to get Hadley off the bus," Jesse explained to Bev.

"Her name is Mandy. She's nice. She lets me play with her hair," Hadley informed the group.

While we waited, Spencer turned to me. "So, is your room officially *open*?"

I frowned and Bev's ears perked up.

With a shrug, I said, "I'd like to keep it for a bit longer. I know that's kinda selfish since I'm pretty much at Jesse's all the time, I just feel like I don't want to completely give up my place with you guys just yet."

"Nonsense," Bev said with a pat on my shoulder. "You'll always be a part of us, but we'll keep your room as *yours* for as long as we can." She turned her attention to Spencer. "Why do you ask?"

"Well, there's someone I know who may be looking for a place to stay. Thought maybe he could take Cooper's room." He twisted his lips. "Or room with Dre?"

"No way, I'm the newest, I get to be last to get a roommate, right?" Dre piped up as he jostled Hadley around on his shoulders.

"That's the way the rules go. Spencer, you know

our home is open. You'll be the next to get a roommate. Would you turn this person away if he had to room with you?" Bev cocked her brow.

"No, not at all. Just thought he'd do better on his own, not with me maybe." Spencer shrugged. "I'll let him know the space is available. Not sure, maybe he's got other options."

Once Hadley was on the bus—after plenty of hugs, kisses, and pictures—we said goodbye to Bev, Spencer, and Dre and headed back to Jesse's house.

"Mmm," Jesse murmured against my neck. "I have no early appointments at the shop. My *boyfriend* —who happens to be opening his dream preschool in just a few short weeks—has at least two hours before he has to go be all business-minded and professional." He teased his tongue against my ear. "I wish I knew what we could do with our time."

I smiled and snaked my arms around his neck. "How about we spend the next couple hours making all of our wishes and dreams come true?"

Jesse laughed as I moved to wrap my legs around his waist. "How did I get so lucky to have such a smart, sexy boyfriend to be madly in love with?"

"I think it was all those coins you threw in the fountain," I whispered against his ear. "Come on, time's ticking and I'm in need of a good dicking."

Jesse snorted. "Smart, sexy, *and* poetic."

I grinned. "What can I say? I'm the whole trifecta."

Jesse delivered on the dicking over the next couple hours.

And we'd spend the rest of our lives working on making our wishes come true.

WANT MORE of the Remington Place crew? Look for Crave, Desire, and Yearn on your favorite book platform. Buying direct from the author is always an appreciated option https://payhip.com/ADEllisAuthor

ALSO BY A.D. ELLIS

Find all of A.D. Ellis's books at https://books2read.com/ap/RWrrNx/AD-Ellis

The *Remington Place* series continues - Crave (book 2) is a steamy, friends-to-lovers, fake relationship M/M romance with a virgin nursing student and a gruff, grumbly construction worker.

Power Struggle is a steamy M/M, age-gap, forced proximity romance set in a small town. A twenty-year history, rival schools and jobs, and a hotel with only one bed make for a hot and heavy, sweet and sexy, HEA-guaranteed love story.

Take Me Home M/M age-gap, opposites-attract romance with plenty of steam and a scene that will make you appreciate camouflage and work boots

Let Love In M/M age-gap, forced proximity, dad's best friend, bisexual-awakening romance. Available on AUDIO!

Let Love Win M/M brother's best friend romance. Available on AUDIO!

Buried Secrets Romantic suspense stand-alone title. Available on AUDIO!

Silver in the City (3 books- meet the Silver crew you read about in Forged in the City) Available on AUDIO!

<u>Forged in the City</u> (3 books- a spin-off series from Silver in the City) Available on AUDIO

<u>The BJ Boys Series</u> (3 books, small town, big love) Available on AUDIO

<u>Forever Better Together</u> (friends to lovers) Available on AUDIO!

<u>His Reluctant Cowboy</u> (age gap, opposites attract, cowboy romance) Available on AUDIO!

<u>What Blooms Beneath</u> (LGBT Fantasy romance) Available on AUDIO!

<u>Sawyer</u>

(this was the first M/M I wrote and you may remember Sawyer and Luke being mentioned in <u>Barrett & Ivan</u> as well as in <u>Ryker & Gavin</u>)

ACKNOWLEDGMENTS

It's always so hard to write this part because I'm worried I'll forget someone without meaning to.

Readers- you are the reason I write. As long as you continue reading my stories, I'll continue writing them. Thank you for your support.

Bloggers- your support, reviews, and promotion are very much appreciated. Thank you!

My author buddies- I don't know that I could keep doing this without our brainstorm sessions, laughter, road trips, meals, wine, and friendship as my support.

Thank you to my alphas, betas, editors, proofreaders, and ARC readers! Your eyes and input are beyond important to me.

Brett and Gage- as usual, I doubt you even grasp how much your support, input, and friendship mean to me. This author journey has brought many wonderful things into my life, and you both are two of the BEST! I'm blessed to call you friends.

My family and friends- thank you for your love and support, always.

ABOUT THE AUTHOR

A.D. Ellis is an Indiana girl, born and raised. She spends much of her time in central Indiana as an instructional coach/teacher in the inner city of Indianapolis, being a mom to two amazing older teens, and wondering how she and her husband of almost two decades have managed to not drive each other insane. A lot of her time is also devoted to phone call avoidance and her hatred of cooking.

She loves chocolate, wine, pizza, and naps along with reading and writing romance. These loves don't leave much time for housework, much to the chagrin of her husband. Who would pick cleaning the house over a nap or a good book? She uses any extra time to increase her fluency in sarcasm.

Find all of A.D. Ellis's M/M romance at https://books2read.com/ap/RWrrNx/AD-Ellis

Sign up at http://www.subscribepage.com/ADEllisNewsMMRomance for a FREE male/male romance book.